Damaged Defender

A Best Friend's Brother Hockey Romance

Anne Martin

Content Warning

This book may contain content that is considered triggering to some. Please take care of yourself.

For a full list, go to: www.annemartinbooks.com

To the real supporting cast—thanks for the tough talks and big laughs. Go team.

Prologue | Zane

Today is my birthday.

But if you ask me, monsters shouldn't get to celebrate birthdays.

And today wouldn't be what it is, if I wasn't one.

A monster, that is.

Maybe I was predestined to have a shitty life just based on the day I was born. March 15th—the Ides of March as some people know it.

According to Shakespeare, it's a day of doom and misfortune. He kind of nailed that one.

The casket containing the life I would've had is slowly lowered into the grave. It feels like an eternity before it finally stops.

I step up first, peering down into the open ground at the mahogany casket her parents chose for her. It's beautiful with floral details carved onto the smooth surface.

Rain droplets start to fall over it and run down the sides. It rains almost every day here, but today, it feels especially fitting. Like the heavens themselves are in mourning.

Behind me, I hear the sobs of my late fiancée's family. I

don't want to look at them. I've been avoiding eye contact this entire time. But as I turn, I know it's inevitable.

Mallory's mom looks at me through red, tear-stained eyes. And everything I've told myself since rushing into the hospital when I got the news—is true.

I don't deserve their sympathies.

If it weren't for me and my bright ideas, Mal would still be here. The life beating inside her would, as well. Today, would've been a celebration.

Instead... well, we're here. And I can't live with myself knowing what I know.

Mrs. Bennett takes my hand and looks at me solemnly. "You would've had a beautiful life together, Zane."

I don't know what to say to this woman. "I-I..." I stutter.

"It's okay," Mal's brother says next to her, placing a steady hand on my shoulder.

I just nod. There are no words for a family that has lost someone so dear to them. I make my way to the back of the crowd where my dad, Frank, and sister, Libby, wait for me under black umbrellas. I don't bother to open mine. I want to feel the raindrops hitting my skin.

At least feeling them will remind me that feeling anything is possible.

My dad leans over as I'm looking skyward, letting the rain attempt to wash away my guilt.

"We can't all win in this life, Zane. Some people just have all the luck... or the means to get lucky." I look over at him and he's staring out past the the family mourning in front of us. "I'm sorry for your loss," he says, before casting me a cold glance and strolling off.

Lucky? As if getting to live or die lies solely on a person's luck?

As soon as the service is over everyone disperses to their

vehicles. The rain has let up a bit. But the ground underfoot is wet and mushy. Mallory's brother comes up to me just as I'm about to get into my car.

"Hey, Zane. Wait up!" I sigh and turn to face him. "Mom just wants you to have this."

He hands me a yellow envelope with the letter Z scribbled on the front. I take it and look at him.

"For what it's worth, I think you would've made a great husband...and father, Zane."

I huff out a small laugh.

"I'm serious," he says with stern eyes.

"For what it's worth... thanks," I say to him.

He gives me a sad smile and places a hand on my shoulder, then turns to meet his family in their vehicle across the street from mine.

I see a few of them wave at me as they drive past. But Mrs. Bennett doesn't look at me. She has her eyes on the small plot where her daughter now rests as they pull away.

Maybe she senses something is off. Maybe she blames me too. Maybe Mal told her.

Once they're gone, I sit in my car for what feels like forever before I finally reach for the envelope and open it.

Inside, is a note. A short one.

It's not your fault. Live a great life for them.

I crumble the note in a fist and toss it onto the passenger's seat. The rage that bubbles up out of me needs an escape so I hit the steering wheel in front of me over and over again. Grunting with each hit.

The passenger door swings open and Libby climbs in shutting the door loudly behind her.

"Zane..." she whispers.

"I'm done, Lib," I say, jaw clenched.

"Today's been rough. But we're going to get through this, okay? I promise you, it won't always be like this. It won't always *feel* like this."

I rest my forehead on the steering wheel and don't say a word. Libby picks up the wrinkled paper and smooths it out. I assume she's reading it.

"She's right you know," Libby says softly.

I look at my sister. "It's not your fault, Zane. You can't blame yourself for something that was an accident."

Why does everyone feel the need to tell me that? Unless they're trying to convince themselves, too.

"Libby, I'm done, ok. I'm done trying to live up to what Granddad wanted for me. Tell Nana that Frank... he can just have it all."

Libby's eyes widen. "I'm not going to do that. You still have time, Zane."

I open the door and step out, turning to her, "I don't care anymore. It's not worth it."

"Zane!" Libby calls out, but I'm already slamming the door shut.

The rain picks up again and I can feel the cool drops seeping into my suit as I start walking toward the cemetery exit. I want to get as far away from here as I can. I pick up speed and start jogging.

My car pulls up next to me with Libby in the driver's seat. She's rolled down the window.

"Would you get back in here, Z? You'll get sick," she yells out.

I never want to be in a car again.

I might have Irish blood, but I've come to accept that I might be the unluckiest Irishmen to ever exist. It's best if anything good, just stay away from me. My sister included.

I sprint toward the headstones where vehicles can't reach.

And I run.

I run as fast as I can... from everything.

Chapter 1
Kesley
Seven Years Later

I hate him.

I hate his friends.

And I especially hate him and his friends on nights like this.

The photos on my wall shake again. The one with me holding my baby boy jostles on the nightstand from the roughhousing coming from next door.

I groan and roll over in my bed for what feels like the thirteenth time in the last five minutes.

He can't be serious.

I knew when my best friend announced that her pro-hockey-playing brother was moving into the apartment across from us again, it spelled nothing but trouble.

But this... this is just ridiculous.

Another loud bang and I hear the muffled voices of men shouting at each other followed by boisterous laughs.

Everything in my room vibrates from the bump of the bass coming from the speakers.

There's no way Libby is asleep right now with all this noise.

I throw the covers off of me and toss my legs over the side of the bed, sliding my slippers on, and reaching for my phone on my nightstand to check the time.

It's 1:32 am and I have to work in the morning. For the last few years I've been able to sleep peacefully every night. Now, there isn't a week that goes by that Zane O'Connor doesn't throw a stupid afterparty at his place.

The amount of half-dressed women and beefy hockey boys that I've seen over the last few months is enough to keep me from ever stepping foot into the Space City Arena where Libby's brother plays for the NHL.

The apartment I share with my best friend is dark right now. When my son is here, we usually leave at least a hallway light on for him. But right now, it's almost pitch black. All except for the small slither of light coming from the front door that is slightly ajar.

I hear a noise coming from Libby's room. *Either she's awake or...* I feel a jolt of adrenaline shoot through me.

What if we're being robbed? Or maybe someone's trying to kidnap Libby?

A million possibilities are running through my mind as I tip-toe to the coat closet, my heart pounding, and pull out the first thing I can find that can be used as a weapon.

My son's hockey stick... *sure.* That works.

I hear strange noises coming from Libby's room that sound like a woman being restrained. She's muffled.

Padding down the hallway, I push open the door to her room with the end of the stick and call out to her. "Lib, you ok?"

The noises suddenly stop. And I hear someone whisper, "Shhh."

"Lib, are you in there?" When I hear what sounds like a

man clearing his throat, I instantly panic. Libby *never* has a guy over. *Ever.*

Screaming, I push the door open and flip on the lights, wielding the hockey stick like Excalibur in the direction of the movement on the bed.

But it's *not* my roommate. It's one of the Houston Heatwave players rolling around with a busty blonde in Libby's bed.

He looks unfazed as he rolls off the woman and cocks his head at my weapon. "Sorry, did we wake you?"

"What are you doing in my apartment, you creep?" I spit out shaking my stick at him. Though I'm relieved it isn't a kidnapper at least.

The player has his hat turned backward and he smiles saying, "Zane said his sister lives here."

"So Zane put you up to this? Unbelievable." I yell out for Libby. But there's no answer.

"Chill," the player scoots off the bed frantically. I pull the hockey stick back ready to swing. "She's at the party," he says with his hands up.

Libby? *My* ride-or-die, bestie for the restie, is partying... with the enemy?

I throw the hockey stick at the player and he catches it with ease. "Hey! Where are you going?" He follows me down the dark hallway leading to our open living room.

"I'm shutting it down," I say through gritted teeth.

"Joshy!" The blond calls out to him from Libby's bed. "Hello... aren't you going to finish what you started?"

I roll my eyes in disgust halfway to the front door. "You're lucky my son isn't here right now, or I'd be calling the police to escort you out."

"You can't shut down the party," the one called Joshy says, ignoring my threat.

9

I pull open the door and the music blasting from next door sounds like it could be coming from a full-on nightclub.

Josh follows me begging, "Please, whatever you do. Just please don't tell Zane I was at your place."

I turn to look at him in the light of the hallway and the guy's charming smile is dazzling. It's almost enough to make me swoon, but not nearly enough to win over my char-broiled heart.

Turning away from him, I kick the half open door to Zane's apartment, ignoring the player's pleas behind me.

"Zane!" I yell out. Inside, the lights are off, strobe lights fill the space with color and patterns. The music drowns out any chance of being heard.

My head jerks in every direction in search of the six foot five owner of the apartment.

In one corner, the furniture is pushed back and shirtless men are wrestling on the ground. They're surrounded by girls in low-cut dresses cheering and spraying beer on them.

In the middle, there's a dance battle taking place. People are surrounding the two guys in the middle; oohing and ahhing.

And there to my right, sitting like a king of chaos perched upon his kitchen island, surrounded by beautiful women and pounding down a beer... is Zane O'Connor.

His wavy brown hair is disheveled and a fallen piece swoops just above his eyes. Those eyes—deep blue, danger-ous, and full of so many secrets.

He's wearing a Heatwave t-shirt with his number eighty-two in large bold letters in case anyone forgets who he is—the Houston Heatwave's resident bad boy.

His eyes meet mine as he brings the bottle down from

his lips and a wicked grin stretches across his face. I'm frozen in place as his eyes slowly rove my body and now I realize I'm dressed in nothing but a silk negligee and some slippers. I'm not even wearing a bra.

I quickly cover up by crossing my arms over my chest. He looks pleased with himself. His smirk pulling just one corner of his mouth. And for the tiniest moment, I feel like the only one in the room.

But that grin he has disappears the moment he sees Josh-i-locks behind me trying to get my attention.

"Seriously, Zane didn't say I could go in there. I just assumed it would be ok. Please..." Joshy pleads.

This place is chaos. *Zane* is chaos. He thinks he's so big and bad.

Well... I'll show him.

I can feel Zane's gaze on me. Ignoring the women surrounding him. Even the one spinning around like an expert on his bachelor pad stripper pole to his left. I turn to the cute hockey player pleading with me.

"Kiss me," I tell him.

His bright eyes go big. "Uh... ha," he chuckles nervously, then his brows cinch. "Wait, are you serious?"

"Now, hurry up."

His eyes shift to Zane watching behind me and he shakes his head before pulling me to him by the waist and pressing his lips to mine.

I don't know why I think this will work. Why I think it'll get Zane to shut down the party. Maybe it's a hunch. But the second I pull away from the hockey boy's kiss, the lights come on and the music stops.

Everyone groans and there are people booing all around us.

Personally, I couldn't feel more satisfied.

"Party's over," Zane says, his voice gruff. He's no longer perched on his throne. Instead, he's at the DJ booth with a solid finger pointed to the door. "Everyone out."

Joshy looks at me and drops his hand from my waist in awe, "How did you do that?"

I give him a smirk. "Pleasure doing business with you... what's your real name?"

"Joshua. The boys just call me by my last name, Hicks."

The blonde girl from Libby's bed is now at his side, "Joshy, there you are. Come on a few of us are hitting up downtown."

"I'm never gonna hear the end of this," he whispers to me, before turning and throwing an arm over the blonde's shoulders. She looks back at me with a glare. And I don't know if he means from her or from my neighbor.

I turn to face Zane just as Libby is coming in from the balcony.

"Hey, what gives?" she says loudly to her brother, holding a cigarette out the door.

Zane nods over in my direction and I see when her lips form the word *shit*. She quickly puts out the cigarette and kicks the butt outside.

I walk over to them and Libby talks first.

"Ok, Kes, just... hear me out. We're celebrating a Heatwave win!" she says it like there's no arguing her logic.

"It's a Heatwave win *every* night there's an earsplitting afterparty like this."

"Yeah, but none that happen when Liam is at your parent's place and I'm about to leave for a really, really long time," she expounds.

I look at Zane who's now standing arms crossed behind her watching me through slitted eyes.

"I wasn't the one who shut it down, Lib. So if you wanted to party with the rowdy Heatwave crew then you can blame the caveman behind you."

People are shuffling out around us. Girls are picking up their tossed heels and making plans to hit up other places. The chatter around us only dies down when they walk by Zane, and picks back up as they exit.

Libby looks back at her brother.

He shrugs. "I'm tired."

I know he's not tired. He's saying that because he doesn't want to admit that me kissing one of his teammate's irritated the living daylights out of him.

A few of Zane's teammates come up to him to say good-night. "You good, Z?" asks the one who I think might be the team captain.

"All good, Landry, just tired... from the game." Zane glares at me.

I wish I could say I understand our dynamic. I wish I could say that it makes sense. But it doesn't. Not to me—and most definitely not to him.

I also don't understand why after so long he decided moving back in next door would be a good idea when we both can't stand each other.

But if I were to take a wild guess, the answer is standing two feet in front of me with her dark red hair flowing over her shoulders and her pouty lips showing us her disappointment.

"You coming, Libby?" One of the boys next to the team captain asks. He's shorter than the other guys, which is still taller than most guys. But he has a softness to him.

She looks at me and then at her brother. "No, Fergie, you boys go ahead. It's getting late." They pat Zane on the shoulder and follow everyone else out.

Once the apartment is empty. I turn to Zane.

"This has got to stop."

"From what I can recall... I lived here first," he says.

"And from what I can recall, you weren't always such an asshole," I snap back.

Libby groans and plops into the nearest chair. "Enough already. You two drive me insane with all this hostility. We're neighbors. She's my best friend," Libby throws her hands in my direction. "And he's my one and only brother," she says tossing them toward Zane.

"And none of those things are going to change. So if we want to co-exist... something's gotta give."

"He has a party every week. It's a Thursday. Some people have real jobs. It's inconsiderate."

Libby wouldn't know. She parties a lot. Having a trust fund gives her the distinct privilege of not having to report to a boss every morning.

"I *have* a real job," Zane growls out. "And you call what you do a real job? You write headlines for a gossip site and moonlight at a bar three nights a week. Those are hardly *real* jobs."

I can feel the rage boiling into my chest. How dare he judge my life like he has everything together. "I'm doing the best I can to support me and *my* son, ok. And I know they're both shitty jobs with shitty pay, which is why I'm not able to afford a place *and* keep my son in private school *and* pay off all my debts... but at least I'm trying. And for you to just stand there and judge me when your daddy's been the one to give you everything you own," I scoff. "You're a real piece of work."

I turn on my heel and my slippers slap the floor with each step. I open the door and slam it shut behind me. When I get to my room, I slink down to the floor in tears.

Damaged Defender

I need to get out. I can't live next to this man anymore. It's too much and I'm at my breaking point.

Chapter 2
Zane

"**G**o away," I yell to whoever is pounding on the door of my condo at this ungodly hour. It's probably one of the guys wanting to grab beers since we have the day off.

"Open up, you big oaf!" The female voice calls out from the hall.

Nope. Not one of the guys.

I groan, rolling over in my sheets and covering my head with a pillow. The pounding continues. And when I still don't get up, my phone starts vibrating. Incessantly. It keeps vibrating until it falls off the nightstand with a loud thump.

"Ugh, Libby!" I growl out, tearing the sheets off of me. I grab a pair of underwear from the top drawer of my dresser and slip them on before heading down the winding metal staircase that leads to the main living area from my bedroom.

The windows are all wide open and I squint realizing I forgot to draw the shades last night before plopping down on my bed. When I get to the last step, my heel slips on

16

some spilled beer from a bottle left on the floor and I land right on my ass.

Grumbling out obscenities, I rub my backside and finally make it to the door. I leave the chain in its place and open it only slightly to peek through the small slit.

"What do you want, Lib?"

My sister waits with her arms crossed and a scowl on her face. "Took you long enough. Open up."

"No."

"We need to talk," she says moving a hand to her hips.

"If this is about last night, it can wait," I say, moving to shut the door. But she places a boot in the door jam. "It can wait," I growl out again.

"Zane. It's not about last night." She holds up a stack of papers and pushes it closer to the door so I can read the words before saying sternly, "It *can't* wait."

I don't have the energy to deal with this right now. I roll my neck eliciting a crack and take a quick inventory of my space.

The boys left the place a mess. And I'm sure at some point we held an amateur wrestling match because there are chairs turned over and my coffee table in the open living room is pushed off to the far corner.

I huff out a sigh before kicking her shoe away and closing the door. A second later I open it wide and step behind it for her to walk through, gesturing for her to come in and bowing sarcastically for the princess.

She jerks her designer purse closer to her body as she steps through, "Didn't look this bad in the dark. Your place is disgusting."

"You're disgusting," I fire back.

"Oh, grow up, Shrek. You can drop the whole ogre act. I know you just do that to get me to stay away." She pushes some pizza boxes aside, takes a seat on one of the leather barstools at the kitchen island, and turns to face me. "Still running around in tighty whities? Some things never change."

I look down at my choice of underwear. Not my best option, I'll admit that. She grabs the hoodie that is lying on the barstool next to her and tosses it at me.

I tie it around my waist and turn it around to cover my junk.

"Zane," she says seriously. My tired eyes meet her pleading ones. "It's been seven years."

I wipe a hand over my face and groan. "That's what this is about?"

"Of course it is. You told me—"

"I know what I told you, Lib. But it's too late to do anything about it now."

Libby glares at me and then takes a swift look around the condo that I've made my own again over the last few months. Her eyes meet mine.

"Do you seriously want to just play hockey and retire a penniless man with no family? Nothing to live for except to replay your glory days in the NHL?"

"You're being dramatic."

"Zane, Granddad's estate—that's *our* home. Not this sad consolation prize Dad tried to convince us was a huge win," she waves a hand around my apartment. "We can't let our home just get donated. He wanted us to have it."

"Yeah, well... his stipulations are a bit over the top. You've said so yourself. Besides, it's too late anyway."

"There's a grace period and you know it. Regardless if you follow through with his stipulations or not; I'm done letting you drink your life away. It's been *seven years*," she emphasizes. "You told me to help. That you just needed some time and you'd be okay. Well, time hasn't changed you, Zane. So something has to change since you won't." She's exasperated.

I guess I would be too if I had to deal with me as a brother and now neighbor, too.

"What do you want me to do, Lib? The team needs me. If I lose focus, they lose games. Bottom line. I can't be distracted by..." I point to the papers in her lap. *"That,"* I say.

She crosses her arms where she's sitting. "That's what you've told yourself for years, Zane. The team comes first. And I get it, trust me, I do."

"I don't think you do," I roar at her.

"Take it down a notch, Hulk. You're disturbing the neighbors," she says picking at a nail, unfazed by my outburst.

Oh sure. *She* can storm into my place anytime she wants and rile me up, but God forbid I disturb her best friend.

"I don't care who's around... you're the one disturbing your neighbor. Now can you please leave so I can get back to sleep?" The pressure building in my head makes it feel like it's about to burst.

"Zane, listen to me for once. You're a grown man. And right now, you have grown man problems, my friend."

"Problems?" I deadpan.

"Yes, problems. Whether or not you want to admit it. You drank away your twenties. You pushed aside any responsibility except your duty to the Heatwave. And now, we're at risk of losing everything Granddad worked for because you want to keep running away and pretending like *this* doesn't exist." She picks up the will and shakes it at me.

I huff out a laugh. The nerve of this woman. She wakes

me up. And dares to point fingers at me like she's some kind of saint that's got it all together.

I cross my arms ready to be done with this conversation. Libby doesn't know the first thing about problems or the responsibility of people counting on you.

"Look, I'm packing up right now. We've put off this conversation long enough." She leans back on the butcher's block kitchen island behind her and waits for my reaction. "I need to know you're going to be okay, Zane... to deal with all of this... without me around to pick up the pieces."

"We're a shoo-in for the playoffs. We got our friends and family game this weekend. We have an actual chance for the cup this year, Lib."

"I know, Z. And trust me when I say I want to be here for you. But all I've done is be here for you. Put aside my career and my dreams to be here for you," she says with a sigh. She holds my gaze and I nod. Libby, as aggravating as she can be, has always been my number one fan.

She was the bored sibling who would come up with chants for the families to practice for game days, as a kid. She came to all my games. All my practices. And she didn't have to.

"I know. And I know that's not fair for you."

"Thank you," she says.

"But I'll be honest, I don't think I'll ever be able to do what Granddad wanted."

"You gave up a long time ago," Libby says softly. "But if you'd just drop the whole bad boy who doesn't give a shit act... maybe someone will be able to see what I see in you."

I drop my arms, "And what's that?"

"Somebody who really is husband material. Someone who fights for the ones he loves. Someone who's more like Granddad than he thinks he is."

"I'm nothing like him," I admit. "Not me, not dad... Granddad was a different breed."

Our dad, Frank O'Connor, isn't our biological father. But he's the only *dad* we've ever known. Our real father, Finn O'Connor, was mugged downtown when I was only two. He died of injuries from stab wounds. Libby was still in our mother's belly at the time.

But Frank, well, he owns half of Houston thanks to a legacy of hard work and good business sense that he picked up from our grandfather. The man who's will is now sitting on my kitchen counter. Taunting me. Reminding me of how I've fallen short. How all the O'Connor men have. Despite all our accomplishments.

Libby grows somber and stares at me without saying another word. I purse my lips knowing she just wants me to confirm that she has nothing to worry about while she's away. That I'll still fulfill my duties. Step up and save what our family has built over generations.

"I'll be okay," I assure her.

She closes her eyes and breathes in deeply, letting it go in one big rush of air. I don't think she believes me. I hardly believe me. But if this is what she needs to permit herself to go follow her childhood dreams of fashion shows and exclusive parties full of opportunity and expensive champagne, then fine, I'll give it to her.

At least she'll be out of my hair for a while so I can drink in peace, without the party police coming for me. I just have to figure out a way to get her roommate to want to leave. The parties alone haven't been enough.

She reaches for my shoulder. I watch her through glaring eyes as she looks up at me. "I know I can't be here when you need the most support. The playoffs. The inheritance. It's a lot for any person. But Kes is right next door if you ever need anything. You're not alone. Just stop being such an asshole and maybe she'll actually warm up to you again."

There's a warmth in her gaze as she searches my face. Libby's the closest person to me other than my hockey brothers. Our parents aren't the most dependable people.

One, because when our father passed, our mother was never the same again. She gave up her parental rights and our father's younger brother took us in. And two, Frank's priority was never me and Libby... it was always acquiring more. We weren't his real kids, after all. His real kids are the businesses and properties in his ever growing portfolio.

But Libby's best friend and roommate, Kesley Brooks, would prefer I be the one to leave to Europe if she had her way.

"I think you and I both know your best friend can't stand me."

She chuckles. "No she can't. But give her a chance, Zane. She's just a little..."

"Opinionated? Uptight?... Square?" I finish for her.

"She's not square," she says in defense of her girl.

I think about the way she kissed Hicks in front of me last night. She did it to piss me off, I'm almost sure of it. And it worked. So maybe she's right, not square. She's cunning.

But I am right about the first two things. We both know it. Libby and Kesley have been friends for a while now. They didn't meet until they were teens but they helped each other grow.

Kesley has turned Lib into a responsible, somewhat thriving adult human. And Libby... well she reminds Kesley to let her hair down every once in a while. Not that Kesley ever does it. But the reminder is there nonetheless.

"She thinks I'm nothing more than an Irish-American thug."

Her brows cinch together. "That's because you kinda are."

I shove her shoulder lightly.

Libby laughs. It's light and airy and all Lib. And I already miss her knowing she won't be in the crowd screaming at the ref at the top of her lungs the next time I get shoved into the penalty box.

"Like I said, just give her a chance." Libby's hazel eyes plead with me. She looks so much like the pictures of our mom now. I don't know how I missed it before.

After a moment, I say, "I'll think about it."

She shakes her head as she steps over scattered bottles and cans, finally reaching the front door. "But she's right you know. You're kind of a heathen. It's time you get your shit together. And you better do it fast, bro."

I cross my arms over my chest and cock my head to the side. "Go take your stupid pictures all over Europe. Let me handle the will."

"Fine. Go win your stupid cup," she says with a wink before walking out the door. Leaving it wide open.

I shake my head and cross the living space to go close it behind her, "It'd be nice if you could close the door on the way out."

"What?" A familiar voice says from the hall. And it isn't Libby's.

Chapter 3
Zane

I open the door wider and see Libby's best friend locking the door to their unit just a few feet from me.

"Kes," I nod to her, composing myself and preparing for her impending wrath.

"Zane," she acknowledges back with an assessing glare as she takes in my attire. "You... ok?"

"Yep," I lean on my doorway. "Couldn't be better."

I know she's only asking because she knows what today is. Otherwise, she'd probably just ignore me and leave to work.

She drops her hand from the doorknob and turns to lean on her door facing me.

"Well, you're wearing a hoodie like it's an apron and I'm pretty sure you don't have on any pants. I'd say you could probably be better." She tilts her head, studying me.

I take in her black blazer and matching pencil skirt. "You going to a funeral?"

She shakes her head, "I told you. I have a real job."

"Tell me, is part of your job requirement to have a giant

stick up your ass at all times? Or did one just happen to get stuck in there?" I cock my head at her.

She looks at me through slitted eyes, "You've got a lot of nerve, O'Connor." She says my last name like it's coated in poison and needs to get the taste out of her mouth immediately.

"Where's Liam?" I ask, changing the subject. "Libby said he wasn't here."

She breathes in deeply, aware that I'm trying to change the subject. She pulls her favorite local bookstore tote forward; the one that says *I'm all booked* in whimsical letters, and drops her keys into it. "What's it to you?"

"Well, of the three of you who live next door, he's by far my favorite."

"And the world just exists to make you happy. Right?" she says sarcastically. "Get over yourself."

Kesley reaches for her perfectly arranged ponytail and tightens her golden locks even more. As if the woman needs to be wound up any tighter.

"Get over myself? Kesley, nobody can say a word to you without you twisting it and making it into something bigger than it is. Loosen up."

"Ever think that maybe it's just *you* I don't like exchanging words with, caveman," she says with a bite.

The door opens behind Kesley and she takes a step back as Libby pokes her head out.

"Are you two serious right now?" Libby hisses. "Can't you just talk like normal humans? At normal human decibels?"

"That would require your brother to be a normal human," Kesley retorts. "And maybe if he kept his music at normal human decibels last night, then I wouldn't be cranky from lack of sleep thanks to our inconsiderate neighbor here." She throws her hand in my direction.

I give my sister a death glare that communicates, *See what I'm talking about?*

Libby throws her head back and groans. "Ok, look. I'm going to need the two of you to not kill each other while I'm away. I've put this Euro trip off *for years.* And I can't play referee to your stupid little catfight from thousands of miles away. So you're both going to have to get over yourselves and love thy fucking neighbor. Got it?"

Kesley and I don't say anything. We just scowl at each other.

"Ok. Looks like you're going to need a ref after all," Libby says into our awkward silence. "Z, when's your friends and family game again?"

My eyes shoot to my sister. "Saturday, why?"

"Great. Kesley, what are you doing Saturday?" Libby turns to her friend.

"Oh, no. We're not doing this," Kesley says with a sarcastic chuckle and both hands up.

"Kes, Liam is with your parents for Spring Break, right? So unless you miraculously found a date for Saturday. I know you're free."

Kesley shakes her head in disbelief.

"So it's settled. Kesley will go to your game in my place," Libby announces.

I say, "I don't want her at my game." At the same time, Kesley says, "I'm not going to his game."

Libby raises a finger, "Uh-uh. You're not doing this for each other. You're doing this for *me.*"

And with those words she catches us both. Because despite how we might feel about each other, Kesley and I share one thing in common. We both love Libby.

We stare at each other from our respective places in front of our doors.

"Kesley, I'll leave you one of Zane's jerseys to wear—"

"Oh no, not a chance. She can't wear my jersey," I protest.

According to my grandfather's will, I have thirty days to find a wife. I can't have my sister's best friend throwing off potentials by showing up wearing one of *my* jerseys.

"*She* is standing right here and can speak for herself, caveman. I don't want to wear your stupid jersey anyways," she barks back.

"Guys... guys." Libby rubs a hand down her face. "Wear the jersey. Don't wear the jersey. I don't freakin care. Just... don't kill each other. Okay?"

Kesley plasters on a fake smile. And I return it with one of my own.

Libby looks from me to Kesley and just shakes her head. "This is going to be so great."

She's being sarcastic. But I'm not when I say with a glare toward Kesley, "Don't wear the jersey."

Kesley Brooks has been a staple in our lives ever since Libby took her under her wing when she moved to town as the new girl in our preppy high school.

Kesley had two loud, fast-talking sisters that I never cared to get to know. But she was the quiet one amongst them. And I would've been a total idiot not to try to shoot my shot with the beautiful green-eyed, blonde-haired bookworm. Every guy did at the time. Even if she was two grades below me.

But in her very Kesley way, she laid it on me pretty thick, "*I don't date jocks, sorry.*" And just went back to reading her book. I took the hint. Ever since then, she decided I wasn't someone worth her time.

And I've made it known, I'm not one to put up with her sass.

So yeah, the last thing I want is for her to show up to a friends and family game wearing my jersey.

Kesley looks at the watch on her left wrist. "This has been so much fun. But I have work to do." She sidesteps Libby and stalks over to the elevators.

"Try not to bite anyone's head off, Simba," I say waving to her as the doors close in front of her. She pushes a button and the doors open again, Libby and I both watching her.

"If you ever watch the movie, Zane, you'd realize that's not the correct reference." Then she disappears behind the elevator doors.

The woman always has to get the last word.

"Her ponytails too tight," I say to Libby who is still standing in the doorway.

"Yours would be too if you had a son to keep in private school while working two jobs and barely making ends meet," she says to me.

"She has Liam in private school? Pearson Prep?"

Libby nods.

"How?"

I know all too well about that private school. It's the same one we all met in. The one Kesley and her sisters went to before they disappeared because their family couldn't afford the tuition one year.

"I told you... she works for it. Now, I gotta finish packing. Please, whatever you do... don't fuck that up," she says pointing to the closed elevator doors.

"Me?" I say, grabbing my chest.

"Yes! She's a good friend if you would just let her be one."

I don't need Kesley Brooks as my friend. I need her as far away from *friend* as she can possibly be.

"I don't need another friend, Lib. But thanks," I say turning back to enter my apartment.

When I step back inside my place I whip off the stupid hoodie and start climbing the steps to get back under the covers. I take a nosedive into the bed and pull the sheets back over me.

What feels like seconds after I close my eyes, I hear the familiar words, "Hello, big boy. Muah. Muah. Muah. Come give me a kiss."

"You have *got* to be kidding me," I groan. "Muppet, shut up!"

The squawk comes from the far end of my apartment.

"Oh, shut up you big Oaf," the bird starts its broken record.

I pull the pillow back over my head and try to silence the noise of the squawking parrot that has been my companion for way too long. How long are these things even supposed to live? If they're anything like sea turtles, I'm done for.

My phone buzzes on the floor where it fell earlier. That's it. I give up. Today is the day nobody wants me to sleep.

I hear you all loud and clear.

I reach down to pick it up. The name *Captain Lando* pops up on the screen along with Keelan Landry's close-up selfie of his face with his mouth open wide and sticking his tongue out. He had saved it to my contacts over Christmas when I left my phone unattended at the team party at his place. When I get drunk, I'm an open target for these guys. And that happens pretty often.

I hit answer, "If this is about brunch... I'm not going."

"Pfft. That ship has sailed, buddy. We have new and improved plans," his voice rings out through the speaker of my phone.

"Landry, not today, man. I just want to sleep. We partied enough last night."

"For the win. This one's for you, O-zone."

That stupid nickname. My team calls me that because I'm known for helping them keep the play in the offensive zone with my defense. That, and somehow in Keelan Landry's mind, Zane O'Connor somehow translates to O-zone and it just stuck.

"Well, I don't want it," I huff flipping onto my back and bringing an arm over my head to block out the light.

"*Well*, that's too bad because..." he trails off.

"Because what?...Keelan? Because what?"

There's another knock on my door. This time it's much louder and much more annoying. It must startle Muppet because he squawks from across the loft, "Hello, big boy! Hello, big boy!"

Fuck. Me.

I reluctantly make my way to the door, for the second time this morning. And when I open it five of my teammates greet me with a cake in the shape of a penis. A very aggressive-looking penis.

"Uh, what the hell is this?"

"Blow it," Landry says motioning to the lit candle at the head of the penis cake.

"I hate you guys so much." They all chuckle.

"You love us," says Michael Ferguson, one of our first-line forwards. He goes by Fergie, for short.

"You gonna let us in so we can eat this incredibly detailed cake that some blushing bride refused to have at her bachelorette party?" says Joshua Hicks, his counterpart on the first line. The empty space from his chipped tooth that he's been sporting for months is now closed. No wonder Kesley didn't hesitate to kiss him. He actually looks normal.

I step aside to let the boys through.

"Why are you guys up so early? And when'd you fix your tooth, Hicks?"

Ryker Balinger, our starting goalie, walks in last slapping a hand onto my shoulder, "It's almost noon. You never showed up for brunch."

What? I look at my watch. He's right. I must've passed out after all.

"And it's been a week since I got the new chiclet. You just noticed?" Hicks says smiling brightly.

Damn. I've been out of it. How much did I drink this week?

"We couldn't let you be alone on your birthday," Landry says from the kitchen, taking down some plates from a cabinet. "How old are you now anyways?"

I rub my face, trying to wake up.

"It's been seven years," Libby's voice from earlier echoes in my head.

"Thirty. I'm thirty," I tell them, still in my tighty whities as I approach the now-cut penis cake.

Our team captain hands me the head of it on a plate. "Well, here's to your dirty thirties, big boy," he announces.

"Here, here," Hicks says, grabbing whatever beers are left in my fridge.

I look to the only player who hasn't said a word. Trevor Sincaid, the newest defenseman, just shrugs. "I tried to stop them," he admits.

"Well then you really suck at defense, Rookie," I say with a smirk.

The boys all sucker punch him in the shoulder and he takes it like a champ.

I should be happy. Happy that they care. Happy that I'm not alone.

But that deep, dark sinking feeling in the pit of my stomach is more overwhelming than anything else at the moment. And I get the urge to drink and just be left alone.

Maybe then I won't have to think about the inheritance clause my late grandfather left in his will that's currently being covered up by an empty pizza box.

Or my late fiancee and the tiny life that was snuffed out along with hers. There would have been a seven-year-old today to celebrate a birthday with.

Instead, it's just me.

In tighty whities.

Surrounded by empty beer bottles and excited faces that could never understand.

And for them, I swallow down my pride... and take a bite of the stupid penis cake.

Chapter 4
Kesley

"So how's it going with that sweet *Latino* boy you were seeing?"

I cringe at the way my mom says *Latino*.

"Well, Mom. It's not. It was just a date. We weren't seeing each other, per se."

I hear the tsk on the other end of the line.

"Mom, I'm twenty-eight. I still have the rest of my life ahead of me."

"Kes-ley," she says displeased.

"What do you want me to do? Pull a husband out of my ass?"

"Kesley Marianna Brooks," her voice is stern. And I suddenly feel five again. "Of course, not. I know you're trying to do right by Liam. It's just..."

I pinch the bridge of my nose as I look around at the empty cubicles surrounding me. Most of my colleagues work from home or coffee shops.

I like to come in, mostly because nobody else is here this early. And it's easier to work outside of the chaotic apartment I share with my best friend and my son.

"It's just what, Mom?"

"If you ever want to—I don't know—give him a sibling..."

I groan.

"I'm just saying it's not going to get any easier with age. You've seen how John and Kira have struggled for their third," she continues.

"You know what else doesn't get any easier with age, Mom? More kids."

She's silent on the other end. She had three of us. She's more of an expert than I could ever hope to be. But she says a million things with her silence.

"Look, Mom. If or when the right person comes along, we'll decide what's right for us in terms of marriage, kids, and houses. Right now, I'm just trying to—"

"Build a career," she answers. "Yeah, yeah. I know."

The disappointment dripping from her doesn't make it any easier. Ever since I graduated college five years ago, with a little boy to also take care of, I've been hearing the same thing. Every phone call. Every family gathering. They worry for me.

But I know it's more for Liam to have a dad. A father figure that is present and able to be there when he needs it the most.

"Did you already get the time off for the long weekend?" She changes the subject and I'm grateful for the relief. For now, at least. The annual Spring Break trip with my family will be a whole other ordeal.

"Always do. You know I wouldn't miss it."

"Good," she says, sounding more chipper. "We have a room with a spare bed for you if you want to... you know, invite someone."

"Mom, I'm not bringing anyone."

I don't know what's more embarrassing, being the only

sibling out of the three of us to still be single. Or to be *so single* my own mother is practically begging me to bring somebody, *anybody*. A stranger off the street would work for her at this point.

"I just don't want you to be lonely, honey. That's all. You work hard. You care for Liam. You deserve good love too."

Good love. That phrase sticks with me for some reason. Have I ever had *good love*? Not from a man that wasn't my flesh and blood.

No. From the men I've dated, I've had broken love. Left-over love. Unprioritized love. And I guess none of those should be considered *love,* to begin with.

Just in the nick of time, I see my boss walk in. I look at the clock. It's only 8:15. A little early for him. But I'll take the distraction.

"Mom, I gotta go. Jeremy's here," I whisper into the phone.

"Oh. Jeremy Clark? As in, editor in chief, Jeremy Clark?"

She sounds way too excited about the prospect of me and my boss being alone in the office together.

"There's nothing there, Mom. This isn't one of your spicy romance novels," I whisper into the phone. "I gotta go."

She chuckles, "A mother can only hope. Bye Kessie."

I quickly disconnect and get back to pretending I'm typing just as Jeremy is approaching my work area on his way to his office.

"Ms. Brooks," he nods his acknowledgment. His scent hits me before I can even get a word out.

"Hello, Mr. Clark. Good morning," I say returning his nod and attempting to blink away the tears that start to form along my lash line from the sting his fragrance invokes.

"You know, I'm glad you're here. I was hoping to get

your help on a little project we've been discussing with the creative department. Would you please follow me to my office?"

My heart sinks.

I've never been considered for any of The Houston Pulse's special projects. As an online news media company, The Pulse, as it's known here in town, is at the cutting edge of journalism. And they only brought me in a few years ago for my very specific set of highly attuned skills.

Clickbait. Yep, I write clickbait.

My sole job is to create captivating and sensational headlines that entice weary internet users to click on our links.

So am I a journalist? Not really. So far, all I've been tasked to do since taking this job a few years back is churn out headlines like it's nobody's business. And it's my headlines that lead readers to the stories my colleagues are tasked to write.

It's okay for now. But of course, I'd love to be taken more seriously as an *actual* journalist. Then maybe I could put that degree I worked so hard for to good use. And maybe then, my family could drop this ridiculous notion of wanting me to get my life together in the only way they know how. *Marriage.*

But *this*, this might be my big break. So I grab a notepad and pen and follow Jeremy down the sea of empty cubicles.

His cologne wafts into my nostrils as we walk and though it smells expensive it's almost—what's the right word... *screechy?* I don't know if a cologne can smell screechy, but somehow his does.

Screechy cologne aside, someone like Jeremy must have a slew of potential wifey candidates just pining after him.

Wealthy. Accomplished. Confident. He'd be a catch

any mom would be happy to welcome into the family. And he's not bad looking. He has perfect, pearly white teeth. His hair is dark and pushed back in a suave style.

Jeremy is put-together, unlike the disheveled caveman I'm forced to now live across thanks to his relationship with my roommate. No, Jeremy is polished. I'll give him that.

I watch the back of his head as he walks, back straight, like a man who has walked into plenty of board rooms in his lifetime and commands attention.

We make it to his office. There he switches on the light and motions to the chair across from his desk.

I've never actually been inside Jeremy Clark's office. People here have a better chance of getting a meeting with the president of the United States than being invited into the bright corner office of our editor-in-chief. I don't say anything. I just take in the surroundings as I make my way to the seat.

The big mahogany bookshelf is full of thick hardcovers. There's one sole painting of what looks like a heartbeat in multiple colors next to a cacophony of awards lining the shelves near his window. They're all carefully selected to show just how big and important the man who summoned me is.

He sets his messenger bag down on the couch and unbuttons his suit top before taking a seat on the cushy desk chair.

I try to look... accomplished. Straighten my posture. Hold my neck up more than usual.

I write for a living and my posture is atrocious. My mom never hesitates to remind me of it when she's around. No doubt thinking it's a contributing factor as to why I have no prospective husbands.

"So, Ms. Brooks," he folds his fingers together and puts

his hands on top of the desk as he leans in toward me. "I'm just going to cut to the chase here."

"Okay," I gulp.

Suddenly, it feels like he just called me in here to fire me and I'm starting to feel somewhat deflated and a whole lot less confident.

"You write the stuff that gets eyes on our work."

I don't know what he wants me to say. It's not a question. I just nod.

"And that's great. It is." The way he feels the need to reassure me, it doesn't feel like it is.

"*But* as a news media company," he continues. "The Pulse is seen as a unique news source with unique angles on all current events. I take the product we put out very seriously if you can't tell." He motions to the shelf full of awards.

Ew. Even if dating Jeremy *were* an option, his arrogance is an absolute no for me. There's a fine line between a confident man and an arrogant one, and though I don't know him well, I can already peg him as someone who would ride that fine line daily.

I'll be sure to bring that up to my mom next weekend so she can put to rest the Kesley and Jeremy fantasy she has in her head.

"That being said, we're hoping to elevate the reader experience. Take them into the various worlds we cover daily. Give them an in-depth, first-hand experience."

"Sir, I-I don't think I'm following. Are you suggesting more in the field kind of journalism?"

"Not just field journalism, Ms. Brooks. I'm talking about a virtual *experience*. I want the readers to feel like they're a part of the story. Like they have a front-row seat into their favorite topics."

I'm still not tracking. And if this man says experience one more time I might roll my eyes without even considering the consequences. But I hope the cinched brows and gentle nod of agreement I'm giving him say something else entirely.

"Here's what I need from you, Ms. Brooks." He gets up and walks over to his bookshelf and thumbs through a row of hardcovers until he lands on one and plucks it out.

He walks to the front of his desk so that we're only a few feet apart and lays the book down next to him as he leans back.

I lean forward to read the title. It's an encyclopedia of sports.

"Sports, Mr. Clark?"

He waves a finger in protest, "Na-ah, not just any sport. He opens it and turns to somewhere in the middle of the book. "What do you know about..." he turns it to me.

There on the page in bold black lettering is..."Hockey?" I ask. I'm sure I can't hide the scrunch of my nose when I say the word.

If it wasn't for Libby's brother and the teammates who frequent his place, I would say zero. I know *zero* about hockey.

Ever since Zane was selected to play for the Heatwave not long after they became an NHL expansion team, Libby has rarely missed a home game. So I live with a hockey expert... who is not going to be home for quite some time thanks to Fashion Week in Milan.

And Jeremy picked me for this which means he must know about my connection to the team.

"I-I honestly don't know much," I admit hoping he'll assign me something else. Seriously, *anything* else.

"Perfect," he beams shutting the book. "You don't need

to. But you do have an in, don't you Ms. Brooks? Somebody who can give you unrestricted access to what it is to be a hockey player in Houston, Texas? What it's like to play for a team that is working on recovering their reputation and garner respect in the league after years of failures."

Just as I suspected, Jeremy's been doing some digging into me.

"What are you asking, Mr. Clark?"

I'm getting nervous. This doesn't just feel like a news story. This feels like an infiltration. *Am I to be some sort of spy for The Pulse?*

"I'm asking you to dive in, Ms. Brooks," he says calmly. "Dive into the world of Heatwave hockey. Learn everything you can about Space City Arena. The players. The... management," he hesitates a moment when he says that. "And bring our readers along for the ride."

"Like an exposé? On the team?"

He shakes his head, "Not an exposé, we're not trying to get anyone in trouble here," he chuckles. Maybe it's in the small inflection change when he said that. Or how he's trying so hard to make it seem like that's not the purpose. But something feels off.

He must see the speculative look I can't hide because he adds, "I'll have in-depth journalists just like you in every area of Sports, Finance, Business, Politics, Entertainment. You name it, we're on it. And we're going to go from being the trusted source of news to one that brings the facts in a way that gives people an—"

"Experience. Yes, so you've said."

He places his hands in his lap looking rather pleased with himself. *Does he even know how annoying he comes across?* Nobody's ever told him, I'm almost convinced of it. If my pay wasn't at stake, I wouldn't mind informing him.

"Mr. Clark, I'm sure there's someone that's better suited for this particular project. Someone more familiar with the topic?"

He doesn't say anything. He just studies me. My fight or flight mode is about to kick in. The back of my head prickles. "Besides," I add. "Who's going to write the clickbait?"

It takes him a moment, but out of nowhere he just laughs, waving away my remark. "Oh, ha. We're doing away with your position, Ms. Brooks."

My heart skips a beat. Maybe two. And my face falls. "Um... excuse me?"

Shit. I just said that out loud. To the editor-in-chief. He returns to the seat at his desk and leans in again. The humor is now gone from his tone. "We need to be taken more seriously amongst our media peers. And sarcastic *churnalism* just isn't going to cut it. Besides, we have A.I. now so..." He waves a hand in the air as if that's that.

I shift uncomfortably in my seat and try to process what he's telling me.

"So... let me try to understand, Mr. Clark. If I don't take on this... project, then I'm out of a job. And you'll be having a robot do the work I do instead. Am I hearing this right?"

I'm doing a horrible job of hiding the disgust at my current predicament.

He tilts his head and with a smile says, "Well, a computer, not a robot. But yes, precisely."

I can't believe this. I don't have any other opportunities right now. Bartending thrice a week alone sure as hell won't pay my bills. Not to mention this is the last thing I need going into Spring Break with my family.

I can hear it already. *"No husband. No real job. Oh, Messy Kessie. Never can get her life together."*

I shake away the imaginary voices of my siblings and

their perfect families, with their perfect kids and their perfect houses. While I'm over here a single mom rooming with her best friend from high school. I have to do something.

"So? What do you say, Ms. Brooks? Are you up for the challenge?"

I shut the notepad in my lap. I haven't scribbled anything into it. But if this is how I can make a name for myself. Do something I can be proud of. Then I guess I have no other choice. I'm backed into a corner here. And when I get backed into a corner... I fight.

"I'll do it," I say with a nod.

"Excellent," he says, a grin stretching across his face. "You start today."

"Oh," I breathe out nervously.

He slides the sports encyclopedia to the edge of his desk. "You have two weeks to get me something good to run with."

I gulp. Two weeks to learn everything I can about a sport I've never even watched. *Awesome.*

"Ms. Brooks, The Heatwave are expected to make it into the playoffs for the first time in franchise history. So after your initial article, if all looks good, you'll become my official Heatwave hockey correspondent. No more clickbait. So make it good. Give our readers an experience," he says waving his hands over his desk like he's a magician.

"An experience," I repeat when really I just want to throw up. "Okay."

"That'll be all, Ms. Brooks." He opens his laptop and starts typing away without another glance in my direction.

I get up quietly and nearly trip over myself.

"Don't forget this," he taps on the book in front of him.

"Right," I chuckle nervously, sliding it off his desk and into my shaking arms.

"Oh, and Ms. Brooks?" I turn to look at him. "It's best if you keep this project between us," he urges.

I nod and walk out of his office feeling like my legs have turned to jello as I slump into my seat and groan.

So he *does* want me to be a spy. I just agreed to be a spy for The Pulse.

To keep my job, I remind myself. *For Liam. For a better life for him.*

I open my notepad to the first blank page and write the one word that will now be taking over every thought for the foreseeable future.

Hockey.

Chapter 5
Kesley

"You know you suck right?"

Libby laughs and tosses a pair of underwear at my face.

"You do!"

"Oh stop being such a baby! I'm doing you both a favor," she says as she lifts up a shirt to fold into her luggage.

"Please, oh wise one. Do explain to me how forcing your brother and me to hang out together is a favor."

She tilts her head and looks at me. "Do you seriously think I've been oblivious to the way you look at him?"

My jaw drops. "What are you talking about? My utter annoyance?"

"Or about how ever since he moved in you've been wearing grown-up clothes to go to work? Not just your jeans and Doc Martens. It's like you want him to see you in your pencil skirts and collared shirts."

I cannot believe the audacity of this girl. "I don't dress up for Zane to notice me, Libby. I dress up for myself. So that I feel better about myself and the fact that I went to college for four years, got my degree, and still somehow barely make enough to pay back my student loans."

She tosses another pair of underwear at me and this time I catch it before it hits my face.

"Bullshit. I know you, Kesley Brooks. Far better than you even know yourself. I know you take your coffee with oat milk because real milk gives you gas and almond milk makes you want to gag. I know you prefer to read the classics in paperback so people can think more highly of you but your Kindle is full of smut—"

"It's not smut... it's... colorful romance," I protest.

"And I know that when Ryker announced he was moving and Zane was taking back his penthouse, you cleaned for three days straight before you even commented on it. And when I finally asked you how you felt about it you replied, *'It's fine. I'm fine.'* Which is classic Kesley code for 'I'm *not* fine.'"

"I *am* fine. And that had nothing to do with your brother and everything to do with the fact that Christmas decorations were still up and we needed a good deep clean."

I throw the underwear back at her and she catches it in her hand and drops it into the luggage, shutting it and zipping it up. She moves the big black luggage bag to the corner of her queen bed and takes the empty seat next to me.

"If you're so fine... then why do you keep sending Liam to stay with your parents, Kes?"

My heart sinks. He has been spending most weekends away.

"And if you say it's because you have to work so hard and he needs childcare I will tie you up and hang you upside down until the truth comes out."

I give her a sidelong glance. "You're kind of evil."

She shrugs and tosses her long hair over her shoulder. "An evil genius maybe."

"Nope," I say getting up. "You're just evil."

"Well at least I'm not in denial," she says pointedly.

Denial. I'm not the one in denial. If anyone is in denial, it's the oblivious caveman next door she calls her brother.

I cross my arms and glare at her from the side of the bed.

She sighs. "Whatever your reasoning for sending Liam away nearly every weekend—"

"It *is* because I'm working two jobs and he deserves to have some fun."

"And what am I? Chopped liver? I am the most fun that kid will ever know," Libby says, the offense dripping off her lips.

"I didn't mean it like that, Lib. You are a fun aunt. The fun*est* aunt. Even more so than my own sisters."

"Thank you," she says, blinking slowly at me.

"It's the truth."

"No, I'm well aware. I've met your sisters."

That makes me laugh and she finally cracks a smile herself.

If people think I'm uptight, it's only because they haven't met the other Brooks sisters, Kira the oldest who runs her household like a small army. And Becka, the youngest and the highest achiever. She gives both Kira and me a run for our money with her three degrees and multiple six-figure earnings as the chief financial officer of one of Houston's newest and biggest alternative energy companies.

They may be high-strung, but unlike my sisters, I'm the only one who isn't settled down with a husband, a thirty-year mortgage, and multiple children. They may as well call me Lambchop and die my wool black because that's what I am, the black sheep of the family.

I look at Libby. My best friend in the entire world. She's never seen me as anything less than a boss babe who is killing it as a mom and as a career woman. Even when I told her I needed to pick up a second job to make ends meet. She never made me feel less than. Instead, she just offered to care for Liam on the nights I had to pick up shifts at the Breakaway Bar downtown.

She did offer to cover my expenses, but that would make me a freeloader and I am anything but that. But free childcare, yes, please. There's nobody better to watch my son.

"I'm going to miss you," I say under my breath.

She clears her throat theatrically and puts a hand up to her ear. "I'm sorry. Did you say something? Because for a second there I thought you said—"

"Yes!" I say louder. "I'm going to miss you and your stupid jokes. And your late-night chicken nuggets and Housewive binges."

She gives me an appreciative half-smile. The golden flecks in her eyes shine even more with the light pouring in through the cracks in the blinds.

"I'm going to miss you too my girl. Which is why..." She stands up and takes my hands. "I want you and Zane to try to get past your differences. You both need people. And you're both stubborn asses that need a good kick in the pants."

She swats my backside as she walks through the door and I just shake my head following her out into the kitchen.

"Fine. But only for you," I lift a finger in her direction.

"Great, then let's celebrate the end of an era."

"What era is that?"

"The one where I'm stuck playing referee between you and my brother. It's been a long road, but there's finally a light at the end of the tunnel." Libby reaches into a cabinet and brings down two wine glasses.

"What are you doing, Lib? It's only noon."

She purses her lips considering it. "You're right. A little early for wine." She puts the wine glasses back and reaches into the fridge, pulling out two beers instead. I stare blankly at my best friend.

"Oh, come on! It's my last day here for the next three weeks. Be bad with me, Kes."

I roll my eyes again and grab the bottle she's offering me. We crack them open and clink our bottles before taking long draws of the beer.

I bring the bottle down and wipe my lips on my sleeve, "But I'm not going to make it easy on him."

She rolls her head back and groans.

"I just mean... I'm wearing that jersey. Where is it?"

Libby perks up like she's totally on board with the idea of me getting under her brother's skin. She sets her beer on our kitchen island and grabs my hand. "Come and have your pick of number eighty-two's jerseys," she says leading me to her walk-in closet.

And I laugh to myself imagining my neighbor's face when he sees me in it.

Chapter 6
Zane

"She forced the girl that hates you to come to the game tonight?" Landry whistles. "Gotta admit, my sister's pretty savage. But Libby... she takes the cake."

"I told her not to bother." I move my bag from the bench to the floor of our locker room and take a seat.

"So what are you going to do if she does come?" Ryker asks as he puts on his gear.

I puff air out of my cheeks. "Are you kidding me? Kesley Brooks wouldn't step foot inside this arena if she knew I was here. It would take an act of God."

"Wow, that's surprising considering you're just so pleasant," Fergie teases me.

I roll my eyes at him.

"Does anyone have ball deodorant?" Hicks calls out from the showers.

I look over at Ryker and Fergie. Both of whom are shaking their heads in embarrassment.

"Your roommate," I remind them.

"Ex-roommate in my case," Ryker points out. "And for good reason."

Hicks strolls out of the shower buck naked, his junk out for all to see. We all shield our eyes.

"Pu-lease, like you guys haven't seen this package a thousand times?" He does a helicopter motion and puts his hands behind his head and I feel like we just time-warped back to my high school locker room.

"Why are you the way you are?" I say, throwing a towel at him.

Hicks just shrugs and walks over to the bench at his stall.

"Trust me, it's in everyone's best interest for me to have my ball deo. Lando, you got any?" he asks our team captain.

Landry rolls his eyes as he bends down and digs through his bag. He tosses a black tube in Hicks' direction and the forward catches it with ease.

Technically Landry's not even supposed to be here since he's still on long-term injured reserve. But we couldn't keep him away, even when he still had a cast on his leg. Hockey and family are everything to Landry. Which makes us all family to him.

He's a better man than me. I seem to be more in the habit of creating enemies. I'm surprised these guys even stick around.

"Are you serious? Sharing scrotum deodorant?" I cock an eyebrow at Hicks.

"A team that stays fresh together plays fresh together, O-zone," Hicks recites like it's a common phrase as he squeezes some of the fragranced gel into his hands.

"That's not even a thing," Fergie tells him with a raised brow.

"It is now," Hicks snaps back at him. "And you'll thank me in the future when you're walking by a girl you like and they go 'You have got to be the best-smelling hockey player I've ever met. Is that from Paris?'"

Chuckles erupt throughout the room.

"Hicks, no girl ever would say such a thing about your ball deodorant," I inform him as I pull on my shin guards.

"How would you know, O-zone? I haven't seen you with a girl the whole time I've known you."

"Not even on dating apps," Fergie confirms.

"Because *you* have such a great track record with girls from dating apps, don't you, Ferg?" Landry says sarcastically, slapping him on the back as he walks by him.

"That was one time," Fergie grits out. The guys laugh. Fergie's been known to fall prey to a catfish or two.

"I don't need dating apps," I say. "I've... got personality."

"Yeah, that's what he calls his right hand," Sincaid chimes in next to me making a crude gesture. The guys burst into a fit of laughs.

I shove him with my shoulder, "You've got a lot of nerve, Rookie. You're lucky we play for the same team. Anyway, I don't need any girl jacking things up for me. I got everything I need."

Though, that's not entirely true. I *do* need a girl. Specifically one willing to marry me within the next thirty—*nope*—twenty eight days, so that my family doesn't lose the enormous inheritance that's now riding on my shoulders. The thought of the task makes me sick to my stomach. Especially considering the final test of approval is my keen-eyed grandmother. She'd sniff a ruse out from a mile away.

Landry squints at me. "What?" I say to him, knowing he's got something on his mind.

"They're right, O-zone. You haven't had a girlfriend the whole time I've known you," he says deep in thought. "Wait, are you... do you not like..." He's struggling for the right words.

"Are you asking me if I'm gay, Landry?" I rise and slip on my pants. "No, I very much like women. But if I *were* gay... there's probably a better way to ask," I say sternly.

"Right, my bad. No judgment, I'm just trying to understand," Landry says.

"Maybe," Ryker offers. "He's scared that he's got no game." He cocks his head to the side and grins at me.

The guys all stop what they're doing and look at Ryker and then at me.

"He snags a girl, and suddenly he's the king of charisma. I've got game, Balsy. But thanks for your concern."

"That's exactly what someone with no game would say," Hicks teases.

"I've got game," I say again trying to assure them. Or myself... I'm not sure who exactly.

"Then prove it," Ryker says folding his arms over his chest and glaring at me.

"Yeah," some of the others chime in.

I look around at my teammates. "I don't have to prove anything to you bozos."

"It's cause he's got no game," Hicks and Fergie say together. And the guys all burst into laughs.

A knock at the entrance interrupts us as Coach Murray pokes his head in. "Everyone decent?"

"Are we ever?" Hicks and a few others reply. It's become our standard response anytime someone asks. They should all know better by now.

The Houston Heatwave players aren't your run-of-the-mill, bring-home-to-meet-mama types. We're the rowdy group that gets kicked out of restaurants and has a tendency toward bar brawls and time in the penalty box. Rules are more like suggestions to us. So decent? Nah. We meet the bare minimum requirements. Except maybe Fergie. He's the only straight arrow I know.

But Hicks does at least have the *decency* to pull a towel around his waist when he spots Coach.

Coach Murray walks in flanked by his assistant coaches. He runs a hand through his salt and pepper hair, most of which has come about from leading us the last few years. He places his other hand on his hip; his usual stance right before he delivers his pre-game speech.

"Well, boys... I," he pauses and the locker room bustle starts to die down as my teammates take their seats at the benches. "I'm... I'm kind of at a loss for words today." He laughs nervously.

He takes in the faces around the locker room. And slowly meets the eyes of all twenty-one of us.

"Look, we've all been through some serious shit this year," he continues. "Challenges in our personal lives. Changes in our professional lives. Players we love traded. New faces who we've had to grow to trust out there. But despite it all, you didn't let any of it stop you. You boys have given it your all this whole season and we're... well, we're finally here. We got one team to beat. One team to finish off. And we've earned a spot in the playoffs."

Heads are nodding around the now quiet room.

"This is the closest we've ever been. But I want you to know that no matter what happens tonight; you should be damn proud of how far you've come. I know I am."

Coach is usually dressed to the nines by now in some form-fitting suit and wearing a tie representing the team colors. Looking every bit like the silver fox that he is according to the whispers from the women on staff.

But tonight, he's here in his orange Heatwave tech tee, some workout pants, and tennis shoes. A retired player himself, he's just as much invested as every single one of us in this locker room. Coaching this team isn't easy. He's dealing with some major hotheads on and off the ice.

But now we've built up just the team we need to make it happen. We have fast-skating forwards who don't hesitate to take shots on goals. We have a goalie who's making it a habit to deny the other team access to our net. And then we have Sincaid and me, defenseman who make it our life purpose to check any player that tries to steal a puck.

I rub some topical anesthetic into my shoulder before putting on my pads.

"You'll make your families proud too, boys. They'll be cheering for you from the stands. Don't forget it."

Family. Pfft. The only family I have that I can count on is Libby. And she's left me high and dry during the turning point game of the season.

"You play for them," Coach continues. "You play for this city. But more importantly, you play for the person to your right and to your left. So that being said... Heat-wave," he yells out.

"Yes, coach," we answer in unison.

"Who's ready?"

"We're ready," we reply together sounding like a pack of rabid dogs.

"That's what I like to hear." One of the assistant coaches hands him a clipboard. "Starters tonight. We got our alternate captain, Hutchison as center."

"Fire on the ice, Coach," Hutchy replies on the other side of the room. We all give a single clap and an "Ah-oo."

"Hicks, left winger," Coach announces.

"Scorching the scoreboard, Coach," Hicks replies, swinging a towel over his head.

Clap. Ah-oo.

"Right wing, we got Ferguson."

"Making 'em sweat, Coach," Fergie replies with a fist pump into the air.

Clap. Ah-oo.

"Left defense. That's you, Sincaid."

The rookie always screws this part up. We all look at him, hopeful he'll get it right for once.

"Too hot to handle, Coach," Sincaid shouts.

Clap. Ah-oo.

I do a double-take as some of the guys cheer. "Way to not fuck it up," I clap him on the back. The young buck gives a side smile and nods with pride.

"O'Connor," my eyes snap to meet Coach Murray's. "You're Right D."

"Bringing the heat, Coach," I reply.

Clap. Ah-oo.

"Net-minder, we got Balinger."

"Access denied, Coach," Ryker's voice calls out.

Clap. Ah-oo.

"Fuck shit up, boys," Coach answers back. He turns and slaps a hand on the shoulders of his assistant coaches as they leave the room.

I look over at Landry who's now leaning on the back wall, arms crossed. Normally he'd be the one to lead our little pre-game hype up. And I gotta admit. I miss his energy. Right now he's just sulking. And if anyone needs to be sulking in this room, it's me.

The red lollipop bounces from one side to the other in Landry's mouth as he looks around the room. Even though he's been cleared to join us for morning skates. He's still got a ways to go with physical therapy before he's back in a game.

Hutchy slips his sweater on over his protective gear. He's sporting the A for alternate captain on his left side. I watch as Landry stares at it. He shakes his head and pushes off the wall, facing me.

"Back to your girl problem," Landry says.

"I don't have a girl problem," I groan, slipping on my jersey.

"You know what I've always wanted, Ry?" He turns his head to look at Ryker, his best friend.

Ryker looks up at him, "What Kee?"

"I've never had a motorcycle," Landry answers as he rubs his chin. "And I wonder if our boy O'Connor here, might be willing to make a little bet."

The boys are all still getting dressed but they look over at me as I'm lacing up my skates.

"Are you that bored with your life, Cap?" I ask him as I focus back on my laces.

He scoots onto the bench next to me and smirks. "You get a girl to fall in love with you or... I get your 'Busa."

"Have you lost your mind?" I scoff at him. "Just go buy yourself a bike."

Landry purses his lips and rises from the seat saying, "You hear that boys? O-zone doesn't think he can get a girl."

I'm not the kind to be easily played. Especially not with Keelan-prankster-Landry. He's a hell of a forward and a top-tier captain, but never one to take too seriously off the ice. But I'd be lying to myself if I didn't admit I'm a little insecure in the opposite-sex department. I mean, what woman would want to be with a drunk NHL player that still wears tighty whities?

But I need a wife stat and this might just be the boost I

need to get things going in that department. I finish tying up my skates and stand up.

"Just pick the girl," I say with feigned confidence.

Landry looks at me through squinted eyes, "You serious?"

Crossing my arms in front of my chest, I say, "If I don't get the girl, you win my bike."

"And if he does win the girl?" Sincaid asks, no doubt stunned that I'd even entertain the bet.

My family keeps all the properties in my grandfather's will, I answer in my head.

Landry thinks about it, "I'll give you whatever your bike's worth... in cash."

Hicks whistles, "I don't think you know what you're saying, Lando. That's a custom bike."

"What's it worth?" Landry asks.

I smirk extending my hand out to him, "Two hundred grand. Now, name the girl."

His eyes widen but he quickly recovers with a smirk of his own. He extends his hand out.

"Kesley Brooks," he says proudly. "And you gotta get her to agree to be your girlfriend before the playoffs. Make her an official WAG."

Fuck. He could've said anyone. Anyone else and I might have stood a chance. And Keelan—*the dick*—he knows that.

I think about my all-matte black speed bike. I bought it just after getting my contract with the Heatwave. A present to myself for making it into the big leagues.

Welp. It's been a nice five years with it.

We shake on it. And the boys all hoot around us.

Two weeks. I've got two weeks to get Kesley Brooks, my sister's best friend who hates my guts to agree to be my girlfriend and twenty-eight days to wife her up.

Ok... I can do this.

"Pleasure doing business with you. Be sure to give it a full tune-up before handing me the pink slip," Keelan says to me with a confident wink.

I respond with a middle finger in the air.

"Alright well, I'll be out there cheering you boys on," Keelan says, ignoring the gesture and pulling out his lollipop to point it at us. "Don't let me down."

* * *

My eyes keep landing on the two empty seats next to Balinger's family. *Where the hell did she go?*

When I saw Kesley Brooks sliding into her seat wearing *my* jersey, I couldn't help the grin that tugged at the corner of my lips. I know she only wore it to piss me off. It was a big *fuck you* to me. And she couldn't have picked a better day to do it.

I hope Keelan saw it. I hope he's shaking in his boots at the prospect of losing two hundred grand. Maybe then he'll learn not to mess with me.

But having to focus on this game with those green eyes watching my every move has been nearly impossible. She was talking to Rowan, Ryker's older brother, for a while. And now they've both disappeared. Making it even more impossible to focus?

Where are you, Kesley?

The defensive pair we're replacing is skating toward the boards, drawing my attention back to the game.

This is it. I snap out of it and look at Sincaid. He nods just before we both jump out at the same time.

We have less than two minutes left in the game and we're tied, 2-2. The puck is suddenly in Georgia's control.

As soon as we hit the ice, we both sprint toward the net in our defensive zone.

Sincaid checks the forward against the glass and the puck goes loose. It gives Hicks just enough time to take it back as he makes his way across the neutral zone and onto the other side of the ice.

The Georgia right-winger snatches it back and starts heading back down into our defensive zone. I backward skate, following him as he barrels toward Balinger in the net.

He attempts a deke but I'm able to free the puck out from under him as he does. He's pissed. I hear the growl of his frustration as he turns and comes for me.

I can sense what he's about to do. And I'm ready for it. It doesn't help that the girl I'm supposed to be winning over disappeared from my sight with another guy. I use the unwelcome rage to fuel me.

I pass the puck to Fergie who takes it into the offensive zone.

"Hey, O'Connor!" He chirps at me. "You play dirtier than your mom was last night in my bed." I roll my eyes. *He's coming for my mom? Is that the best he can do?*

"Almost as dirty as your girl was handling my stick, Devo," I smirk at him. "Heard she's writing a song about it."

Number Forty-four of the Georgia Thunderhawks, Devin Matthews, has been in an on-again off-again relationship with a very well-known pop star. And it's rumored she may have a thing for hockey players.

"Listen here, you son of a—" Matthews tosses his stick and throws down his gloves. I do the same as the play stops and he comes barreling toward me.

I grab him by the jersey and pound a fist into him as hard as I can. My hand screams as it connects with his rock-solid face. He's pulling back and scrambling, trying to get his jersey loose, like a wild animal trapped in a potato sack.

"Don't you ever talk about her," he yells as we keep battling it out. He lands a blow on my face that has me seeing stars for a moment.

Note to self, don't talk about Matthews' girl unless you want to get pummeled and forget where you are.

Sincaid comes up behind him and grabs him by the neck to try to pull him off of me. "Let him go, Matthews, or I'll drop you like the piece of shit you are."

Two more Thunderhawks come up behind me pulling my arms off their teammate and the Heatwave players start dropping their gloves and joining in on the brawl. There might be three, maybe four, individual fights taking place as the ref blows his whistle to get us to stop.

Nobody does.

We're all too close to a win. The energy on the ice is charged with testosterone, adrenaline, and the need to come out on top.

The linesmen and ref get involved, blowing whistles and putting their arms in between us to get us to stop fighting. The fans are on their feet screaming, cheering, and booing.

Chirps are spat out all around.

"You skate like a drunk squirrel," someone shouts.

"Your mom handles a stick better than you."

I can't even make out who's saying what anymore. But our teammates are finally able to get me and Matthews loose only for him to come charging at me and tackling me to the ice.

My helmet gets knocked off my head and I feel the boards behind me when I land on my ass, Matthews tripping over my skates. I feel it when my unprotected head bounces off the boards and the warmth of the blood trickles down my neck.

Matthews scrambles up to his feet and looks at me before he cries out, "Oh shit, O'Connor!"

Chapter 7
Kesley

"It looks so much worse than it feels, Kesley. I swear." The big bad hockey player tries to convince me he's fine as I get the door to his place unlocked.

"What the hell were you thinking chirping Matthews, O-zone?" Keelan says from under his right side. He and Ryker are both holding him up from either side. The bandage around his head looking rather ominous.

"You know that guy's a ticking time bomb just waiting to explode," Ryker adds.

I get the door open and step in turning on the lights. He left his windows wide open so we're able to see the entire lit-up Houston skyline from our place on the eighth floor of this building at the city center.

I turn and hold the door open for them to scoot him in.

"Where do you want him, Kesley?" Keelan asks.

"Put him on the couch. He won't be walking up any stairs tonight," I say assessing his winding metal staircase to get to his bed. When Liam first saw it when Lib brought him here not too long ago to feed Zane's parrot, Liam thought it was the coolest thing in the world.

Then, he took one look at the firemen pole on the other side and took it back. Because *that* was the coolest thing he'd ever seen in a grown man's place.

What my darling son doesn't know is that the stupid pole he finds so fascinating is *not* meant for firemen.

"Guess he won't be using that tonight," says Ryker, eyeing the pole.

I much preferred Ryker as my neighbor. He was quiet. Kept to himself. Nothing like its current occupant.

The rest of the units are occupied by high-end business professionals and more than a few Heatwave players because of the proximity to the Space City Arena. Not many families though. In fact, Liam might be the only child in the building now that I think about it.

But after the accident that claimed Zane's fiancee's life, he just couldn't bear to live here anymore. He gave the place to Ryker and took a unit near the bottom floor. He only moved back in recently when Ryker bought a home and offered it back to him.

It's weird having him back after so long. So much has changed.

"You sure you don't want us to stay," Keelan asks. "He's kind of a handful."

Zane grunts as they plant him on the sofa across from his giant screen TV.

"We'll be fine," he insists.

"I can handle him," I assure his friends putting my purse on the kitchen island and dropping the keys next to it. I turn back to them. "You guys, go. Celebrate. You deserve it."

Ryker and Keelan both look at each other still considering it and then back to Zane who's now propped up on the armrest of the couch with a pillow behind him.

"Uh-uh," I say to the defenseman. "Doc says you need to sit up. Twenty-four hours."

He grumbles but ultimately obeys. Slapping the pillow as he gets back into a seated position and grabs the remote like a pissed-off toddler.

"See?" I say turning to his teammates who are still hesitating near the door.

"Okay, but if you need anything," Keelan says shaking his phone.

"Let me see your phone," Ryker says extending his hand out to me.

"Mine?" I ask confused.

"I'm going to give you Izzy's number. She's my fiancee and a little easier to reach after hours than her brother here," he motions toward the team captain who rolls his eyes.

Zane cranes his neck and watches the interaction as I hand Ryker my phone and he types in the number.

"Feel free to spank him if he misbehaves," Keelan says from the doorway with a wink. Ryker laughs and Zane grins from his place on the couch. "Then again, he might like that too much."

"There will be no spanking," I point to each one of them as his teammates step out into the hall. The boys close the door behind them and I lock it, turning to the bane of my existence who's staring at me with rapt attention.

"What?" I ask him.

"I don't mind being spanked," he says now that we're alone. His voice, a low rumble.

"What are you doing, caveman?" I say drily, crossing my arms.

"Nothing," he says with a shrug turning back to the TV. It's on the sports network and they're giving a recap of tonight's game. "You look good in my jersey, Simba," he says without looking back at me.

I groan, looking down at the jersey that was intended to make him mad. But he must've bumped his head too hard. Or maybe the punch from Matthews left him with a concussion and he's forgotten who I am.

Twenty-four hours. I have to put up with Zane O'Connor and his ridiculously good looks and heated stares for twenty-four *freakin* hours. We're going to need some ground rules.

I ignore him and go to the kitchen, snapping the kitchen towel off the oven and grabbing some ice from the freezer to stick inside it. Then I head to my purse and dig out the small pot of arnica I keep there for Liam just in case.

I sit in the empty seat beside him and push his foot away until it's touching the ground. "Put this on your face," I say handing him the ice and arnica.

"I've got a better idea, Nurse Kesley," he says with those piercing ocean-blue eyes dancing over my features play-fully. "How about you do it?"

"You're a big boy. You can take care of your own injuries."

"Then why are you here?"

"I'm only here because I promised Libby that I'd be here if you needed anything. So she could go and do what she needed to do without worrying that her brother would be getting into trouble of any sort."

He squints at me in thought.

"What?"

"The boys could've stayed. Are you sure it wasn't that you wanted me all to yourself, little lion?"

My stomach does a weird flip flop when he says my old nickname. And I can't help but think he might be a little right. I didn't *have* to stay the night. His hockey bros were way more than willing to have the after-party here making sure he didn't fall asleep like the doctor ordered. They pretty much insisted on it. The hit was bad enough to draw blood but not bad enough for him to stay in the hospital overnight. That technically leaves me playing Nurse for the toned athlete.

"I think," he continues, scooting a little closer to me and throwing a tattooed arm around the back of the couch making our skin touch. "I think you wanted to stay here." He lowers his voice to a husky whisper, "Tell me I'm wrong, little lion."

I can smell his woodsy and *very* intoxicating cologne. My nostrils flare as the scent dances into my lungs and takes hold of me. It's nothing like Jeremy Clark and his screechy aftershave and cologne combo that left my eyes watering. This one is manly and intriguing. Leaving me wanting to smell more of it.

I shouldn't be here. Not alone with the dark-haired eye candy that is Mr. Tattooed and dangerous, Zane O'Connor. I knew this man before all the fame. Before he was anything but Frank O'Connor's son, the mega investor whose face was plastered on billboards across the city. But this broken man sitting next to me isn't some sweet boy next door.

No. He's Mr. Fuck-you-and-leave-you... and I will *not* be falling for his type. Not ever again.

Even if it's been a long time since I've been with a man. A *very* long time.

I work. I take care of Liam. I don't have time for my own needs. Not that I've felt any needs for a while. Not until the muscled man with the bandaged head next to me moved back in a few months ago sending alarms ringing through my head reminding me constantly to stay away.

But here I am... ignoring every alarm bell.

I swallow hard and move away from him a few inches. He holds back his grin, biting the inside of his cheek. That jawline of his is so pronounced that I can see the muscle in his cheek twitch.

"How about we play a game," he says, his voice husky and playful. "It'll help us pass the time."

"If it has anything to do with that stripper pole back there, I'm out," I say throwing my hands up.

He throws his head back and laughs. It's deep and hearty. "It wasn't going to. But since you mentioned it..."

"I only mentioned it to let you know I'm not interested in any of your games that might require it."

"Oh, what? Is the single mom too much of a prude to try it?"

"I am *not* a prude!" I fire back, crossing my arms over my chest.

"Oh, no?" He cocks his head to the side like a sly fox. "Prove it."

I scoff. "I don't need to prove anything to you, caveman."

"Kesley." The way his gravelly voice says my name, slides past his lips like a dare. And I feel the thrill of it down my chest and right between my thighs.

I hate that he does this to me. It was so much easier when I didn't have to see this devilish man every day. Resisting temptation is easier to do when it's not staring you down as you leave your apartment day after day making your cheeks flush uncomfortably. Infiltrating your dreams when you least expect it.

"Oh my god... of course," he says bringing a hand up to his head in a facepalm.

I glare at him, "What?"

"You don't know how to use it... do you?" His eyes shoot me a daring look.

This jerk.

"It makes so much sense. Remember that one party downtown with Lib and Mallory? When we were all still in college, you were dating that one dude... the guy with the nose piercing and the weird name."

"I remember it."

"You were the only one who wouldn't jump at the chance to dance on stage."

"That doesn't mean I don't know how to do it. Just that I didn't *want* to. On a stage. With all those eyes watching me." He blinks at me. "And that dude's name was Radley, by the way. He was Australian and gorgeous."

He chuckles to himself and looks around the empty penthouse before his eyes land back on me. "Nobody here now but you and me. Unless you'd like me to call up Radley, the gorgeous Australian."

I glare at him and he laughs. He *laughs*. I hate him.

"It's okay, Kes. I get it. You're not a stripper pole kinda girl. Probably why *Radley* didn't last. Let's just watch a movie—"

"Put some music on," I order him.

His eyes widen, "What?"

I get up from the couch. "Now, before I change my mind, caveman."

He thinks I'm a prude? That I can't let loose?

I'll show him. I can do this. I can be wild. Spontaneous. Sexy. Like those flashy girls the Heatwave boys always have around them. Like my best friend, Libby who models for a living.

Like Mallory.

That's what Zane liked about her anyway. She was carefree. Fun. And if she were alive today, she wouldn't bat an eye at this request.

He's stunned for a split second before he reaches forward and grabs his phone. "Any requests for DJ O-zone?"

"Surprise me," I say, pulling his jersey up over my head and wriggling out of it. The camisole I'm wearing underneath rides up my abdomen and he stares at me before returning his attention to his phone. I toss the jersey next to him.

He selects something and then gets up and takes a front-row seat at a barstool at his kitchen island. His bedroom loft is just above the kitchen, so the firemen—I mean *stripper* —pole lands you right in front of where he's positioned himself.

The song comes on through the speakers in the loft and I give him a tilt of my head. He returns it with a controlled grin that sends shivers down my spine.

His eyes darken and I close my eyes so I don't get intimidated as I start to sway to the rhythm of Ariana Grande's song, *Positions*. I walk up to the pole and look at the shiny metal leading up to the floor of his room above me. My first thought is, *I wonder if this pole's been disinfected.* But I shake off the thought, fully aware that he would rub it in about how I should loosen up if I mentioned it out loud.

I'm still in my jeans and Doc Marten boots and I'm honestly not sure if that'll be a hindrance on the stupid pole. He's right. I've never done this before. But I've seen my friends do it. It can't be *that* hard.

"Helps if you have less clothes on," Zane offers when he sees my hesitation.

I look over my shoulder at him and now he's wearing a full-on grin. I turn back to the pole and I don't know how long I'm standing there staring at it before his barstool scrapes across the hardwood floor. He goes to a cabinet and pulls down a bottle of tequila.

He shakes it at me and I'm almost about to give up and just go watch a movie when I remember Libby's parting words to me before she left on her European tour. *"Have fun, Kes. Try new things. Live a little."*

Ugh. Why do her words always come to me at the worst time convincing me to do things I normally wouldn't? I shake off my nerves and nod at him.

The smile that spreads on his face is all the encouragement I need. I'm going to have fun. I'm going to enjoy this. I won't let my thoughts, my guilt, or anything else get in the way.

I walk up to him, as he's pulling down two shot glasses.

"You're not supposed to be drinking," I tell him as I snatch the bottle off the counter and pop the cork off bringing the bottle to my lips as I take a long swig.

The alcohol burns my chest to the point that I might be able to breathe fire. I cough and Zane watches me with amusement.

"Woah, little lion. Careful there," he warns, hooded eyes on me.

The song is still playing through the speakers and I place the bottle down hard causing some of the liquid to splash out of it.

Without another thought, I grab his hand and lead him back to the barstool he was on. He leans back, one leg propped on the ring of the stool, the other planted on the ground.

I can feel him watching my every move as I approach the pole again, this time with a little liquid courage swishing in my stomach. I walk behind it and reach down to unlace my boots, kicking them and my socks off one at a time and as I rise I swipe my hand over the smooth silvery surface.

Zane's smile starts to falter into something more. He licks his lips and turns his head to the side, slowly crossing his arms over his muscled chest, and taking in my every movement.

I walk around it again until I'm facing away from him and bring my hands to the buttons of my jeans. I toss a look over my shoulder at him and now he's dropping his arms and leaning forward in the barstool. I notice the small movement as he adjusts himself in his jeans. His eyes watching me intently.

I unbutton the top loop, zip it down, and lean forward as I slowly drop my jeans down to my ankles and step out of them. I kick them to him and he catches them before they hit his face. The look in his eyes is feral and the dark grin returns.

I'm not some perky little bunny anymore. I'm a woman. I've had a kid. I don't do things like this.

Which is exactly why you should. The thought is almost audible.

I breathe, now only wearing my camisole and panties. I wrap a bare leg around the bar and swing my body around it like I used to watch my friends do. He's right. Less clothes means more grip. I use my upper body to pull me up and my legs to hold me in place as I do, slowly inching over the pole until I'm just a few feet above the ground.

I look down at him and his lips are parted, hands on his knees ready to step in if I fall. I position my legs the way I remember the girls doing and if I let go I'm either going to slide down the pole irresistibly sexy or...

"Kesley," he calls out just as I let go and almost fall to the floor before he lunges forward and catches me in his waiting arms. "Are you crazy?"

He sounds like a concerned parent and I can't help the laugh that escapes me as he holds me there on the floor at the bottom of the stupid stripper pole. Zane O'Connor, worried about me? Oh, how the tables have turned.

He stands up with me still in his arms and sets me on the barstool with very little effort. The song is nearing the end and he's staring into my very soul.

When it changes to *Dangerous Woman* he leans in and puts a hand at either side of me on the kitchen island. Caging me in. I lean back. My eyes run over the length of his body in front of me. He's lean and strong. He always has been. I've seen him shirtless more times than I care to admit. Sneaking peeks at him when I'd gone to visit Libby after school. Watching him swim when we'd lay poolside during those hot Texas summers.

I've always seen him. But right now, with his eyes boring into me and his intoxicating cologne filling my nostrils, I feel like the only thing he sees.

And I can admit, it feels amazing.

Chapter 8
Zane

Those green eyes are looking at my lips as I lick them.

Seeing this woman who I've known for so long, stripping in front of me, is making me just about lose my sanity.

I've never seen this side of her. Kesley is careful.

Measured.

Everything she does is for a reason.

Keelan and his bet aside though. She's something. And I get the feeling she might feel something for me. Maybe something she's denying herself. And if this that's the case... then I have her exactly where I want her.

My eyes drop to her lips. I'd be stupid not to admit that I want to take that perfect pouty mouth into my own and taste her. Tease her until she's coming undone for me.

"It's been seven years." Libby's voice creeps into my mind.

That's seven years of mourning. Seven years of grieving. Seven years of holding back and stopping myself from the pursuit of happiness. That's why I've never moved on. Why my days are spent with hockey and booze on repeat, day after day.

It's time, is what Libby was trying to tell me.

I reach for Kesley's waist and hoist her up off the stool and she yelps in surprise.

"What are you doing?" she says in a high-pitched voice. But her legs wrap around my waist like they know exactly what they want.

I look up at her, "Something I've wanted to do for years, little lion."

Her eyes are hooded as she swallows hard and brings her arms around my neck to hold herself up on my body.

She leans her face close to mine and our lips are about to touch when Muppet screeches from the guest room, "Hello, big boy! Muah. Muah. Muah. Come give me a kiss."

Kesley's eyes widen and at the same time I mumble, "Fucking bird."

She scrambles off of me and slides down until her feet are back on the ground. I can feel the moment instantly pass.

Stupid. Fucking. Bird.

"That's freaky," she admits. And I rub the back of my head annoyed.

"He's hungry," I say, reluctantly going to the pantry to get the bird seed that I have stashed.

Kesley stays staring down the hall.

"Does that happen a lot?" she asks.

"Every day," I say grabbing a fresh bottle of water from the fridge. "Wanna say hi?"

Her face contorts into an expression I can't pinpoint. Disgust? Curiosity?

"I mean... you think he'd recognize me?"

I shrug, grabbing the bird's sustenance. "Come and find out."

I brush past her, the hairs on my arm sticking up as I feel her warmth, and make my way down the hall. She hesitates but then I hear her small footsteps following behind me.

I open the door to the spare room where I keep the bird most days.

"Hey, Muppet."

"Hello, big boy. Hello, big boy," the parrot replies.

Kesley chuckles from behind me, "That's what Mal used to call him, right?"

It is. The stupid bird that my late fiancee insisted on getting has now been my roommate for years.

"She could've had any animal that wasn't a dog or a cat. A quiet little hamster if she wanted. And Mal picked a parrot."

And now I'm the one that has to take care of it. I don't have the heart to get rid of him. I shake my head, removing the sheet over the bird's cage and letting it float to the floor.

The grey and white parrot tilts his head to the side and watches my every move with his left eye. Its pupil dilates as it takes me in.

"It's just me, Muppet. Sorry to disappoint you." I unlatch the door to the cage and give him my arm to climb onto.

Kesley is standing next to me as the bird takes one tentative step onto my arm and then another. I slowly pull him out from the giant cage and bring him up to my face.

Muppet tilts his head left and right in rapid movements, looking nervous.

"Hi Muppet," Kesley coos next to me. She reaches a

finger up to the bird's neck and softly rubs downward against its feathers.

Muppet closes his eyes and stretches his neck out for her to keep doing it. The air escapes through my nose as I chuckle.

Looks like I'm not the only one craving her touch.

Kesley drops her hand and gives me a sidelong glance. *Yes, I'm jealous of a stupid bird.*

"You ready to eat, bud?" Muppet shakes himself out of his Kesley trance and starts bobbing up and down excitedly.

"How often do you have to feed him?" Kesley asks as I reach for the food I placed on the small table next to Muppet's cage.

"Usually just in the morning, he snacks the rest of the day. Guess he's just hungry tonight."

Or maybe he's as excited as I am to have this beautiful woman here in my apartment.

Kesley picks up one of the snacks on the table and wags it in front of his face. Muppet pulls back eyeing the stick for a second before snatching it out of her hands.

She giggles. And I watch a rare smile spread across her face. This is weird, right? I have a half-naked Kesley Brooks petting my late fiancee's parrot in the apartment we were supposed to be sharing.

And I want it. I feel a sharp pang in the pit of my stomach. Like I'm doing something wrong.

"Liam would love to have a pet," she says softly as she pets the bird again and breaks my downward spiral.

"Is he... into animals?"

"Just the unconventional kinds. A parrot is right up his alley. He didn't stop talking about Muppet for days when Libby first introduced him," she drops her hand and I can tell Muppet misses it already.

"Sounds like Mal. She wanted so many pets. But Dad insisted on giving us this penthouse. And most pets aren't allowed in this building. She found out that parrots weren't in the fine print so..." I motion to Muppet.

She nods. And a moment later asks, "How is Frank? He used to visit Libby pretty often, but it's been a few months."

Oh, Frank... our pseudo-dad.

"Who knows, he's always too busy closing the next deal to have any grip on what's going on with the people around him."

I've seen Frank all of two times since Mallory's funeral. Once for Christmas at Nana's before she took a turn in her health and stopped hosting them. And the second, on accident, shopping at a local sports store. Maybe if I count all the billboards with his face on them that I pass daily, then maybe that number could be higher.

I get it. Some people don't know how to act or what to say to someone who has lost so much.

When Mal's accident happened, I was out of it for months. It's hard to grapple with losing someone in a matter of mere seconds. People did the best they could to be there for me. For Mallory's family, too. Others just slowly faded away.

Never thought it would be my own dad, though. He should know the pain of loss—he lost a brother. He should understand better than anyone.

Staying away just became easier for some after the accident. But not Kesley. Even if we didn't talk much. She was still there. Still willing to be in my world. She'd drop off food and swing by just to say hi and make sure I was still—I don't know—alive, maybe?

And she was grieving too. Mallory had become a friend

of hers. Not as close as Libby, but they did spend a lot of time together. The three of them.

Maybe she was the only one there because she was the only one, other than Libby, who could see what I was going through. But even she started pulling away after a while. Especially when Liam needed more and more of her attention. When she took on the second job, I stopped seeing her altogether.

I offered her money to help. But she wouldn't take it. Eventually, I felt deprived by her distance and chose to just move altogether. This place just held too many memories. And moving in again definitely brings them back to mind. But it's not the same place it used to be.

Now it's a Heatwave hangout spot. Whether the woman standing next to me likes it or not.

Kesley repeats my name and I shake off my thoughts. "I'm sorry. Did you say something?"

"Yeah, you zoned out on me. I said, do you still want to watch a movie? We have about," she checks her watch, "nineteen hours of awake time to go."

I place Muppet back into his home and give him the food and water, latching his door and turning to her.

"Should I order some pizza?" I ask her.

"Only if you get one with pineapples on it."

I scrunch my nose. "I hoped you had grown out of that."

"Some things are good the way they are, caveman." She winks and walks out of the room, still in nothing but her camisole and panties. And as she leaves I lift a silent prayer that it stays that way.

* * *

"What? Simba's the king?!" I yell out tossing popcorn at the TV.

Kesley leans over and laughs into the pillow that was sitting on her lap. "Zane, it's called *The Lion King.* I've told you since high school not to call me, Simba. If anybody's a Simba, it would be you."

"And what would that make you? Nala?" She tosses the pillow at me and I fall back onto the couch exaggeratedly.

"You wish. And stop moving so much. You're supposed to be sitting still," she scolds me.

"Says the woman who just launched a pillow rocket at my face."

"I thought you took hits for a living," she teases as she pulls the blanket off and stands up.

I sit up, "Where are you going?"

She cocks her head to the side. "Bathroom. Which one can I use?"

"There's one down the hall," I say motioning with my head in the direction of it. "And there's one upstairs right off my bedroom." I waggle my eyebrows and she shakes her head.

"Down the hall one works just fine," she says, tossing the blanket over my head so I don't stare at her as she walks away.

I quickly remove it to do *just* that. And I catch her perfect ass just as she rounds the corner of the hallway.

I groan tossing the blanket back over my head. It's three in the morning. And in a few hours, the sun is going to come up and I won't have her all to myself.

Our time alone in my apartment feels like it's zooming by. Not to mention the extreme case of blue balls I'm toting. One can't simply sit next to a half-naked woman like Kesley without experiencing it. Maybe I can just...

I sneak a peek down the hall and slip my pants down to my thighs. Using the blanket that was just covering her beautiful body I release my erection from its imprisonment, slowly stroking it.

I think about her sitting next to me. The way her nipples perked up through that camisole from the chill of the apartment. I on purpose didn't turn on the heater just so I could catch glimpses of it.

Then her stripping in front of me earlier. She didn't go all the way. She didn't have to. I would've spilled into my pants if she would've gone another minute dancing in front of me like that. She didn't even have to touch me. My hand picks up speed.

I'm lost in thoughts of her, stroking myself when I hear her soft voice from in front of me. "Zane."

Oh shit. Fuck.

I scramble to cover myself with the pillow she threw at me.

Welp. This is just fucking embarrassing. "I-I'm so sorry, Kes. It's just been so long... and you're just so... you. I..."

"Shhh," she leans forward and puts a finger to my lips. "It's ok."

It's okay? Is it okay that she just caught me touching myself? That is not okay! That is... weak. This woman is making me weak.

But she stays there with her finger over my lips. God I want to suck it into my mouth and pull her into my lap. "It's okay," she says again.

She straightens up and reaches to her waist and pulls off her camisole. Those nipples I was watching poke through earlier are now on full display in front of me.

What the hell is happening?

She wraps her blonde hair into one of her hands and

holds it up over her head. Her body stretches up and those beautifully round breasts taunt me.

"Kes-ley," I say gulping.

"Keep going."

Am I dreaming right now?

I watch her as the finger she had on my lips trails down the length of her body disappearing under her panties. She's.... she's touching herself.

Maybe I *did* get a concussion from that hit earlier. Maybe this is some kind of fever dream and I'm still in the hospital bed. That's the only logical explanation for my neighbor to be naked and touching herself in front of me. My erection twitches underneath the blanket at the sight of her and I know I'm definitely awake.

"Kesley," I say again, my voice cracking from the attempted restraint.

Her head is rolled back and she lifts her leg and plants it on the sofa at my side. Her fingers still moving underneath the fabric. She is... unlike anything I've ever seen before.

"Go ahead, Zane," she says through parted lips. "Touch yourself."

My eyes stay glued on the temptress before me. But my hand now has a mind of its own. I swallow again as I take hold of my cock and stroke it under the blanket.

She looks down at me and watches me move. "Mmmm. Do you like how that feels?"

"Yes," I grit out. The strokes get a little faster as I watch her.

"What do you think about when you touch yourself?"

Fuck. Me. Don't do this to me, little lion.

"You," I say through my clenched teeth. "I think about you, Kesley. Having you all to myself. Your skin on mine. Tasting you."

Her own strokes increase and she throws her head back again, licking her lips. The softest of moans escapes from her.

"Do you want to know what I think about?" she asks. I might as well come right now from the jolt of pleasure that question sends through me.

"What do you think about, little lion?" My eyes can't tear away from her even if I tried. She looks back down at me, still stroking herself.

"I think about... you kissing me. Pushing me up against a wall or bending me over a couch, just like this one. And claiming me over and over again."

I imagine doing just that and gulp.

She slides her fingers out from below her panties and places her foot back on the floor. I stop moving my hand.

I think she's going to stop. But instead, she puts a knee on either side of me and straddles me. "Doctor says no strenuous activity," she whispers into my ear.

"Right," I say turning my face to her.

"So I want you to sit there and stroke yourself while I kiss you and rub myself."

"Kesley, what the fu—"

She pulls my lips to hers and we kiss. While I'm stroking myself under a blanket as she straddles me and touches herself.

Where the hell did Ms. Prim and Proper go? Did she get replaced by a body double in the bathroom?

I don't hold back. I ravage that vicious mouth of hers. Wanting to taste every bit of it. My body instantly reacts, my movement gets erratic and it's the sound of her release as she screams into my mouth that has me letting go on the blanket between us.

Our mouths are still locked when she takes her hand

out from beneath the fabric of her panties and she sits back on my thighs. We stare at each other without saying a word.

"How often do you think of me when you stroke yourself, Zane?" Her head is tilted to the side and the smirk on her face tells me she knows the answer.

"Every. Single. Time," I say.

And it's the truth. Because Kesley Brooks is the woman I love to hate. And everybody knows there's a thin line between love and hate.

And that thin line is called desire.

Chapter 9
Kesley

I can feel his eyes burning holes into the top of my head. So I look up. "What?"

He laughs, the air escaping through his nose. "Your move, little lion."

I look back at the checkerboard in front of me, finally picking up a red piece and jumping one of his, claiming it for my tiny win pile of black pieces.

He nods his head as he picks up one of his black pieces and jumps three of mine. Silently adding my red pieces to his growing pile.

I sit up straighter and cross my arms over my chest announcing, "I hate this game."

His lips quirk up. "Why? Because you're losing?"

"No... yeah." I shrug, rolling my eyes.

"Then you'd make a terrible hockey player. Losing's a part of the game. You learn more from the losses than you ever do from the wins," he says, rising from his spot in front of the coffee table.

"Well aren't you just a wealth of knowledge," I mumble. That's when I remember... *Hockey.*

Shit.

I need to be learning everything I can. Instead, I'm getting swept up in lazy rainy afternoon games of checkers with the hot, tatted-up defenseman across the hall.

I yawn for the fourth time in a row. The sleep deprivation is hitting me hard though.

"Uh-oh. Looks like my nurse won't make it through her shift." He opens the fridge to retrieve some oat milk for the coffee that just finished brewing.

"You take your coffee with oat milk?" I ask him.

He closes the fridge and looks at me. "And brown sugar. Why?"

"Since when?"

He squints like he's trying to remember. "I guess since... I actually don't know."

I shake it off. Probably just a coincidence that we take our coffee the same way. It's not like we haven't grabbed coffee with our old friend group before.

We've spent the last seventeen hours together, awake. We're both tired. Soon the people in our worlds are going to start bombarding us with check-in calls, no doubt.

As soon as the thought leaves me, my phone rings on the kitchen counter.

"Can you toss that to me?" I say through another yawn. But he's already answering the call, "This is O'Connor."

I jump up instantly awake whisper-yelling, "Zane! That's my phone!"

His eyes widen and he looks at the caller ID on the screen before bringing the phone back to his ear. Staring at me he chuckles nervously to the voice on the other end.

"Who is it?" I mouth to him, moving closer. He puts a hand up to stop me.

"Yes, the very one. And no worries at all, Mrs. Brooks.

Kesley's right here," he bites his lip as the voice chirps on the other line.

My mom. Oh, great. I reach a hand out wiggling my fingers for him to pass me the phone. "Right. Right, yes," he says, giving me his muscled back instead as he grabs a mug from the shelf and pours some coffee. "I can see why you'd think that... Mmhmm."

He keeps the phone tucked under his ear in between his head and his shoulder.

"Zane! Gimme the phone!" I whisper.

"Well, I would say it's pretty serious ma'am," he says to her, quickly turning to catch my reaction and giving me a wink.

What the hell is he doing?

"Is that right? Well, that sounds lovely, Mrs. Brooks... no, Kesley hadn't mentioned it. I'm sure she just... forgot. She's been pretty busy with work."

I drag a hand over my face. "I'll be sure to check my schedule. Thank you... Uh-huh. Yes, you too. Here's your daughter."

He hands me the phone with a smirk and slides me the piping coffee mug at the same time.

I snatch the phone from him and bring it to my chest, "What the hell was that?"

He bites his lips as he holds back an adorable smile that just works to infuriate me more. I hesitate a moment before I hear my mom's, "Hello? Kessie?"

"Uh... ha!" I chuckle nervously. "Hey, Mom."

"Zane O'Connor, Kes?" She all but shrieks into the phone.

Oh my god. She thinks we're together. And Zane just confirmed.

"I obviously invited him for the weekend since you didn't have the guts to do it," she adds.

My jaw locks up. I don't know what to say, "Mom... we're not..."

"I already told your father and he's so excited to see him again."

"When did you even—"

"He has a thousand and one questions about his time with the Heatwave. You know your dad. He's a huge hockey fan!"

Wait a minute. That's true. And bringing Zane would mean I'd get more insider access. This... this might actually work.

"Right, right," I say thinking through it. I look over to Zane who's now leaning against the counter sipping on his coffee looking rather smug if you ask me.

I know why I'd want him there, but what's his angle?

"Well, like he said... if it works with his schedule, he'll be there," I say to her.

Mom squeals with excitement, "Liam will be so happy."

Oh my god! Liam!

"On second thought... maybe this is all a little too soon. Liam doesn't," I look at Zane. His eyes clock my every move. "He doesn't know," I say with great hesitation.

"Well, I figured as much, Kes. Sounds like you've been trying to keep this little secret to yourselves."

"Just, please don't say anything to him. Please, mom," I urge her.

"You're just friends," she plays along.

But honestly, that *is* the truth. Zane and I *are* just friends. Frenemies maybe. *Just frenemies that made out while pleasuring ourselves like lust-filled teenagers last night.* But that was a one-time thing. That won't be happening again.

"That's right," I say.

"I can't wait to tell your sisters that you're bringing someone. They won't believe it. This is the best news I've got all week. Oh, there's Kira now! I gotta go. Bye Kessie."

"Mom! Mom, wait. Nothing's set." She hangs up on me.

I drop the phone from my ear with a huff and Zane sets his coffee mug next to me before taking the phone from my hands and placing it on the counter.

"What have you done?" I grit out.

"Parents love me," he assures me with a cocky smile. The old Zane maybe. But this unhinged version of him... yeah, I'm not so sure. Though I'm starting to feel a little unhinged myself.

"Like I'm going to bring home the hockey heathen that drinks, smokes, and gets around in a speed bike?" I shake my head. We're both delirious and sleep-deprived. We're not thinking straight. "You're not coming on my family's Spring Break trip, Zane."

He takes a seat on his leather barstool and pulls me into him by the waist. "Oh, come on. Like you wouldn't like to rub it in your sister's faces that you're sleeping with a hockey star?"

Oh, absolutely not. We are not doing this. I push back off of him.

"What happened last night cannot happen again," I say sternly.

He drops his head to the side and assesses me. And I suddenly feel extremely uncomfortable wearing the clothes that he let me borrow when I got cold earlier. It feels too personal.

I turn and pick up my clothes still in a pile on the floor next to *the* pole.

"Is it because you're talking to Rowan?" he asks, the playfulness gone from his voice.

I straighten up and turn back to face him, "What are you talking about?"

"You guys sure seemed to hit it off at the game yesterday. Or is it Hicks you're into?" He crosses his arms.

"I don't know either of them. And that was the first time I'd ever spoken to Rowan. So no, we're not *talking*."

"Then where did you two go?" He looks genuinely hurt.

I finally realize why he's giving me the third degree."Zane O'Connor... are you jealous?"

He leans back on the same barstool he sat on when I was dancing for him last night. His elbows are tucked behind him, trying to portray himself to be as confident as ever, even if I can see right through his facade.

"You're jealous," I point at him with the shirt in my hands.

"Pfft. I've just never seen you so animated talking to another man," he admits.

"Well, if you *must* know. We were just checking out the renovations going on at the arena."

He suddenly sits up. "The ones behind the plastic tarp?"

"Uh, yeah. Are there any other renovations?"

"Kesley!"

"What? We didn't get caught."

He shakes his head but a smirk crosses his face.

"What?"

"If you wanted a private tour of the facilities, you could've just asked me," he says with a hand on his chest.

A private tour. A private tour with him would surely mean us winding up in some dark corner of the arena doing unspeakable things to each other based on what happened last night. Though, if I want to keep my job, a private tour is exactly what I should get.

"I don't know," I hesitate.

"Got what you wanted already then?" he says licking his lips and toying with me. "With Rowan?"

"Oh my god. Nothing happened with Rowan," I say again. "Not that I owe *you* an explanation."

"No, you don't. But if I'm going on your family trip..."

"That's *not* happening and you know it," I glare at him.

He looks up and sighs, "Your mom seems to think otherwise."

"My *mom* would be happy if I brought an escort who I paid to claim to be in love with me like some freakin' nineties rom-com."

"Well, then this is a step up, isn't it? I require no fee for my services," he says. "Except..." There's a long pause before either of us says anything.

"Except what?"

"Ok, well, you want to get your parents off your back, right? Give them some peace of mind that you're not a lonely spinster?"

"I'm not a lonely spinster. I am an independent woman taking care of myself and my son," I say with bite.

"And I respect you all the more for it," Zane adds with a hand to his heart. I can't tell if he's mocking me or genuine. "But what if I told you we might be able to help each other out?"

"I'm not having sex with you, Zane. No matter how much you think you can pay me. What happened last night will never happen again."

"I'm not offering sex, Kesley," he stands from his barstool

and stalks over to me. "I'm offering you... a marriage proposal."

I must be hearing him wrong because it sounded like he just said the word *marriage*.

"A marriage proposal?" I deadpan.

He nods, "A limited time. No strings attached. You get something that you want and I get something I want. And in a few months. We can call the whole thing off... marriage proposal."

Chapter 10
Kesley

I stare blankly at the muscular man.

"How hard did you hit your head?"

He grins. "I haven't been more clear on something I've wanted in a long time, little lion."

"I can't just marry you, Zane."

"Why not?"

I scoff. "You say *no strings attached* like there won't be any consequences. I have a son. I can't just bring you on a family trip like '*Hey everyone, meet my neighbor and oh yeah... husband, Zane. He just so happens to be Libby's brother. The same Libby who I live with,*'" I say sarcastically playing out the scenario.

"Well, when you say it like that it sounds ridiculous."

"Because it *is* ridiculous! And when it's time to call it quits... Liam will be devastated. By some miracle, he actually likes you. And what am I supposed to tell him when mommy is no longer hanging out with the guy she claimed to love and he has to see you every day?"

"I can leave. If it makes things easier."

I stare at him without saying a word.

He drops his hands to his thighs and rubs them down as he thinks. "Ok, ok. I hear you."

"Do you? Because you really don't seem to take life too seriously, Zane. And marriage... that's pretty freakin' serious for most people."

"I'm not most people," he shrugs. "Tell you what..." he pauses. "I'll throw in two hundred G's."

I can't believe the words coming out of this man's mouth. I grab the phone off the kitchen counter and search for the saved contact Ryker gave me.

"What are you doing?" he asks, eyeing the phone.

"I think it's time I called your teammates to come take care of you, because what you're saying right now..." I look up at him. "It's crazy talk."

He reaches out for my phone and plucks it out of my hand, "Just... hear me out, ok? There's a way we can make this work for everyone involved."

I cross my arms unwilling to hear another word from him. "Give me my phone."

"Kesley." His eyes soften. "Please."

It's a soft cry for help. And it punches me right in the gut. I don't owe him anything. But he's not the man he used to be. I can see right through the mask he puts up in front of everyone. And for a moment, I catch a glimpse of the brokenness underneath the facade. And my heart breaks for him.

When I don't make another move. He sighs deeply, grabs his coffee mug off the counter, and takes it with him to the couch.

"I need to find a wife, and I have less than thirty days to do it."

I shake my head. *This is insane.*

He pats the space on the sofa next to him and I roll my eyes but oblige.

"My Granddad, Francis O'Connor. He passed away almost a decade ago. The man was a legend. A first-generation immigrant. He worked hard for everything he earned. Before he passed, he had amassed a huge portfolio of properties. Beautiful one-of-a-kind properties throughout Texas and even some in other countries."

I sip my coffee and listen. I've heard a lot about Francis from his sister. She was very fond of the man. And has photos up in her room of them all together when they were little.

"Francis was old-school. He and Nana were married sixty-three years by the time he passed away. He believed marriage was the bedrock of society. And that for any bloodline to gain strength and generational wealth... marriages—long-lasting marriages—had to be forged. In marriage, there's dynasty and legacy. That's what he believed, anyway."

"Sixty-three years is a long time to be with someone," I admit. "It's no wonder he felt that way. He must've loved your Nana."

"More than anything in the world. But in his will, he left her with his most prized home back in Ireland along with the big house they lived in together here in Houston. It was all she wanted. And the rest of the wealth would be passed down to the youngest O'Connor male to be married before the end of his first thirty days after turning thirty."

"What? Why?"

He straightens up on the couch and pauses to look out the window of his apartment a moment before answering.

"It's his way of showing that he believes in our family

lineage. That he believed love and longevity go hand in hand with success."

"But, why thirty?"

Zane shakes his head, "Grandpa Francis was convinced that by the time you're thirty, you've already met the woman you're meant to share a life with. Anything past that and you're just stalling."

I nearly spit out the coffee in my mouth. "That's ludicrous."

Zane only shrugs. "I can find the flaws in his thinking all day. Or... I can embrace that Granddad was a wise man and almost everything he believed has turned out to be true."

"And you're the youngest O'Connor male. Your dad... er, Frank, he doesn't count?"

"Frank would've received the inheritance since my real dad passed. But he's never stayed married. He's had three wives and counting."

I join him in staring out the giant window. We're both quiet for a moment. Finally, I turn to him. Staring at his profile, he's still focused on the world outside.

"What happens if you don't marry?"

He licks his lips and glances at me before returning his attention to the city outside.

"Every last thing will be donated."

"Just like that?"

Zane snaps his fingers. "Just like that."

He's not wrong. We can help each other. And as much as I hate to admit it. I need him. And it sounds like he needs me.

"Fine," I say, barely above a whisper.

He turns his head from the couch where he's now seated. "Fine, what?"

"Fine, I'll... think about marrying you."

He stares at me for a moment before saying, "I'll marry you under one condition..."

Is he serious right now?

"I said I'd think about it."

We hold each other's gaze for far too long. Neither of us relenting. But that look on his face has my body reacting.

"Ok, fine. What's the condition?"

"I want you..." he pauses.

"Is there an end to that sentence?" I ask when he doesn't continue.

He chuckles to himself, "I want you to make it convincing, little lion. You need to be head over heels for me. Nobody can know about our little... arrangement."

"You want me to play the doting girlfriend?"

"Doting wife," he corrects me.

I scoff. "Not happening, O'Connor."

He hasn't been in a serious relationship since Mallory passed. And I'm not some rebound for him to try to get back on his feet after being out of practice for so long.

He takes a sip of his coffee as he watches me.

"What?"

"You've already lost your bargaining chip in that department, Kesley. I already know what you think about when you're alone in your room at night," he lowers his voice an octave. "Touching yourself to thoughts of me."

He smirks from behind the coffee mug.

My cheeks feel red hot all of a sudden. "I just said that in the heat of the moment."

"You're a terrible liar, little lion."

"Well, you're asking me for something I can't give you, caveman."

He stiffens, as if my words affect him.

"I know you've had a rough go in life. I know you're still

working through some things. But I can't promise you *head over heels*. I'm here. I'm willing. Anything other than that," I shake my head. "I'm sorry."

He bites the inner parts of his cheeks and nods his understanding. "Okay."

"Okay?" I repeat.

"Yep. I hear you loud and clear. I'm way too broken. Way too damaged to be anything more to you."

"Zane, that's not what I said."

"But that's what you mean, isn't it? All I'm saying is, I get it. I wouldn't want me either."

I sigh. I would want nothing more than to give him my affection. To see if the electric pull I've felt toward him all these years could be something more than just sexual attraction.

But it's not just me I'm living for. Every decision I make affects my son, too. So for now, I need to keep him close enough that I get the intel I need to keep my job. But at an arm's length, because Zane isn't healed. And I don't know if he ever will be.

I grab my purse and keys.

"Wait, where are you going? We still have..." he checks his watch. "Five hours."

"I need a shower," I tell him. "This is a lot to think about."

"There's plenty of showers here," he points out.

Let me clarify, I need a shower sans beefy hockey player with icy blue eyes in my vicinity wearing down my defenses and making me agree to something so ludicrous as marriage.

"I need my stuff," I say instead.

"Alright," he pushes himself off the couch and follows me.

"What are you doing?"

"I'm coming with you," he says with a tilt of his head.

* * *

An hour later, I'm walking into the living room of my apartment. The TV is blasting. Zane is nowhere in sight.

"Zane?" I call out. Maybe I took longer than expected. Taking extra care to groom myself properly before being back in this man's presence. Maybe he finally passed out. "Zane? You asleep?"

There's a knock on the door. And I jump from the scare.

The door is already unlocked. I look through the peep-hole and see Zane's head dropping as he leans onto the door frame. *What the hell?*

I quickly pull the door open. "Where'd you go?"

He laughs but looks totally out of it.

"Are you okay?"

Those bright eyes beam. "Well, hello there. Didn't expect to see you here?"

"Very funny," I say putting a hand on my hips. "Are you feeling ok?"

"Better now that you're here, girl," he says slightly slurring. I smell the alcohol on his breath.

"Zane, you're not supposed to be drinking," I say pulling him into my apartment.

He stumbles in. "I'm sorry, Mal. I just... Libby convinced me to give her a chance." My heart sinks.

Did he just call me... Mal?

"Zane, I'm... I'm Kesley. What do you mean Libby convinced you?" I take his face into my hand and make him look at me. "How much did you drink?"

"I'm gravy, baby. I just needed a little something to take

the edge off. You know we made it into the playoffs? It's kind of a big deal." He pulls away and walks over to the couch plopping onto it and reaching for the remote in front of him.

Is this from the hit? I knew all this marriage talk had to be a result of the incident. I close the door to my apartment and look around for my phone while he flips through channels.

I quickly dial the number Ryker left for me. It's late but he told me she'd answer.

A soft female voice answers, "Hello? This is Izzy."

I hold the phone tight against my ear and walk into the hall leading to my bedroom. "Hi, Izzy. It's Kesley, I'm sorry to be calling so late. Ryker gave me your number."

"Hi Kesley, yeah I told him to. I saw you in O'Connor's jersey at the game yesterday and wanted to make sure you had a way to get in touch with another... uh... teammate's... person."

"You mean girlfriend?" I ask.

"I wasn't sure what to call you," she admits.

"Yet to be determined. Listen, I have a question."

"Shoot," she says.

"Are you familiar with concussions?"

"Unfortunately, yes," she says solemnly. "You think he has one?"

"Well, is it normal for someone to... imagine things?"

"In my experience, yes. Very much so. He took a pretty big hit last night. Is he acting strange?"

"Very."

"What's he doing?" she probes.

"Uh, well, he's just saying a lot of weird stuff. Calling me someone else's name. And... he's slurring his words. But I think he might have been drinking."

"You want me to send Ryker over?" I hear a man's voice on the other end whispering to her.

"It's O'Connor," she whispers back.

"No, no," I say. "I'm sorry to bother you guys. You must've been sleeping. I was just worried that maybe he's having a bad reaction to being hit."

I walk back into the living room. The noise from the TV is overpowered by the snoring defenseman taking up my couch.

"Honestly, we've been up for over a day. He's probably just exhausted," I admit.

"You sure?"

I walk up to Zane and kick him lightly in the leg. He snores louder and swats at me before flipping over on the couch murmuring to himself.

"Yeah, I'm sure."

"Ok, well, if anything changes. Just drop me a line."

"Will do. Thanks, Izzy. And sorry to bother you, again."

"Kesley, it's no bother. If there's one thing you should know it's that these boys are like family. If you or Zane need anything, they'll be there at the drop of a hat. Seriously."

I smile at the thought. "Thank you. Goodnight, Izzy. And goodnight, Ryker." The grumpy goalie says something unintelligible on the other line.

"What he means to say is *"Goodnight Kesley. Thanks for staying up with Zaney boy so I don't have to.* Right, Goalie-zilla?"

I chuckle.

"Yeah, thanks for putting up with him," Ryker's voice comes on the line. "On behalf of the Houston Heatwave. You've done us all a great service." It's sarcastic but I can play.

"It's hard, honest work. But somebody's gotta do it," I say before hanging up.

I drop my phone onto the coffee table and grab the remote to turn off the TV. Then taking the throw that's on my reading chair, I toss it over Zane's deep-breathing body.

He cuddles into it and mumbles to himself, "You're so warm, little lion. Just like I imagined."

For a moment I think he's awake. But the snoring continues and I know he's just talking in his sleep.

"Goodnight, Zane," I whisper to him before turning the lights out and padding through the apartment back to my room.

Married... to Libby's brother.

What would Libby have to say about this?

Chapter 11

Zane

10:21 AM CAPTAIN LANDO:

Earth to O-zone.

10:25 AM CAPTAIN LANDO:

O'Connor...If you're alive out there, send me a thumbs-up emoji at the very least. Sheesh.

10:26 AM FERGIE:

Zane. Just say something, man. Anything.

10:27 AM BALSY:

He's not answering his phone. Izzy's calling Nurse Kesley.

10:30 AM HICKS:

No need. His hot neighbor is here with me playing nurse now. *peach emoji**eggplant emoji*

10:55 AM ME:

middle finger emoji

10:56 AM CAPTAIN LANDO:

Wrong finger, asshole.

10:56 AM BALSY:

There he is.

10:56 AM FERGIE:

Call off the national guard.

Wait…where's the rookie?

I turn to Sincaid who's in the driver's seat. "Thanks for taking me. You didn't have to do this."

He looks at my profile before putting his attention back on the road with a shrug. "You would've done it for me."

He's right. I would've. Though it wouldn't be a car I'd be lugging him to and from doctor's appointments in. I hate cars. I hate planes too. But taking a few pills before a flight helps take care of that phobia. Driving though? Hell no. Unless it's someone else behind the wheel. And even then…

"You okay, Z?" The rookie's brows are furrowed and his eyes are bouncing from the road and back to me every few seconds.

Change the subject.

"I'm fine," I assure him. My clenched fists in my lap uncurl as I try to breathe. "The guys are going to flip their lids that I'm out for a few games," I say, sounding more like myself and not like someone straining to get control over what surely might be a panic attack.

"And Matthews is likely facing a suspension," Sincaid adds.

"He deserves it. He can dish it out but he can't take it." *I'm okay. I'm okay. We're almost at my place.*

"You did go after his girl," he smirks. "Sore subject. Everyone knows it."

"He came for my mom." Not that she would care. *Red light. Shit. This is taking forever.*

"Fair. So who do you think Coach will call up to play while you're out?" he asks, looking at me while we're stopped. The concern on his face doesn't falter. But I've become a pro at hiding.

"We have plenty of good D-men on the roster." I sit up more and try to not look so threatened. "They'll figure it out. And gives you a chance to play with someone that doesn't wind up in the box every game," I grin. "It's a win for you either way."

Sincaid shakes his head. "Doesn't feel like a win, Z. Not with the playoffs coming up. How long did they say you might need to heal?"

It's true, this isn't great timing. Then again, my schedule for the week has suddenly opened up. So maybe not all is lost. "Doc says it's minor. Maybe a week or two before I'm back on the ice."

"The guys aren't going to like this. Matthews will have a target on his back from here on. They already can't stand the Thunderhawks."

"Long-standing rivals. Thunderhawks were pissed when we entered the division. A few of their guys got offered contracts early on to join us. It was like a slap in the face for them."

He pulls up outside of my building and the car comes to a complete stop and I can finally breathe normally.

"So, what are you going to do for a week with no hockey?" He pries some more.

I smirk, "I've got a few ideas."

* * *

It's late when I pull up to the bar. Coach and the boys took it hard when they found out about my lingering condition.

We have three games this week alone. And just like the rookie predicted, Matthews now has a 'Wanted Dead or Alive' poster up inside our locker room with his face on it. A little overkill if you ask me, but the boys didn't waste any time expressing their fury.

I shut off my bike and pull off my helmet. Shaking out the hair that likes to stick to my forehead on these humid Houston nights. I pull the ball cap out of my back pocket and slap it over my head.

The bar is already alive with music and movement inside. I lift a leg over the side of my Hayabusa; the matte black helmet with the mirrored visor tucked under my arm as I stroll into the bar.

I shouldn't be here. She's busy at work. But I want Kesley to see that I'm okay. And not some hurt puppy that constantly needs to be watched.

And I need to know if this woman will agree to be my wife.

The boys are playing tonight which means the Heatwave faithful are all gathered here at The Breakaway to catch the game. If I can't be playing, then there's no place I'd rather be than amongst our screaming die-hard fans who like to drink too much.

I spot her in the corner tapping away on the POS with one hand and a stack of bills in her other hand. The register pops open and she tucks away the cash where it goes and pulls out the change her customer needs.

I stroll up to her and lean over the bar. "Hello, wifey."

Her eyes flicker up to my face and then go back to the register, ignoring my comment. She closes it with her hip and hands the change over to her waiting patron.

"No, no. Keep the change, sweetheart." The older man winks at her.

I don't realize I'm staring at him but I must be because Kesley calls my name in a strained voice.

"What?" I say turning to her.

"Stop scaring my customers," she motions with a quick jerk of her head towards the older gentleman who is now staring back at me.

"I'm sorry," I say to the man as I take the empty barstool next to him. But he's still staring back at me, and now with an open jaw.

"It's you. You're Zane O'Connor." His lips quirk up.

"Guilty," I say.

He taps the man next to him, whose eyes are glued to the screen until it goes to a quick commercial break. The second man turns to me, too. And I see the realization cross his face.

Great. There's no hiding under my cap, now.

The man guffaws and fumbles for his phone. "This is crazy. You're here. You're really here. Can I get a selfie, man? Hey, how's the head?" he asks as he fully turns his body in my direction.

Suddenly the entire bar is turned away from the TV and leaning toward us to hear my update.

I can't let the fans down.

"Fit as a fiddle," I announce proudly. "Couldn't be better, just need the all clear from the doc and I'll be back on the ice in no time."

I'm sure our PR manager, Rina Lopez, would be proud of that answer, considering she's the one who fed me the line.

Kesley stares at my fan club with fascination. At least I think it's fascination. It could be irritation. It's hard to know the difference with her.

I turn to her. "In the meantime, I find myself with a little time off." I wink.

She rolls her eyes and crosses her arms in front of her. "What's that supposed to mean?"

"That means... looks like my schedule has suddenly cleared up for a certain weekend trip," I say, popping the P.

She drops her arms, "Yeah, I've been thinking. I don't think that's such a good idea."

"Hey Kes!" A man with blonde hair tied up in a man bun calls from the other end pointing at two waiting customers in the middle of the bar. I think Ryker told me once that this guy owns the place.

"We're not done talking about this," she says, grabbing a dish towel and throwing it over her shoulder as she goes to attend to the waiting customers.

The man next to me leans over and whispers, "Word of advice, kid?" He's dressed in a suit, with his white shirt and tie loosened. He looks like he just got out of an important meeting and came straight to the bar.

"About?" I ask him.

"Don't be coy. Tell her what you want."

I cock my head to the side. "And what exactly do you think I want?" I ask the probing stranger.

"Or don't," he says putting his hands up. "There's just a big difference between a man that lets things happen and a man that *makes* things happen."

His eyes are back on the screen above our heads, just as Hutchy hits a one-timer into the goal of the opposing team. We all jump up out of our seats shouting and high-fiving each other for the Heatwave goal.

"Your boys are playing well tonight," he says.

"They are. But back to your observation..." I say to him, wanting to find out what this complete stranger is seeing.

He turns his attention back to me. "It's written all over your face, O'Connor."

"What is?" I ask.

"That you want her, son."

This guy doesn't even know me. And he's able to read me like a book. "So... you think I should just make a move?"

He looks at me and then back to the game, "I think you're a man who's probably withheld because he's too afraid of what could be."

How is he doing this? "How could you possibly know that?"

He finally leans back on the barstool and turns to me, "Because, O'Connor. In another life, I was you. I've read about you. I read up on all my favorite players." He smiles and it touches his eyes. "I lost my wife of twenty years almost a decade ago. Worst pain of my life. It took me forever to finally come to grips with the idea that even though my wife wasn't alive anymore, it didn't mean I couldn't live for the both of us."

I shake my head. "But isn't that... unfair? She's gone and you still get to live?"

The man whose name I still haven't caught furrows his brow. "What you're talking about sounds a heck of a lot like survivor's guilt, son. And if you go the rest of your life holding on to that belief. You'll always be miserable. Nothing will hold the sweetness you crave. Guilt has a way of robbing us of all the joy life has in store for us."

The man looks back at the game. Fergie takes the puck around the net and shoots a wraparound goal during a Heatwave penalty kill.

The bar crowd jumps to their feet and high fives are served up all around again for the shorthanded goal.

When we're settled down, he looks over to me. "You ok, son?"

I blink at him. "I'm living my dream. I play for the NHL. I have teammates that are like brothers I never asked for but they're there. I have a sister that cares for me more than she needs to. A place to call home. A city that loves me even if I don't deserve their admiration. And I still..." I shake my head. "I still can't feel much of anything most days."

The man takes a swig of his drink and places it down in front of him, turning to me. "The goodness of life isn't something you can just wait to experience. Sometimes we have to chase it down. Make it stay. And let go of the guilt that keeps us from enjoying that goodness."

I look up at Kesley still serving up drinks on the other side of the bar. She has no idea how I feel about her. She can't possibly know the depth of it.

"You're looking for permission to live, O'Connor," the man says. "And people who look for permission for every little thing they do in life, end up wasting a lot of time on something they're never going to get."

I blink at him some more.

"Anyway, I'm sure I've talked your ear off," he says turning back to the TV.

I turn to face the register in front of me. Kesley is slinging drinks on the other side of the bar like it's nobody's business. And I'm sure if we get a win tonight, the boys will be coming through for a quick celly later making her even busier.

When she starts walking in my direction balancing cards, cups, and plates I jump into action. Kesley freezes as she sees me pop open the bar-top and grab a few plates out of her hands.

"Zane, what are you doing? You can't be back here," she grits out.

"Sure I can," I say with a grin.

She whips her head back over to the bar owner at the other end of the bar and he's busy taking orders on that side. "Fine, take these to the kitchen. Through those doors," she motions with her head.

I nod and catch a glimpse of the wise man smiling as he takes another swig of his drink.

It's midnight when the bar is finally settling down. The Heatwave surprisingly lost the game in overtime. So the guys didn't show up. They tend to sulk after losses. A bad habit of ours for sure.

I'm in the back washing dishes with the silent guy whose name tag says *Wayne* when Kesley pokes her head in.

"Wayne, is this guy bothering you?" she asks, leaning on the door frame with her arms crossed.

Wayne looks up, sees her, and takes an airpod out from one of his ears. "I'm sorry did you say something, Kesley?"

"Wait, did you have those in the whole time?" I ask him pointing at the earpiece, dumbfounded.

"Have you been talking to yourself this whole time, Zane?" Kesley asks playfully.

Wayne shrugs and puts the airpod back into his ear. His long stringy hair covers it again.

"Wow, Wayne. And here I thought we were hitting it off." I toss the drying towel I was using onto the counter and walk over to Kesley.

"Why are you still here? Shouldn't you be resting?"

I place a forearm above her head and lean in. "If you want me to leave, just say so, little lion."

Her breath hitches slightly as I wait for her rebuttal.

"I liked having you here," she admits.

"You did?" My growing grin can't help itself.

"Yeah, it's easier to make fun of you with the customers when you're right there to point at and laugh."

I scoff. "You're a mean, little lion."

"Well, you're easy to roast. So I guess we're even." She ducks out from under my arm and goes to the small employee break room.

"Wait," I say catching up to her. "We're not even."

She turns to me with a glare.

"You took care of me the other day. It's my turn to return the favor."

She grabs her bag and keys from a cubby and turns to face me again. "And what exactly do you have in mind?"

"Well, you wanted to see the arena didn't you?"

She pauses as if I just piqued her interest.

"Yeah?"

"So let me show you the arena. It'll be you're own personal tour."

"Okay... when?"

I look at my watch. The ice should've been leveled out already by the Zambonis.

"Right now," I say with a smirk.

Chapter 12
Kesley

'm fun. I'm sexy. I can be spontaneous.

I'm repeating the words like a mantra in my head as the unusually cool night air whips through my hair under the helmet Zane insisted that I wear. I tighten my hold around his waist as we zoom through downtown Houston.

It didn't take much convincing on Zane's part to get me on the back of his bike to ride out to Space City Arena. I'm just curious enough to see what I can learn that I didn't bat an eye when he slipped onto his bike and patted the seat behind him.

He parks in the area where the players and staff park and shuts off the bike.

"You shouldn't be riding without a helmet," I tell him.

"Well, I don't feel comfortable with you riding without one so..."

I slip off the heavy full-face helmet and hand it back to him.

"I'll buy you one that fits," he promises.

He turns to me and holds out his hand to help me off the back of his bike. "You don't have to do that."

"Sure I do," he says with that husky voice that I don't want to argue with. "Come on."

He swipes his card and the door beeps with green lights as it opens.

"So the players have their own entrance?"

"Players, staff, management. Yep. We all have special access."

"And you're allowed after hours like this?"

He holds the door open to slip me through and his amused smile crosses his face. "Not necessarily."

He shuts the door behind us. And places a hand on the small of my back to lead me down the dark hallway. My body responds to the touch with a bolt of electricity down my spine.

"Zane? Are you telling me we're breaking and entering? Can we go to jail for this? I have a son, I can't go to jail," I freak out.

"Shhh," he stops my rant and places a finger on my lips. "Nobody's going to jail," he whispers. "Now, follow me."

He takes my hand and leads me into another hall that is only lit up by the red emergency exit signs above the doorways.

"Where are we going?" I whisper behind him.

He keeps pulling me along until we get to a door in the middle of the dark hall. He swipes his card again and it opens. Pulling me in, he shuts the door behind us before switching on the lights.

I blink at the sudden change and look around.

"A closet? You brought me to a closet."

He chuckles. "It should be somewhere around here."

He drops my hand and goes to a storage box, lifting it to

see what's inside. When he doesn't find what he's looking for. He moves to another box.

"Care to clue me on what we're looking for, Sherlock?"

He doesn't stop but continues pushing aside some things and searching through more boxes.

"Zane."

"Here it is!" His face lights up as he holds up a pair of pretty pink skates lined with what looks like soft wool.

"Those look... expensive."

He looks down at my shoes and then back at the skates. "And they should fit you just right. They're Libby's."

Of course, they are. I hesitate to grab them. "I don't know how to skate," I admit.

He lowers the skates to his side. "Really?"

"Really," I tell him.

"Well, then... lucky for you, little lion. I'm an excellent skater. I'll teach you. Come with me."

He opens the door again and pokes his head back out into the dark hall. He switches off the light and takes my hand again to lead me down further until we get to an orange door.

"What's in here?" I whisper.

He plugs in a key code and the door beeps open. "You'll see."

When we step inside the lights automatically switch on revealing row after row of black metal storage shelving each with a Heatwave logo on the end and a glowing keypad with buttons pointing right or left. They're lined up back to back with no space in between them.

He walks to the very last one and presses the right button on it. Suddenly mechanisms whir to life and the first shelving unit moves followed by the second and the third each clicking into place behind the other until it reaches the last unit and stops. There's now room enough for him to walk down it.

"This is some high-tech stuff," I say in awe.

"It's the NHL," he shrugs, before disappearing down into the space between the shelves. I poke my head around it and see him grabbing some skates from a box that has his last name printed on the front.

"So after each game, you guys put your stuff away in here?"

He grabs a few extra pads and walks back down the aisle toward me. "We have EMs. Equipment managers. Their whole job is to make sure all the gear is taken care of and ready to go for game day. They usually handle the care of the equipment so we can focus on training."

I hold the pink skates in one arm and offer to help him with the other.

"I've got it, Watson."

"Watson?"

"Yeah, if I'm Sherlock then you must be Watson."

"No," I correct him. "I'd be his fascinating and far more entertaining sister, Enola."

Zane halts as we're making our way to the door leading back to the hall with all of the collected gear. "Sherlock has a sister?" he says surprised.

"Hockey doesn't leave much room for streaming movies I presume?"

He just blinks at me.

"Yes, Sherlock has a sister who is twenty years younger than him. In the new franchise. The one with Henry Cavill."

"Huh," he says turning back. "People say *I* look like Henry Cavill you know."

"No, they don't."

He stops again and I bump into him. "Yes, they do."

"Who says that, Zane?"

He thinks about it before turning around again and saying, "People."

I roll my eyes. But for the first time. I can see it. The dark hair. The strong jawline. The Superman-esque chin. If he had heterochromia instead of those ocean eyes of his... yeah. I can see it.

But I won't be admitting that to him. He has enough ego for him and Henry both.

I follow him down the dark hallway until we meet a set of double doors. Before he pushes through he turns around to me and says with theatrical flair, "Are you ready for one of the most memorable experiences of your life?"

Experiences. Ugh. He sounds like my boss. I glare up at him, "Seriously?"

"Not many people can say they've skated on NHL pro hockey ice, Kes. It's kind of a life goal for some people."

"You're really talking this up, caveman. You better deliver."

"Oh, I deliver," he says with a smirk.

I push past him and swing the door open myself. And when I do, I'm met with the coliseum that is an empty twenty-thousand-seat indoor hockey arena. The smell of the ice is the first thing that hits me. It's chill. And I shiver from the cold air that hits my skin.

"Here," Zane motions to a random seat in a dark corner near the entrance. "Sit here and lace up while I go grab some sweaters."

I sit down and kick off the boots I've been wearing for the last eight hours since starting my shift at The Breakaway. I yawn. Remembering it's super late. Zane and I are slowly making late-night hangs a habit.

I'm finally at the point of lacing my skates when he comes bursting through the set of doors. In his arms is a parka accompanied by a Heatwave pullover that matches the one he's now wearing with the number eighty-two sprawled across the back.

"Which one?" he asks, raising each one up, one at a time.

"The parka's a little overkill. Don't ya think?"

He shrugs and tosses it to the side looking down at my work so far.

"Need some help there?"

I try looping the laces into one of the little holes and tug on it. "I think I've got it."

"Here, let me." He slowly takes a knee in front of me and reaches for my leg, taking it into his lap. He undoes the laces. Pulling and tightening with expert precision. He stops to rock my ankle back and forth and then continues until he gets to the top of the skate and he does some trick with the laces pulling them into bunny ears and tying them with finesse.

He looks up at me. That muscle in his jaw ticking again as he licks his lips. The look on his face sends my insides whirling. But without warning he drops my now laced-up foot and takes the other one. I struggle to balance on the seat with his aggressive movement.

"Careful, little lion," he warns.

"You're so rough."

"You telling me you don't like it rough?" he asks, cocking a brow.

I look down at him. At the way he's holding my leg balanced on his own. He wraps a big hand around my ankle and slides it up toward my knee.

I watch his movement. My heart rate picks up speed.

He wraps his other hand around my leg and drags it up

to my thigh. I gulp, watching him caress me over the leggings I'm wearing. His hands feel so warm to the touch. They heat my leg the entire way. He stops just short of my upper thigh before he looks up at me through his dark lashes.

A dare lingers in that look. I reach forward, taking his face into both hands, and pull him toward me. Without any hesitation, his lips meet mine. A low, pleased rumble escapes him as our lips move gently. Erotically. Ever so slowly over each other. It isn't hurried. Instead, it's painfully measured. He brings one knee down and lifts me out of my chair.

And before I can register what he's doing, he's replacing me on the chair and sitting me on his lap.

"I can't tell you how many times I've imagined doing this."

"Zane," I rasp against his lips. "There could be cameras." I look around in a panic.

He grins. "I'm just kissing you, Kesley."

He has one hand on my lower back and the other is traveling up my thigh. He moves his lips from my mouth and onto my neck and whispers, "Unless you want me to do more."

He spins me around so that my back is flush against him and he puts a hand on either of my thighs and spreads me open wide for him. I'm hanging onto the edge of the chair for stability as he strokes the inside of each thigh tenderly. I breathe deep and relax into his touch. My body relaxes with each breath as he massages me.

He whispers against my ear, "You're always so tense, Kesley. Do you need me to help you relax?"

He leans forward and swipes his tongue along my neck and I moan from the contact.

"You've been holding out on me, little lion. You taste divine." He swipes his tongue over me again and this time I roll my head back onto his shoulder giving him full access to it.

His mouth goes back to my ear, "I wonder what else you'll let me taste." He squeezes my thighs and the heat at my core is so intense. I want him to move his hands higher. To relax me like he's promising. Instead, he's just winding me up.

"Now, tell me, Kesley..." His hands are still on my thighs. Holding me open for him as he reaches forward and makes slow, tantalizing circles with his thumb over that sensitive spot between my legs.

I close my eyes and cherish the sensation. Wanting more. Needing more. I swallow hard.

"Do you like it soft and gentle and sweet?" he asks into my ear in a low rasp.

He keeps working me over my leggings. It's not nearly enough for what my body is craving.

He stops stroking me. And lifts me up off his lap until I'm standing. Still with only one skate on my foot. He rises from the chair and looks down at me, grabbing me by the chin and pulling my face up to meet his hooded gaze. His other hand is on the small of my back holding me up to him.

"Or do you like it hard, fast. Rough?" he asks, his head cocking to the side as he waits for my response.

"I-I... I can't even think," I admit to him.

He hums in satisfaction. "Maybe a little both then?" He uses his thumb to pull down my bottom lip. "I guess we'll have to find out. When I make you my wife."

The way he says the words *my wife* sends the heat that was pulsing through my core into overdrive.

I suck in my lip waiting for him to bend down and kiss

me. The look on his face says that he will. That he wants that as bad as I do.

Instead, he drops his hand. And I instantly miss it.

"Sorry to disappoint you," he says with a sly grin. "But I'm supposed to be giving you a private tour and you're being very distracting, little lion. So sit down, and let's put that other skate on you, hmm?"

I hate him. He knows exactly what he's doing to me and it's driving me mad.

There's a rumble in his chest as he chuckles to himself at my expense and I glare at him.

"You want more? Say you'll be my wife," he says matter of factly.

I scoff. "Are you serious right now?"

He bites on his bottom lip playfully before letting it go. "Dead serious, Kes."

He cocks his head again and I've never wanted to slap a man as much as I want to slap that bemused look right off of Zane right this instant.

"You look like you'd rather murder me than marry me."

I narrow my eyes at him as I sit down and stick out my foot for him to lace up the other skate. He works hard to restrain himself from laughing at me.

When he's done tying up my laces he stands and offers an outstretched hand. I slap it away and push myself off the chair, trying to balance on the skates that are practically boots on top of thick sharpened knives.

"So feisty," he says taking my seat and putting on his skates.

I try hard to balance on the edges of the blades as I make my way to the entrance of the arena and wait for him. He's much faster lacing up his own skates. He grabs the sweatshirt off the floor and stalks over to me like the expert skater he is.

"Here," he says holding out the hoodie. "You're gonna want this. Trust me."

I yank the hoodie out of his hands and pull it over my head. I'm so pissed at him right now. What kind of an asshole leaves a woman hanging high and dry like that? I mean, I know I technically said that us being together wasn't going to happen. It can't happen. But also, why stoke the fire only to put it out?

He's infuriating.

He tilts his head as he assesses me.

"What?" I say moving toward the ice again.

"Don't like the concept of edging, I presume."

I turn to him perplexed. "What are you... wait, you did that on purpose?!"

He comes up behind me and slips a hand on my waist pulling me to him until I'm flush against his rock-hard body. And I can feel the rock hardness in his jeans.

I gulp as the warmth from his breath brushes against my ear. "I want to see you on the edge of coming undone," he says. "Over and over. Until finally you take what you want from me and ride out your pleasure. Coming so hard you pass out in my bed, little lion."

The heat returns to that place between my legs and I can't help but imagine what that would mean for me to ride out my pleasure with him. He notices when I stop breathing.

"But first, I need to hear you say it," his playful voice returns.

"Say what, caveman?"

He reaches around me and pushes open the door to the ice. "Say you'll marry me."

Still in a haze. Still wildly turned on and upset with him, I take a tentative step onto the ice. He's immediately behind me holding me in place. I wobble onto it. Mostly because I'm not used to being on it, but also because the man just turned my legs to noodles with his words.

He steps on after me and effortlessly glides around to where I'm facing. He stretches out his hands for me to take them and as I take sad little infant steps toward him, I slip and he catches me.

He chuckles. "Not such a feisty little lion on the ice. Are you, Kes?"

"You play too much," I tell him.

He shrugs. "You should play more."

He pulls me toward him and I slowly slide up to him until my arms are wrapped around his waist. My face plants onto his chest.

"You ok?"

"I know I'm going to regret this," I tell him, my words muffled by his sweater.

"It just takes practice. All good things do."

I look up at him, his strong arms balancing me. "I'm not talking about the ice skating, Zane."

He cocks a brow.

"I'm going to regret saying yes to being your wife."

A slow smile spreads across his face. "I'll make sure I make you eat those words."

And with that, he pulls me along with him on the ice.

Chapter 13
Kesley

It's a work-from-home kind of day.

One, because Zane had me skating until my legs gave out last night so walking sounds like a horrendous idea.

And two, because just as I suspected, a private tour with him meant we'd be making out in some dark corner of the arena. I was able to make it two months as his neighbor again before I found myself physically incapable of keeping my hands off the man I despise.

Though, we did do a little more than just make out. That slick tongue of his sounds like it might be good for more than just smooth-talking. So when I woke up this morning alone in my bed, I was slightly disappointed. Whatever the girl version is of blue balls, I'm feeling it.

I toss in my bed again and reach over to check my phone on the nightstand. It's nine am. We stayed out until almost four in the morning.

I decide to do some research on hockey and I'm playing a video describing all the positions on a team when my phone lights up and buzzes with Izzy's name.

I jolt up and hit the answer button. "Hello?"

"Oh hi, Kesley! Good, you're up," Izzy says in a chipper voice. She must be a morning person. I'm not a night owl but I'm also not an early bird. I'm more like a lazy caterpillar in a cocoon that prefers not to be disturbed until she's fully ready.

"Just barely," I admit accompanied by a yawn. "Everything ok?"

"Yes! Everything's great. Listen, Kesley, the boys are heading out to Florida tonight for an away game and Rina and I won't be going with them this time."

"Okay," I say, wondering where this is going.

"I'm feeling very pregnant," she continues. "And Rina... well she's my bestie and hates going on trips if I'm not there so she's sending her assistant this time. We were wondering..." She hesitates.

I rub my eyes. "Yes?"

"Well, would you be interested in a girl's night? I have so much wine and I need help getting rid of it since drinking is out of the question for the time being and it's just teasing me sitting there in my wine rack."

A girl's night? I hadn't realized just how long it's been since I've sat and chatted with other girls that weren't Libby or my mom.

"That sounds... fun, Izzy. W-what time are you getting together?"

"Later, around 7:30. I'll shoot you my address. I don't want to seem too forward it's just... most of the guys aren't in serious relationships so when I find someone that is... I get a little excited."

Izzy seems like a girl's girl. The kind of person you want to have in your corner.

"I don't have a shift tonight so I'll be there."

"Oh yay!" I hear her clapping on the other end. "We'll dish about everything you need to know being a Heatwave SO."

"A what?"

"A significant other. A WAG! There aren't many of us."

"Oh," I chuckle nervously, "I'm not a..."

"You are with O'Connor, aren't you? Oh my god, am I reading this all wrong?"

"Um... I mean, I am," I admit sheepishly.

"Totally understand. You haven't defined the relationship. It's cool," she says. "Regardless of what kind of label you want to put on the O'Connor thing, you're a friend of Libby's so you're a friend of ours."

"Your friends with Libby?"

"Oh yeah, we hang out at every home game."

Libby. She hasn't called yet. I'm not sure how I'm going to tell her that Zane and I will be more than neighbors soon. Maybe Zane already did and she's pissed and avoiding me.

"So what do you say?" Izzy asks.

"Count me in."

She squeals. "Yay! I can't wait to give you the inside scoop. See you later."

Inside scoop. Yes, that's exactly what I need. "Me too, Izzy. See you later."

When I hang up, I feel a growing ball of guilt in the pit of my stomach.

Am I a horrible person?

I'm using Zane. Now, Izzy. To get the information I need to be able to put out an "experience" aka *an* exposé for The Pulse's readers.

And for what?

I look around my quiet room and my eyes land on a picture of me holding Liam when he was just a newborn.

His beautiful eyes are gazing at me and the smile on my face is real and palpable.

"I'm doing it for him. For us," I whisper to myself.

It's just a means to an end. Besides, I'm not Zane's significant other. He came to me to help him get his inheritance. Not because he feels anything for me... except maybe the desire to combine body parts.

Once he gets what he wants, he'll be out of my life and back to being the obnoxious neighbor next door. I need to remind myself of that. This is temporary. And once I get what I need too, it might be time for Liam and I to get a place of our own.

The hard knock on my door makes my stomach jump into my throat. I'm not expecting company.

I plant my feet on the ground and stretch before doing a quick mirror check. My messy bun is messier than usual and I most definitely did not wash my face before passing out last night. The runny mascara under my eyes is proof of that. At least I'm wearing pajamas.

I pad across the apartment and peek out the peephole. On the other side of it is a refreshed-looking Zane carrying a cup holder with various drinks in one hand and a paper bag in the other. I instantly panic.

Shit. I look like shit. And he looks like... I check again. *That.*

When did he even have time to go out and grab all that? Unlocking the door I open it, hiding my body and half of my face behind it.

His eyes are bright but a sudden look of confusion crosses his face. "What are you doing?"

"What are *you* doing, you vampire?"

He tilts his head, "Vampire?"

"You must be Dracula. You don't sleep apparently."

He chuckles, "Oh I sleep. Living in the same space as a squawking parrot just makes for unwanted early wake-up calls." He lifts the items in his hands. "Brought some sustenance. Can I come in?"

The smell of hot coffee fills my nostrils and I open the door wider without thinking.

He smiles and steps in. "Another vampire trait," I announce.

"What's that?" He sets the drinks on the table near the kitchen area.

"Having to ask for permission to enter a home."

He looks up from the bag he's rummaging through. "Most people call those manners, Kesley."

"Didn't realize you knew about those."

He whips out a donut and hands me one of the coffees along with it, unfazed by my un-caffeinated comments. I hesitate, but it looks really good. And my stomach rumbles giving it away.

I take the offered items and go to sit on my couch.

"How are your legs?" he asks, pulling a cup of coffee for himself and sitting in the space next to me.

"Like they ran a marathon. Up a mountain. In the middle of winter."

He laughs. "I feel like that after most games."

"Then how do you recover for the next game?"

He pauses to think about it. "Ice baths. Warm massages. And a lot of topical anesthetic cream."

"That's why you always smell like a nursing home," I grin as I take a sip of the warm liquid.

He puts a hand on his chest. "I do not smell like a nursing home. Nursing homes smell better than I do."

Teasing. This is what life with Zane used to be like. He teased me. I teased him. But it never went beyond that.

Especially since by the time I realized I might like the cocky jock, he was already dating Mallory Bennett. But this playful Zane... I haven't seen this version of him since before the accident.

"Izzy called me," I tell him.

He cocks his head. "What'd she say?"

"She and Rina want to hang out with me later. Something about being the newest WAG."

He laughs. "Wait, Rina's not a WAG," he says.

"No, but Izzy seems to think that *I* am," I deadpan.

"It was the jersey," he says with a nod.

"The what?"

"You wore my real jersey at the friends and family game. That's basically like me putting a ring on it."

I choke on the sip of coffee I just inhaled. "Excuse me?" I cough out.

Zane laughs again. "Yeah. You wear the jersey. You're staking your claim."

"But people wear your jersey at every game, don't they? People don't just assume they're dating you."

"Not *my* jersey, Kes. Those are replicas."

"That just seems like an unnecessary assumption."

He holds back a grin and leans further back on the couch crossing an ankle over his knee. "I bet she wants to get together and talk playoff jackets."

"What's that?"

"A quirky tradition the WAGs started a little while back. We've never actually been in the playoffs... or had WAGs so never needed them. But, we're in and you're here." He smiles amused with himself.

"We're not official," I remind him.

"Not yet," he says with so much confidence.

He licks his lips and gives me a smoldering, panty-melting look. The devil.

"Whatever," I say avoiding his gaze. "Besides Izzy, are there any other *real* WAGs?"

"Hutchy has one. He eloped not too long ago. No babies yet. But I think they're trying. Let me see..." He gets lost thinking through his teammates. "I mean if Cap and Rina ever give into their mutual attraction."

"Rina Lopez? The PR manager?" I ask. "They don't seem to like each other much." They snubbed each other at the game I attended on Saturday.

"Nah, they had to have banged. I see it all over their faces of mutual disdain," he says.

I don't know Rina. But I'm assuming that her dating a player, or even just sleeping with one, wouldn't be a good thing for her career.

I watch Zane as he looks around my apartment. Photos of Liam and I are sprinkled throughout the space. Quite a few with Libby, too. And his eyes are roving over each one from his place on the couch. He usually doesn't stay for long. I start to get nervous.

"So Liam," he says.

My eyes whip to his. "Yeah?"

"Smart kid. Does he know what he wants to be when he grows up? Besides a parrot dad like myself?"

"He wants to be a lot of things—he's six. But mostly he wants to be a superhero."

"So I've seen." He smirks.

Liam is known for his very intense superhero obsessions. When he clings to one, he becomes that hero—all day, every day. Except while he's in school.

"So what's the hero du jour?" Zane asks, cocking his head at me.

"The incredible Hulk."

"Huh, interesting choice."

"Why's that?" I ask.

"He's *my* favorite." He says it with a sense of pride. Like he somehow inspired my son's latest obsession. I'm about to tell him I don't mean to burst his bubble and that Liam will be obsessed with a new hero soon enough when my phone bleets from the coffee table.

I set my coffee down and flip it to see the caller ID.

Shit. It's Jeremy.

Zane arches a brow in my direction. "Is that *Rowan?*" he asks.

I roll my eyes. "That's none of your business."

"Technically, you're my fiancee... so I'd say it is."

I glare at him and leave him to take the call in my room, only answering it once I have the door closed.

I clear my throat, "Hello, Mr. Clark.

"Ms. Brooks," he says drily. "How's the research coming along?"

"Uh, good. Really good, sir. I think I'll have some pretty interesting content for our readers."

"That's great to hear. Listen, I have a request, Ms. Brooks."

As if he hasn't already requested enough of me. "Yes, sir?"

"I need you to find out everything you can about the Heatwave PR manager."

I blink back my surprise. "Rina Lopez, sir?" *Does he have my place bugged or something?*

"Yes, Lopez," he says with a hint of disgust.

"Ok-ay, what exactly do you want me to find out?"

"Just what she's hiding. Every PR manager is hired to spin stories to protect their players. I need to get to the bottom of what she's hiding."

Why does this sound like a personal vendetta? "I don't know if that's something I can do, sir."

He stays silent on the other end for a long moment. "Your job is on the line here, Ms. Brooks. If I were you, I'd do whatever I had to do to make sure I came out on top. Wouldn't you?"

I hold back the growl I want to unleash. I hate being backed into a corner. "Yes, sir."

"Good. I look forward to your article, Ms. Brooks." He hangs up without another word.

I shake my head at what I've gotten myself into. Once this exposé comes out, not only will Zane go back to hating me, but I'll lose all faith and confidence from Rina and Izzy. From the entire team. I'll be on the side of the press. And from my observations, you can't stay friends with someone whose sole job is to report on everything they know about you. I wish Libby were here. She would've talked me out of this.

But I have to do it. It's the launchpad for my career. Once I'm considered a true journalist, so many more opportunities will open up for me. I'll be able to move me and Liam into our own place. My parents can stop worrying about me. I've always known this was a cutthroat field. This is just the name of the game.

I go back to a waiting Zane in the living room. He's sipping his coffee and flipping through channels like nothing is amiss.

"Did you say hi to Rowan for me?"

I scoff. "You know, jealousy isn't a good look for you, Zane."

He looks at me and shrugs. "Just protecting what's mine."

"I'm not your property."

"Tell that to the wet spot between your legs last night."

I can feel my face flush.

"You know what, Zane. Yes, you turn me on. Okay. I admit that. I'm a single mom who hasn't been in a serious relationship in... well... ever. I don't party. I don't sleep around. So don't think you're some kind of sexy panty-whisperer. You just so happened to find the one woman who could probably get off on somebody whispering the word *sex* into her ear. Okay."

He sits there, not moving. Just staring at me.

"What? Don't just look at me like that."

He leans forward placing his coffee cup on the table in front of him and he shifts on the couch until he's next to me. He swings an arm around the back of the couch, leans into me, and whispers, "Sex."

I pull back and stare at him. And he grins.

"Are you serious?"

"I think you don't give yourself enough credit, Kesley."

I shake my head confused.

"Any man would give up his most prized possession for a chance to get to be the one to put a smile on your face. You're not some easy lay. You're not a forgettable one-night stand. You are complex. Challenging. So I want you to know something. I do intend to drive you wild and give you the best sex you could possibly imagine. And I would want nothing more than to watch you come undone from my touch."

The room suddenly feels like a sauna.

"But I also intend to make you feel like the amazing woman that you are. To give you the attention you deserve. And not take it for granted when I walk into a room with you on my arm and every man in the vicinity secretly wishes that it was them walking you in. You don't see what I see, Kes. You don't see how other people see you. It's endearing. Because you don't have to walk around half-naked to drive men crazy. You just have to smile. And do you know how I know that?"

I think I'm stunned. Because all I do is shake my head in response. "Because that smile. That beautiful hard-earned smile from you is what's kept me sane during some of the hardest points in my life. I could never admit it before. But it's the truth."

He watches me for a second before standing up and grabbing the coffee cup. "I've got an appointment I need to get to," he announces. "But I'll call you later and we'll talk details about our wedding."

And with that, he walks out my door... and I'm left in even more of a puddle than I was last night.

Chapter 14
Zane

"Zane, welcome. Please have a seat," the stunning Black woman with the grey dreadlocks motions to me. She's warm. Motherly. I get the sense she can make anyone crack with just a few key phrases.

I look around the office taking in the blue color on the walls and the small trinkets she has scattered throughout the space. I go to the area she motioned to. There's a couch that could fit three of me. A chair on the other side of it. And a bean bag.

I look at her with furrowed brows. "Any... seat in particular?"

"Nope," she shakes her head. "Whichever you prefer."

I nod. This is a test. It has to be. The study has commenced and I'm officially a monkey being evaluated for my intelligence. I know what choosing the bean bag would say about me so that's a hard pass. But the chair and the couch? I don't know. Does choosing the chair mean I think I'm some kind of king. A narcissist who thinks himself better than others. And what of that couch? It looks like it was taken from someone's grandmother's house. Does choosing it say that I have repressed memories of growing up that need to be dug up and dealt with? *What does it all mean?*

"Zane," the woman says calmly, snapping my attention back to her. "They're just seats. Pick anyone you like." She smiles.

I take in a deep breath and opt for the couch, sitting in the middle and trying to get comfortable. I cross an ankle over my knee and lean back, placing one hand on my lap and the other across the back of the couch.

There. Open posture. Confident. I'm cool. Cool hand Luke. Totally in control. I've got this.

My phone dings in my pocket and I scramble to turn the volume off apologizing profusely as I stuff it back in my pocket and reposition myself. Clearing my throat as I do.

She purses her lips together. "Zane, are you nervous about meeting with me today?"

"What? No. I'm good," I nod to confirm.

She smiles and nods. "Okay, my name is Ada. And I just want to remind you that this is a safe space. You don't have to worry about anything getting out to anyone you know."

"Mmhmm," I nod my understanding.

"Okay then." She leans back, crosses her ankle over her knee, and places her notebook on her lap. "Let's begin with, what brings you in today?"

* * *

"She's amazing, isn't she? She's like Mr. Rogers and Bob Ross and... and Toni Morrison all mixed up into one beautiful human who can read the depths of your soul like a book," Landry goes off.

I'm still feeling hungover from the emotional session. "Yeah, yeah she is," I agree.

"Well, I'm really proud of you man. That's a big step. You can't change anything until you recognize you have a problem."

I think about Libby's words back at my apartment, *"You've got problems, Zane."*

"I guess so," I admit.

"I know so," Keelan says. "Speaking of problems, how are things progressing with Kesley? You shining up my bike for me?"

"Don't be so convinced you got this in the bag," I tell him. "I think you underestimate my abilities."

"Oh is that, right? Well, Ryker did tell me she's hanging with Izzy and Rina today. Hutchy's wife is going too. Sounds like you might be right, O-zone."

I hear the horns of a stadium going off in the background. "Game's getting started here. I'll check in with you later. Bye, man."

I hang up with my team captain. And look around at the downtown bustle taking place around me. I have the rest of the afternoon to burn. The guys aren't here which means the arena is probably available. Normally, I'd go home and not emerge for a few days, wasted and in desperate need of a shave. But, I don't want to. I don't need to.

It'd be good to burn off some of this anxious energy though. I jump on my bike and head over to the arena. The wind is whipping past me on the road. My mind is still a giant whir of jumbled thoughts.

The therapist Landry suggested I go to for grief counseling gave me a lot to think about. And right now, I just need to clear my head.

When I step onto the ice in the empty arena I feel a rush of excitement like I did as a kid stepping onto the rink.

The conversation in that small office earlier is on repeat in my mind.

"What brought you in today, Zane?"

"I think I need help."

"That's a fair assumption," Ada says smiling. *"Most people don't see a therapist without recognizing they can use some help."*

"Right."

"And what do you think you need help with if you don't mind me asking?"

I sit there briefly. Words flying through my mind as I try to grasp onto the one that stands out the most. "Guilt."

"You need help with your guilt?" she clarifies.

"I think so."

"And what brought you to that conclusion?"

I shake my head. I hate doing this. Talking. Bringing stuff up. I'd rather go home and lock myself away. I hate this feeling of having my chest ripped open. Being exposed. But I think about Kesley. The way she looked at me when I was talking to her this morning. And it gives me the small strength I need to keep going.

I push myself and glide on the ice. My legs wake up and I skate across until I reach the red line on the other side of the rink. I stop and the loose ice sprays into the air at my abrupt stop. I turn and skate across to the other side.

"Zane, where does this guilt come from?"

I hate this question. I don't want to admit it. But I need to. I can't move forward if I keep holding onto it. Leaving it unspoken and buried.

"It's... It's been seven years since I lost my pregnant fiancee in a car accident."

The woman pauses to let that sink in, "I'm so sorry to hear that, Zane."

I reach the other side of the rink and as soon as my skate reaches the red line I stop abruptly. The loose ice on this side sprays onto the glass just as I switch on my feet and skate across the ice again.

"It's okay. It was a while ago," I tell her.

"Is that what you feel? Do you feel like it's okay?"

My brows furrow. Bile rises into my throat. I want to throw up. My heart rate picks up and suddenly I'm not sitting on a couch in a psychiatrist's office. I'm getting off a plane. When my phone gets the message. Mallory and the baby... they're not okay.

"No," I choke out.

"No what, Zane?" she presses.

"No, it's... it's not okay."

"What part of it?"

"None of it. None of it is okay."

She nods. "Why?"

"Because it's not fair," I say, my voice rising.

The sound of my blades on the ice picks up speed as I barrel toward the other end of the ice. My lungs are filling with short bursts of air. And my legs are feeling the effects of the sustained sprints. But I keep going. I keep pushing.

"What isn't fair, Zane?"

I look at her. She can't be serious? I have to explain it to her? "That... that in a few seconds a driver would veer into Mallory's car, slamming her vehicle into oncoming traffic and straight into an eighteen-wheeler instantly killing them both..." I crack. "And I'd have to bury them... on my birthday."

I'm sitting there. My hands are clammy. I'm sweating. When did I start sweating? My face is wet. Tears. I'm crying. I didn't even realize I started fucking crying. How am I crying? I'm not sad. I'm furious.

The woman across from me, motions to the box of tissues in front of me. When was the last time I cried?

"And it's not fair, that I'm the one still here. That I have to pretend to be okay."

She nods again. "You're right. None of that. None of that is fair."

I make it to the other side of the ice and stop abruptly again. Spraying the glass with snow.

"Zane, what are you hoping to accomplish in therapy? What would success look like for you?"

"I told you. I don't want to feel this overwhelming guilt."

"Guilt for what?"

I close my eyes. "For still being here. For still living. For not living. Not fully anyway. For wasting the life I have. The life they don't get."

I cross the red line again and instead of continuing I stop abruptly and drop to my knees. The wet streaks drip down from the corners of my eyes onto my cheeks, spilling onto the ice below me.

The sobs start taking over. I try to breathe and cry at the same time and what comes out is a mix of cuss words intermingled with silent pleas for help.

"Grief is like a song you've just heard for the first time. It's confusing and you don't understand the melody. Then you get to the chorus and it pulls you in. It reaches a crescendo and you feel the full force of the music. And when the chorus returns you remember it. It's not as unfamiliar. You know what to expect now. The second time you hear the song. It's easier on the ears. You recognize the parts and where they lead. And by the third time, you might be singing along to the chorus. Then when someone asks you what you're singing. You're able to share from a place of understanding the words, the melody, the way it's carried you."

I stare up at the woman. The tears have stopped streaming and I take in a deep, full breath.

"There's a beautiful life for you. A new song, Zane. And I'll be here to make sure we get you to sing it."

I place a hand on the ice and bring one foot out, rising on it until I'm standing at the end of the rink. I look at the streaks my blades have left. At the mess of shredded ice. My legs are tired.

But for the first time, in a really long time I feel... *alive.*

Chapter 15
Kesley

"Well, I still can't help but laugh when the boys call Ryker, Balsy," Izzy says drinking her sparkling juice out of a wine glass.

"The boys and their nicknames," Rina shakes her head, grabbing the real wine she has in front of her and pouring herself another glass.

Both women are dressed in pajamas in their respective styles. Izzy's in a set of comfy yoga pants that stretch over her growing belly and a white crop top. Her black hair is in a messy bun on top of her head.

Rina is wearing an all-black ensemble of cozy-looking pants with a matching spaghetti strap top covered by a floor-length duster sweater. She looks like she could just jump out of bed at any moment to answer a call and be camera-ready. Her dark brown hair is tied back in a sleek pony.

"It's always been a thing with hockey players," Candace adds. "The least amount of syllables they can get to say something... the better."

Candace Hutchison is wrapped in a blanket on the other side of the couch. She's wearing Hutchy's Heatwave t-shirt and a pair of biker shorts. She removes her glasses to wipe them on the shirt and for the first time, I notice just how blue her eyes are. The girl is stunning. But she's so casual and down to earth. All of them are. Except maybe Rina, she seems like she could command an army, if the occasion called for it.

The lights in the living room are turned down creating a chill ambiance and Izzy has the fireplace on since it's abnormally cold on this March evening. The cool rain coming down outside made for a gloomy evening that is quickly being warmed up by this room and the company in it.

I forget for a moment that it won't last. A sobering thought.

I keep checking my phone to make sure I don't miss the call from Liam. My parents promised they'd be calling after they took him fishing today.

"Waiting for a certain someone?" Rina asks, lifting an eyebrow at me as I place my phone down again for the hundredth time.

"My son, Liam," I smile. I'm sure they thought it was a certain six-foot-five defender. Though it is strange he hasn't reached out given how insistent he's been lately. I wonder if he's alright.

"You said he's six years old. What's been the hardest age?" Izzy asks, tucking her feet under her and getting cozy. "So far, at least?"

I smile, remembering Liam as a baby and then how quickly he became a toddler with mussed hair and sticky hands. Now he's a full-blown human with thoughts of his own.

"Each stage has its pros and cons," I admit. "When they're babies you wonder how you can ever live without having this child in your arms. Then they grow up and start jumping off of things and getting hurt and you realize that you can't protect them from everything. But that's all you want to do as their mom. To keep them from hurting. Then they grow up and get curious about the world around them and what things mean. They ask a billion questions a day and you realize just how little you know about things because you start saying things like '*I don't know. That's just the way it is.*'"

The three women around me are all watching me like I'm some old sage straight out of an epic adventure novel.

"You learn to ultimately embrace each season. I have a sister whose kids are older. She and Mom always tell me to hold onto the moment you're in. That it'll pass in the blink of an eye."

Izzy's hand floats down to her growing belly. She's more than halfway through her pregnancy and was just complaining earlier about her swollen feet and ridiculous appetite.

"But if you were to ask me what's the easiest stage... I'd say right now," motioning to her belly. "Before they can cry and poop and scream and ask a million questions. They're just... with you."

Izzy wipes a tear from her eye and I look around as Candace is sniffling and Rina is clearing her throat uncomfortably.

"I'm sorry. This was supposed to be a fun girl's night and I just made it all emotional, bleh," I shake my head and take a sip of my wine.

Izzy laughs through her tears. "Oh please, don't apologize. This is what girls do. We talk about boys and motherhood and taking over the world—all in one night."

"That's why chocolate and wine were invented," Rina

says matter-of-factly, taking another swig followed by a chocolate-covered almond.

"Speaking of taking over the world," Candace says excitedly. "Our boys are in the playoffs!"

Izzy groans. "Ryker is *impossible* lately, on his strict diet and workout regimens. I told him the other day that if he doesn't stop doing pushups next to the bed before he goes to sleep, then I'm sending him back to my brother's house."

My stomach sinks again knowing this is the moment, "So what exactly does that mean for them? I know it's a big deal, but..."

"A big deal?" Rina says. "It's a *huge* deal. The Houston Heatwave has had one of the toughest runs in new franchise history."

"What do you mean?"

Izzy sits up. "Well, you know how when a city has a big enough fan base they can request to be an NHL expansion? Well, once they go through all the hoops, the teams get built."

"They pick from college-level players or pick up free agents that aren't under binding contracts on other teams," Rina adds.

I nod remembering all that from what I've read in my research so far. "But when you say they've had a tough run..."

"What I mean is that most of the newer teams are stacked with just the right mix of experience and potential," Rina says.

"And that didn't happen for the Heatwave?"

The girls all look at each other. "It did not," says Rina. "The old owner tried something a little different when he had his GM recruit for the Heatwave. Instead of going through the proper process they kind of made some under-the-table deals to get some of the best players from other teams. Paid off sports agents and other GMs to get things done. And kept it hush-hush. Stratton had a lot of pull."

"Yeah, pull," Candace says rubbing her fingers together, suggesting he had a lot of money.

"And that's bad."

"Very," Rina says. "So bad, you can't repeat that to anybody," she says pointing a threatening finger.

I lift my glass and take a long sip of my wine.

"Anyways, the original owner of the team passed away a few years ago and his youngest daughter, Mackenzie Stratton, took over as owner. Ever since she came on board, she's been cleaning up shop. Firing the bad apples and rebuilding. Some people weren't happy about it. But it was the right call."

"So the Heatwave stole players from other teams?" I ask.

"The original Heatwave owner did, yes. But since Mack's been in charge it's all been clean. The club almost got shut down because of the scandal. Some people think her dad passed from a heart attack stemming from the pressure of the mounting judgments he was facing. He wanted to win at all costs, and it cost him everything."

"Needless to say," Candace chimes in. "The Houston Heatwave is one of the least-liked teams in the league. Our boys are divas. Most of them were the best from wherever they came. Chip on the shoulder kind of dudes."

"But you're all here so they can't be *that* bad," I point out.

"They're not," they all say in unison and look at each other with grins.

"They're passionate. Driven. They're a brotherhood. And that's what makes us want to cheer them on," Candace says.

Is this what Jeremy was talking about? What Rina is hiding? The Heatwave had a less than stellar start but they're making it right. Their hard work is what's taking them to the playoffs, not anything else. I wonder what exactly my boss is hoping to find out.

The video call chime on my phone goes off and I jump. "Oh, I gotta take this," I tell the girls and they motion for me to go. I fumble with the phone to press the start video button as I get up and go to the back patio, shutting the door behind me.

"Hey, Incredible Hulk!"

"Hey Mom," Liam says from behind his green mask. He doesn't sound too happy.

"What's wrong, snooks?"

"I caught a fish today," he says with a little sniffle in his voice.

"But isn't that a good thing? That's what you're supposed to do."

His shoulders are slumped and he looks defeated in his green Hulk costume. "I know."

"Well then, what's wrong?"

"Mom, he couldn't breathe. I tried telling Pop-Pops and he just said 'Fish are meant to be eaten, Liam. They're not supposed to breathe once you catch them.' Mom... that is so messed up. How am I supposed to be ok knowing that this poor fish was just swimming swimming swimming minding his own business and then all of a sudden it gets stuck on my hook and gets pulled out of his safe and happy life and thrown into Pop-Pops dark cooler until it gets back to his house only to get..." his voice cracks. "Only to get fried to death, Mom! I can't. I can't do it."

"Oh, my baby. My beautiful empathetic and sweet,

sweet boy. I am so sorry. Look, fishing isn't for everyone," I try to tell him.

My dad comes up behind him and places a hand on his shoulder. "Listen, Kessie. I just feel like I should mention that I didn't force Liam to eat the fish we caught. I let him throw his back in so he could feel better."

"That's alright Dad. It's just a new experience for him. You didn't do anything wrong."

"No, *I* didn't," Liam interjects. "Because I have a heart." He turns to my dad and crosses his arms. I want to feel sorry for him. But the entire interaction just makes me chuckle. My dad looks at me with a face that says he's at a loss.

"Liam, your Pop-Pops isn't heartless. He let you throw it back, didn't he?"

Liam thinks about it for a moment, "I mean... yeah."

"Ok, baby. So sounds to me like you guys are heroes. You spared that little guy's life and now he can go on living safe and happy."

"And traumatized," Liam adds.

"Liam, where did you even learn that word?"

"From Micah. He said it means you go crazy from something bad happening to you."

"Well, you can tell your cousin to go pick up a dictionary and learn the real meaning of that word before he goes around trying to teach you the wrong one."

Micah's bouncy brown hair comes into view before he does.

"Mom says—"

"I heard her. I heard her. Hi, Aunt Kes!" Micah says pushing Liam aside and waving at me enthusiastically.

"Hi Micah, you're being nice to Liam, right? Remember he's younger than you."

"Yeah, yeah, I am. I'm just teaching the little guy."

I chuckle.

Micah is two years older than Liam and he's my sister Kira's youngest. And he's all Kira, if you ask me.

"I'm happy I got to see you, Micah. Do you mind letting me chat with Liam for a little bit?"

"Sure, Aunt Kes. Oh, Aunt Kes—wait before you go—is it true that you have a boyfriend and he plays professional hockey and he's going to be here with us this weekend?"

My stomach drops out of me. I can feel it when it happens.

"What?" Liam says to him. "Mom doesn't have a boyfriend." The way he says the word *boyfriend* sounds like it tastes vile on his lips.

"No, Micah. I don't have a boyfriend. He's... just a friend."

"Oh, but he does play hockey, right? At that big ice place in Houston?"

Liam looks from the screen to Micah and then back to the screen again.

"Mom, what's he talking about? Do you mean where Aunt Libby's brother plays hockey? Wait, is Zane going to be here with us?"

I rub a hand down my face. "That's kind of what I wanted to talk to you about, snooks. Zane got hurt so I had to take care of him for a little bit since Aunt Libby is in another country. And well, Memaw kind of invited him to come stay with us this weekend."

"Oh," Liam says.

"I-Is that ok with you?"

He shrugs, "Sure, I like Zane. He has that cool parrot."

Micah chimes in, "What? He's a hockey player *and* he has a parrot?"

"Yeah," Liam perks up. "He even has a fireman pole to get from his room to his kitchen. It's the coolest thing ever."

I flush at his mention of the pole.

"Okay, boys. Zane will be very excited to know you like all these things about him."

"Is he like a superhero or something? Does he have a special suit he wears?" Micah continues, ignoring me completely.

"Yeah, it's called a jersey. My Aunt Libby has one. It has the big number 82. That's his superhero number," Liam informs his older cousin.

I watch as the boys talk excitedly about my soon-to-be husband who decided to crash our family vacation. The light inside the pool house across from me turns on and I realize that Izzy must have a guest here.

"Hey boys, I gotta go," I say in a whisper. "I'll check back in soon okay?"

"Okay," they both say, before going back to their Zane hero worship. I disconnect and look up just in time for the pool house porch lights to come on and the door to swing open.

"Rowan?" I ask the figure poking his head out. He steps out even further and places a hand up to try to see better.

"Kesley? Is that you?" He waves.

I get up from the steps I'm sitting on and walk over to the edge of the back patio. "It is. Do you... are you visiting?"

"I live here," he says.

"Oh. I had no idea."

He shrugs. "Still looking for a job. No bites, yet. How's your research coming along?" he asks.

I panic and turn back to make sure I closed the sliding door behind me. The three women are still chatting away and laughing in the dimly lit living room. I step onto the grass and approach Rowan standing at the end of his porch.

"Uh-oh. Did you get fired?"

I laugh nervously. "No, I'm still very much employed for the time being."

I shouldn't have told Rowan about my work dilemma. But at the time I was spiraling. And he seemed so non-judgmental. I just word-vomited on him. He took it like a champ. And promised he wouldn't say anything. That it wasn't his story to tell.

It's weighing heavy on me that this spy work for The Pulse is also not *my* story to tell either.

"So you're still going through with the exposé?" He leans onto the wooden beam of the porch and crosses his arms assessing me. It's non-threatening. More like a genuine interest in the matter.

"Maybe there's a way to keep my job *and* write the exposé without actually exposing the Heatwave? Maybe just telling some interesting facts? Or shining a light on all the good they're doing in the community. Rina was telling me the guys have been really involved this season."

He cocks his head to the side and considers it. "I think an exposé by its very definition is meant to do just that... expose."

I drop my head.

"But sounds to me like you're having a change of heart."

"There's just so many ways to write something, you know?" I put my hands in my pockets and kick at a rock in front of me. "It can come from a place of giving the people some juicy details without actually compromising the team in any way."

"And you think your prick boss is going to be okay with a non-compromising story?"

Who is this guy anyway? How does he know the right questions to ask?

"What are you the in-house therapist?"

"Ryker would say as much," he chuckles, uncrossing his arms and sitting on the steps of his porch.

"Ok, I'm only going to say this because you're a vault and my best friend is not here to bounce this off of."

Rowan bites his lip. His light green eyes dance with curiosity. "Okay, shoot."

"I'm out of a job if I don't write it. I'm swamped during my shifts at The Breakaway Bar. I have every reason to want to make this work. With a promotion, I can drop my night-time gig and just be there for Liam."

"Mmhmm," he says listening. "But?"

"But," I continue. "I like everyone I'm meeting. Zane has some really good friends who care about him. Izzy and the girls are down-to-earth and so fun. And Zane." I think about the way he was so honest with me this morning. He seems so different from even just a few days ago.

"I'm afraid that by going through with this... I'll lose it all."

"Not all," Rowan points out.

"No, I'll have a new position that pays more and can sustain me and my son."

"Well," Rowan says leaning back on his forearms. "Sounds like you got some soul-searching to do."

I nod. "Any tips on how to do that?"

He smiles. I've heard a little bit of Rowan and Ryker's story from Izzy. And they've both had a lot of soul-searching to do in their lives.

"Whatever you choose to do, let it fill you with life and not drain you of it," he answers.

Chapter 16
Zane

I'm pulling up to the location that Kesley sent me.

She walks out of the sky-high building wearing a cute business casual outfit and her book tote. As I pull up next to her, she cocks her head to the side and assesses me.

"Really?"

"What were you expecting me to show up in? A limo?" I ask.

She looks around at the people watching us.

"I mean, no, but... I'm in a skirt," her eyes go down to her feet. "And heels, Zane."

I unhook the extra helmet I bought for her, swing my leg over the bike, and walk up to her. She looks up at me through those dark lashes.

"I like you in heels," I tell her. "You should keep them on later too." I take her hair and push it behind her back, slipping the matching black helmet over her head and making sure it fits her properly.

"There, how does that feel?"

She says something from behind the mirrored visor and

it's muffled. I hit the button that brings the visor up. "Say that again, little lion."

"I said, how am I supposed to breathe in this thing?"

"You don't need to breathe. You just need to be protected." I knock on the top of the helmet and she narrows her eyes at me.

Before she can say another smart remark, I hit the button and bring the visor down over her eyes. She jumps back. "Come on. We don't want to be late or we'll miss the view."

I put my helmet on and start up the bike. The purr from the engine startles more than a couple of people nearby. Our Bluetooth mics in our helmets connect and I can hear her breathing. "You coming or what?"

She pulls her tote to herself and stalks over to me.

"What about my things?" she asks, holding up the tote.

I pop open the back part that lifts up from under her seat. "Slide it in," I tell her.

"Fancy."

When she's settled behind me, I rev the engine. She slips her small hands around my waist loosely.

"You'll wanna hold on a little tighter than that, Kes."

"Oh really? You're not just trying to get me to press my chest into you?"

"Oh, I'm definitely trying to get you to press your chest into me. That's why I'm going to do this." I rev the engine again and look around before peeling away from the big building.

She gasps and holds on even tighter to me. "Told you."

I can feel her rolling her eyes behind me, even if I can't see her and I can't hold back the grin that crosses my face.

We ride in silence out of the city. The constant hum of

the bike seems to relax her a bit. I can feel her breathing start to slow down.

We're on an open stretch of road that I've ridden through more times than I can count. The sun is going down and we're following it to the west of Houston. This is why polarized visors help. It's for the moments like this when the sun would be blinding us. "You okay back there?"

"I'm still holding you aren't I?"

Her hands move up from the place they were resting and it feels warm as she grazes my abdomen.

She feels amazing against me. Like she was made to be molded to me like this.

I growl at her touch. "Careful, don't get me too excited."

She chuckles and takes the dare. Her hand slips under my shirt and travels down below the button of my jeans. My heart starts to race.

"Sorry, did you say something?"

This woman drives me crazy. I lean back, keeping one hand on the handlebar and reach for her thigh at my side, rubbing it with my free hand and going further back to give her ass a squeeze.

"Eyes on the road, caveman."

I laugh to myself.

After a few silent moments she finally asks, "Where are we going, Zane?"

"You'll see. Stop trying to spoil the surprise."

"Well, will this surprise have any food involved?"

I chuckle, "Dinner and dessert. I promise."

"Fine then."

"What were you going to do if I had said no? Jump off the bike?"

"I was considering it," she plays.

"We're almost there."

We're coming up to the entrance of my Granddad's ranch.

"Woah," she breathes out. "This is so beautiful. What is it?"

I pull to the side and she leans back as we come to a stop.

"It's the O'Connor ranch."

I type in the code to the giant metal gate and it whirs open. The big black wrought iron gate coming to life and parting before us. Beyond it are bright green rolling hills lined with acres of trees. The road looks like it disappears into a forest but I know what's just beyond the tree line.

I get back on the bike and Kesley resumes her tight hold on me.

As we roar down the quiet area, the dust from the road kicks up around us. It reminds me that it hasn't been used in quite some time.

Frank brought us to this place when Libby and I were little after our biological dad passed. Even then, he was trying to do things to try to keep us happy. He'd buy anything we wanted if it meant he didn't actually have to raise us.

We pass the mansion Granddad had custom-built for the O'Connor clan to spend our summers. There's the stable. The pool. Frank even had an outdoor synthetic ice rink added to the property so that I could practice during the off-season.

The grounds are amazing. But the most beautiful part of the ranch is something that nobody can just have built. Libby and I used to play in it almost every day that we lived out here.

I pull up to the opening of what looks like a giant fairy

garden. There are string lights that are just starting to come to life throughout the area.

"What is this place?" Kesley asks in awe. She takes off her helmet and takes my hand when I reach back for her.

"It's the entrance to a private vineyard."

"A vineyard? As in a wine vineyard?"

I nod. "It's one of my dad's many businesses."

I set my helmet down on the bike and Kesley does the same. "Wait here."

At the golden gazebo near the entrance, there's a picnic basket that I had asked the estate staff to prepare. Inside is the dinner I promised her.

"Ok, Zane. I gotta admit. I wasn't expecting any of... this," she motions all around her.

"That's because you think I'm some dumb jock that can't think of anything but hockey."

She smirks. "Your words, not mine."

"Come on, we got a ways to go before we get to the spot."

She looks around. "This... this isn't the spot?"

"Nope."

She looks down at her heels and then back at me.

"Lucky for you," I say. "I like you in these heels." I turn around and lean forward for her to jump on my back.

"You're not going to carry me, Zane."

"Yes, I am. Jump on."

When she hesitates I look back at her. "Would you rather I throw you over my shoulder like a caveman?"

"No."

"Then come on. I don't bite... that hard," I grin.

She rolls her eyes and pulls her leather jacket I also bought her closer to her body before jumping onto my back. She hitches up her skirt and wraps her legs around my waist. Her arms secure around my neck from behind us I lean forward to grab the picnic basket.

"You guys grew up here?" she asks.

"Not all the time. Frank owns a million properties. This is just the one we loved the most. And technically, it'll be mine since it's in our grandfather's name."

"I always knew you and Libby were spoiled... but damn. This is next level."

"We weren't spoiled. I mean sure, we had a lot of nice things growing up. But it was only to cover up the fact that we were kind of alone in this world. Frank was our dad, by all intents and purposes, but he had a revolving door of wives and girlfriends. Nothing was ever stable."

Kesley is quiet behind me.

"What are you thinking about?"

"Just how different people can be raised. My parents didn't have much. My dad lost his business and had to take out a second mortgage just to keep us in private school. But our home was filled with so much laughter and love. Sometimes I would think if they could choose between each other or their kids, they'd get rid of us in a heartbeat just for them to get to hang out together."

I hitch her up as she starts sliding down my back a bit.

"Yeah well, I'd pick that over a giant empty house any day."

"I guess I would too," she admits.

I'm walking past row after row of grapevines when I finally get to the end of the field. And there it is. Standing majestically before us.

I place Kesley back down on her feet. "Zane," she whispers.

"It's beautiful, isn't it?" I watch as she takes a few tentative steps toward the giant live oak tree.

I walk up next to her. "Frank had it carbon-dated or whatever you do with giant old trees. It's over a thousand years old."

The tree's huge trunk measures the circumference of an elephant. And its branches shooting out in all directions are thick and bulky as well.

I take her by the hand and pull her with me toward it.

She walks around the tree when we get to it and doesn't stop shaking her head. "It looks like something out of a Tolkien book."

I laugh. "It might be for all we know."

Bending down, I open the basket that was prepared for us. Inside is an assortment of cheese, crackers, meats and chocolate. And two bottles of wine from our very own family vineyard along with a wine opener. "Hmm. No glasses."

Kelsey rips her eyes away from the majestic tree and looks down at me.

She takes one of the bottles and holds it up so she can read it. The picture of the giant live oak is on the wine label as well. "Oh my god. I've seen this bottle before."

I nod. "We sell it to local restaurants and family-owned places throughout Texas."

She looks over at me still in shock. "Why did Libby never tell me about this place?"

I shrug. "Like I said. It was big, beautiful, and very lonely. At least we had each other. Lib and I used to come out here and eat peanut butter and banana sandwiches on the branches and watch the sunset. We snuck a bottle out a time or two."

Kesley's smile is back. The one that makes my heart drop without notice. "Did you have wine glasses back then?"

I think, "No."

"Then from the bottle it is." She hands it back to me, takes the blanket I pulled from the basket, and flaps it open for us to lay on.

She's about to kick off her heels when I tell her, "Uh-uh, those stay on."

She looks at me like I've lost my mind. "You're not the boss of me, caveman."

"Nobody is the boss of you, Kesley. But they need to stay on."

She squints like she's trying to understand.

Just in time, I hear a man's voice calling behind us. We both turn to see him, dressed in a black suit and a clergy collar.

"Hi, Jack."

Jack, my observant stranger from the bar, also happens to be an ordained minister. When I reached out to him about marrying us, he jumped at the opportunity.

"Hi, Mr. O'Connor." He turns to Kesley, "And soon to be, Mrs. O'Connor." He dips his head.

Kesley drops the grape that is about to go in her mouth.

"Oh, this is..." she looks around frantically. "This is a wedding?"

"Party of two," I tell her with a grin.

"Zane this is... oh my god... this is happening way too fast," she says fanning herself.

"Yeah, well, we agreed."

She's shaking her head. "Yeah," she breathes. "I just need a moment."

Jack looks from Kesley and back to me. "We'll just need a moment," I tell him. And he nods, holding his bible and heading toward the vineyard.

"Kesley," I say taking her hand. "Listen to me."

She's breathing in deep and blowing it out quickly

trying to wrap her mind around what we're about to do, no doubt.

"Kesley," I say again. Her green eyes meet mine. "You are opinionated. And uptight. And if you feel some kind of way about something, everyone within earshot will know about it."

"Wow. Tell me how you really feel, caveman..."

"But you're also the sexiest, most authentic, and intelligent human that I've ever met." I take her chin in my hand so she can look at me. "And I can't get enough of it."

Her lips part and her breath is ragged.

"What's wrong? Cat got your tongue?"

She shakes her head and opens her mouth again. "Nobody likes that I'm opinionated. So I find that hard to believe."

She's adorable. The way her green eyes catch the golden hue of the setting sun has me mesmerized. "Believe it, little lion. Because what I want, I get."

"You're too cocky for your own good."

"So you're saying I'm charming?"

"I'm saying you're arrogant and need to be taken down a notch."

I give her a shrug, "Probably. And if anyone's going to do it... I'd like it to be you."

Her eyes shoot down to my lips before slowly coming back to meet my gaze.

"You want to kiss me," I say with a grin.

She narrows her eyes, "No, I don't."

"Kesley."

"Zane," she repeats.

"Are you ready to marry me, little lion?"

She takes in one last deep breath. "Yes."

I nod and turn toward Jack who is waiting just in the

distance. I wave him down. "Let's get this show on the road, Jack."

* * *

"You are so ridiculous. Men don't talk like that," she laughs and pops a grape into her mouth. The ring I got for her is glinting as it catches the last bit of sunlight. She's referring to my on-the-spot vows.

"What kind of guys have you been dating?" I cock my head toward my new wife.

She purses her lips and shakes her head, "Let's just say I'm pretty convinced that the last generation of good men has passed. I'm hoping to revive them again with Liam's generation."

I think of the little boy in the superhero costume heading out to school early in the mornings. He's cute, just like his mom.

"He's excited that you're coming this weekend," she adds.

"Really? So it's official?"

She rolls her eyes and pops another grape into her mouth. "Yeah, he and his cousin seem to think you're..." She waves a hand into the air, "Cool, or whatever."

I smirk. "And what do *you* think?"

"I find you mildly interesting," she grins and looks back to the setting sun. "Wow, this view is stunning."

I can't keep my eyes off her. The way her golden hair swirls at the ends. The way her nose twitches as she notices me looking at her. And I couldn't agree more... the view *is* stunning.

There's a small droplet that falls onto her arm and

makes its way down. We both look at each other before looking up and noticing that a grey cloud is moving in.

"Great," I mumble.

She looks at me as I sit up and start putting away the food. I reach for the open bottle of wine and right before I'm about to cork it, Kesley steals it away from me.

"What are you doing? It's starting to rain."

She brings the bottle up to her lips and drinks deeply. After taking a few large gulps she drops the arm holding it to her side and looks at me. "What's wrong, Zane? You scared of a little water?"

I watch her as the droplets increase. Spotting her cream top with dots of wetness. I watch her as she pulls it over her head and shakes out her hair. She wriggles her skirt up and grabs my hand to pull me back down onto the blanket.

The rain picks up and now everything around us is getting soaked. Her hair turns brown as it catches the water and she straddles me.

"I'm guessing you don't want to go inside?" I ask.

She reaches for the hem of my shirt and I lift my arms letting her tug it off of me. She grabs onto my belt and tugs on it.

I watch her undo the buckle and pull on it hard, releasing it from my jeans as she whips it behind her.

One hand goes to her lower back and the other wraps around the back of her neck as I sit up with her in my lap. Her eyes are hooded and those lips of hers are still slightly parted.

"Zane, I—"

I pull her to me and take her mouth. Our lips move slowly over each other as we savor the feeling. The rain picks up and drenches us. Kesley gasps as we both get soaked. Just barely protected by the giant oak's leaves above us.

I stand with her still wrapped around me and start running in the direction of the pool house. It's the closest structure. The rain pelts our skin and by the time we make it under the wraparound porch and I set her back on her feet, we're both breathless and uncontrollably laughing.

Thunder rolls through the area and we see lightning flash in the distance causing us both to jump. I take her by the hand and lead her into the empty house.

Chapter 17
Kesley

On the outside, the pool house has Texas stone accented by thick cedar wood beams. But inside, it's bright and modern. There's an open kitchen with a giant island to the left and a single king-size bed with an open shower to the right. In the middle is the longest fireplace I've ever seen and a big cozy L-shaped couch in front of it.

Just seeing the fireplace my body shivers.

Zane tugs me closer to it and turns it on. It roars to life, instantly creating much needed warmth. He pulls me to him and we stand there defrosting for a second.

"I'll be right back," he says.

He comes back with thick fluffy white towels, wrapping one around my shoulders. I'm already feeling so much better.

"Wasn't expecting all that," he says looking back out through the open sliding doors.

Texas. If you don't like the weather, just wait an hour. It'll change.

"This place looks new," I say looking around.

"That's because it is," he says taking a seat on the couch and patting the spot next to him.

I walk up to it and sit down facing the fireplace. "Does Frank rent it out or something?"

He looks at me and then back to the fireplace. "No. I did it. I told Nana my plans and she loved it."

I shake my head. "How many acres do they own out here? Like fifty?"

"Closer to five hundred."

I almost choke on nothing.

"Five hundred acres?! And you choose to live in a two-bedroom penthouse in the city?"

He looks at me with those deep eyes of his. The fire dances in them. "That's where you are."

"I'm not what's keeping you there," I tell him.

"How could you possibly know if that's true or not?"

I turn to him. "I'm not the reason you live in those condos."

"What if you are?"

"Libby, maybe. Your history, sure. But not..."

"Kesley," he breathes. "I can live anywhere in or out of the city. I can buy a condo anywhere else. But I chose to live in the one place that honestly, I'd rather just move furthest away from. And it's not because of my sister... as much as I love the brat..."

I'm dumbfounded. This can't be right. What he's saying can't be true.

"I could've left after Mal passed. I could've turned down Ryker's offer to take back my old place across from you. But after all these years... I wanted to be near you."

I shake my head. Registering his words. "How long?"

"What?"

"How long has that been true for you?"

He reaches behind his neck and rubs it. "Long enough."

My heart is beating frantically. To the point where I think it might burst out of my chest.

"This isn't just some crush on the cute girl next door. I want you, Kes. In a way you can't possibly understand."

I stare into the fire. Zane has feelings for me. Libby's brother. The same one I rejected in high school. The same one I've pined over for years after getting to know him. Hoping, wishing, and dreaming that he could finally see me. *He* has feelings for me.

"But Mallory," I whisper.

"We both know there's no use in thinking about that. We're here. We're what's possible, Kes."

"So I'm... what? The rebound?"

"No," he says, taking my chin in his hand so that I look at him. "You, Kesley Brooks, are my end game."

With those words. Whatever icy walls I had built up around my heart all these years, start to melt away.

He sees it in my eyes. And the moment he does he pulls me onto his lap and looks up at me. "Kesley... I'm done fighting this. I'm done pretending I'm ok. What I want is something real and whole. And I want it with you. I'm willing to do whatever it takes to get it."

I look down at those earnest eyes of his. And I feel it in the depths of my soul. I nod. He reaches a hand up to my neck and pulls me to him. He takes my lips into his and with it my very breath. "Give me a chance," he pleads.

I want him too. I have for a long time. And this feels too good to be real. Like the floor will fall out from under us at some point and we won't be able to stand. But all I can do is live in this moment.

Right here, right now. No regrets.

I push off of him to stand. "You know that I'm kind of a package deal, right? You don't get just me."

"I was hoping that would be the case," he smiles.

This can't be right. How is it that he's saying all the right things right now?

Warmed from the inside out. I strip out of my wet skirt. Zane leans forward and places his forearms on his knees. He looks ready to pounce at any moment.

With his eyes glued on me, I reach back and undo my bra, letting it fall to the floor. Then still in my heels, I reach down and let my panties fall to the floor before stepping out of them and kicking them toward Zane.

He catches them in his hand and smirks putting them in his back pocket. I'm standing before him, my husband, completely bare. In nothing but the pair of heels, he insisted I keep on.

He reaches forward and takes me by the hips looking up at me and kissing me right between my legs. My hands go up to his wet hair and I pull it back forcing him to look up at me.

There's a playfulness in his eyes.

"But there's something you should know about me, husband."

He licks his lips. "And what's that, little lion?"

I bend down until my lips are right at his ear and whisper slowly, "I *do* like it rough."

His eyes reflect the fire that is burning in front of him and I can almost see the flames of his own desire in them.

He kisses me again and works his way up my abdomen, between my breasts until he's rising up out of the couch and stands tall above me. I look up at him now as he cocks his head and says in a gravelly voice that makes me shudder, "I knew you would."

My skin is ablaze with the need for his touch. He's so restrained, it bothers me. But before I can say anything he unbuttons his jeans as he kicks off his boots, and lets them fall to his feet. He's in nothing but his boxer shorts. They cling to him as the erection they hold back begs to be released.

My mouth waters as he gazes at me. This beautiful, broken man before me. He wants what I want.

In an instant, he grabs me by the waist and pulls me to him. "Such a pretty mouth you have." He rubs his thumb along my bottom lip before his voice drops an octave, "I can't wait to fuck it, wife."

My heart stops. *Oh... wow.*

His smile widens just before he takes my lips into his again. Without warning he wraps a muscled arm around my waist and pulls me up off the ground, tossing me onto the cozy couch. I sink into it.

"How should we do this?" He thinks out loud. He puts a hand to my chest and pushes me further down onto the couch as he kicks my legs open and sinks down to his knees between them. He brings his mouth to my core and kisses me there again. "Should I start by kissing you here? Licking and tasting until you're begging me to make you come?"

I feel the thrill of that creep up my spine. He places another soft kiss there. Then he climbs over me until his face is in front of mine. "Or... should I..." He kisses along my neck and up to my ear. "Just fuck that pretty pussy of yours right here," he pushes his restrained erection against me. "Right now."

I'm at a loss for words. "What's wrong, little lion? Cat got your tongue again?"

His mouth meets mine and he slides his tongue into my

mouth. I moan into him. "Mmm, I have an idea," he says against my lips.

He backs up and picks me up again. It's like I weigh nothing to this beast of a man. He takes me to the bed in the corner and drops me onto it. I lose a heel along the way and he tsks. "Such a shame, I liked those on you. I was hoping you'd press them into me while I pounded into you... maybe later." He takes my other foot and caresses it with his warm hand, making the other heel drop onto the floor.

"You are..."

"What? Were you expecting a gentleman? I'm sorry to disappoint. I think you and I are past pleasantries. Don't you think?"

My eyes go wide. "Starting with this." He goes to the side of the bed and slides off his boxers revealing quite a sight. He slides into bed next to me, lying down with his head facing up toward the foot of the bed.

"W-what are you doing, Zane?"

"Climb on me, little lion. Ride my face."

Every fiber in me lights up. And I do as he says. I roll over and position myself over his face. He grabs my hips and slams me down onto his tongue. I let out a gasp. He starts slow. Licking and teasing me, then he slips that smooth talking tongue into me and I lose it. Shifting over him creating more and more friction. I watch as his erection gets even harder and a bead forms at the head. I want to lick it and make it mine.

As I lean forward, Zane growls against me, "Don't you dare." Then goes back to ravishing me.

"You can't..." He keeps licking me. "You can't tell me... what to do," I breathe out.

He locks me in place over his mouth. Not letting me

lean forward to take him into me. "Zane," I gasp at the pleasure building. "Let me taste you."

He stops just long enough to say, "No." Then goes back to licking at that sensitive part of me.

"Zane."

"Atta-girl. Say my name, baby. But you're not the one in control right now." He swipes his tongue some more, "I am."

Feeling like taking matters into my own hands I reach forward and grab ahold of him, and as I do he slides a thick finger into me as he continues to lick. I let out a guttural moan as he fucks me with both his finger and his tongue.

"Zane," I gasp out.

"Wait. Your. Turn." He orders and slips a second finger into me. My body explodes with pleasure. And he hums his delight. I want to feel him. More of him. So against my better judgment, I lean forward and wrap my lips around the head of his cock and slide him into my throat.

He growls again. It sends ripples of pleasure through me and I ride him even harder. I moan as I draw him in slowly. But Zane isn't having it. He lets go of my hip and brings a solid hand to my ass, swatting me in one brisk move.

"Ah!" I shudder.

"Not." He swats again. "Yet." And again. The sting from his spankings makes my orgasm rip through me and before I know it I'm screaming my release against his cock as I keep riding his face.

The saliva from my mouth drips down as I draw him out of my mouth to breathe.

Zane rolls me over until he's hovering over me. "Now that I have your attention."

Oh, good lord. He notches himself at my entrance and

drives into me. I drop my head back as he fills me. Drawing back painstakingly slow only to drive back into me again.

"Tell me something, little lion," he grits out.

I lick my lips and try to regain my composure as he drives into me again and draws out another moan. "What?" I breathe.

He grabs my waist with both hands as he pounds into me from the side of the bed. "Since you're so opinionated. And want to be in control..." He drives into me some more.

I'm going to lose it again. I bite down on my lip. "Mmhmm?"

"Why don't you tell me where you want my cum?"

With parted lips and my throat dry I try to swallow. "Um... uh"

"Hmm..." he says. "Looks like you're at a loss for words. How about this?" He reaches down between my legs and circles my clit as he continues to pound into me. He draws out a second wave of pleasure that crashes into me even harder than the first. And this time I don't have his cock in my mouth to silence it. I shudder as I come on him.

And only when I stop writhing beneath him does he say. "On your knees. Face me."

I instantly do as he says and look up at him. "Open that pretty mouth for me, little lion."

I part my lips for him and he steps forward and slides his cock now coated in my juices, straight into my mouth.

"You like it rough?" he asks again.

I hum against him as he pushes further into my mouth. He grabs the base of my ponytail and slams into me. "I'm sorry, pretty girl. Can you say that again? It's hard to hear what you're saying."

I choke on him. And I want more. He draws himself out of me to let me speak. "Yes," I say between breaths.

"Ah... that's what I thought you said." He puts both hands at the back of my head and pushes into my mouth as I draw him in. I feel my core contract at the feeling of him filling my mouth. I can't get enough of this man. He does it a few more times until I feel him shudder and growl out his release.

I take every bit of it and swallow him down as the tears roll down my face.

Zane reaches down and wipes them with the pad of his thumb.

And bends down to kiss me. Drawing my tongue into his mouth and tasting the mix of us.

"Mmm... just like I imagined," he says. "We taste good together, Kesley."

I let out a breath and collapse onto the bed as he goes to the shower and turns it on. I'm almost asleep when he bends down to peel me off the bed.

"Before you do that, I'm going to shower and feed you. You're going to need your energy, wife. I haven't got my fill of you yet."

I wrap my arms around him and nuzzle his neck as he steps into the shower holding me against his body. The promise of more to come, hanging in the steaming air around us.

And the thought of it feels so right.

Chapter 18
Zane

K esley rings the doorbell to the bright teal house on stilts. It's right at the water's edge. And the backyard must have some incredible views facing out into the ocean. We hear the sound of excited footsteps and look at each other.

We agreed to take it slow with her family. Nobody needs to know we already tied the knot. Which is why the ring I gave her was left back at the condo.

The door chain is unlocked and a little boy with big bright eyes and curly light brown hair answers the door. "They're here!" He yells behind him and then turns back to us. "It's you! You're the superstar hockey player!" The boy says in awe. I look at Kesley who rolls her eyes.

"I mean... I wouldn't call him a superstar," she walks in and I follow her with a smirk.

I mouth to him "Yes I am." And he giggles.

Kesley waves a hand in my direction, "Micah this is..."

"Zane!" Liam calls from across the room dressed in his all-green Hulk costume.

"Hey!" He jumps into my arms and I catch him. "Woah!

173

Wait a dang second." I set him down. And rub my chin. "Have you got more muscles since the last time I saw you?"

He nods his head excitedly, "Yep! Look at this." He turns and does some bodybuilder poses. The fake muscles from his suit bend and stretch with each move.

"Woah!"

"I know right? I can't wait to show Aunt Libby. She sent it from Milian."

"You mean, Milan, snooks?"

"Yeah!" Liam says still posing.

Micah joins him too, "Zane! Zane! Look at this." He flexes next to Liam and suddenly we have a Hulk vs. Micah fitness competition. I laugh as the boys grunt and pose. They remind me so much of my teammates in the locker room. Maybe us guys never fully grow up, after all.

"That must be our newest guest," a woman with a blonde bob singsongs from the kitchen.

"Hi Mom," Kesley waves at her. "I'd just like to remind everyone that I'm also here."

Mrs. Brooks looks like a more mature Kesley. She wears intriguing red glasses that frame her emerald-green eyes. The same color as her daughter's. Mr. Brooks is a dark-haired man who looks like his outfit of choice might be a polo and golf shorts, even on days he doesn't intend to go golfing. He rises from the kitchen table where he was picking up some cards.

"Mom, Dad. This is Zane... Libby's brother." *Libby's brother, my ass.*

I shoot her a quick knowing glance before turning my attention to her parents who are both coming at me with glowing smiles.

Mrs. Brooks reaches me first and wraps an arm around

my neck like we're family. "Oh, please call me Sherrie. This is David."

David reaches a hand out to me and I shake it as Kesley and her mom hug.

"It's nice to see you, Zane. Libby's told us quite a bit about you over the years. Kesley on the other hand..." Sherrie motions to her daughter.

"That's because there's nothing to tell. This is Zane. Libby's brother. Our neighbor. He plays for the Heatwave. What else would you like to know? Is Kira here?" Kesley gets out all in one breath. She seems frazzled and not at all like the calm confident woman in my bed last night.

She goes to the kitchen in search of her older sister.

Sherrie turns back to me. "She's never brought a boy home," she whispers like she's telling me a huge secret. Though everyone else in the room heard it too.

Micah and Liam are now arguing about each of their respective strengths. And it's turning into a wrestling match.

David watches the brawl like it's a regular occurrence and turns to me, unbothered. He slaps a hand on my shoulder "Come on back, son. I'm just getting ready to grill up some steaks. The guys went on a beer run and should be back soon."

"The guys?" I thought Kesley only had sisters.

Sherrie's already walking back to the kitchen to continue preparing dinner. "John, Kira's husband. And Benny, Becka's."

I let out a small cough, "Oh yeah... Benny." I went to school with Kesley's brother-in-law. He was in my graduating class. He didn't like me much.

I look around in search of Kesley, but she's disappeared somewhere in the house.

"David, why don't you give Zane a tour of the beach house?"

I look at Kesley's dad. "Yeah, sure. That sounds great."

Micah and Liam finally stopped wrestling and are back. "Zane, just wait until you see my room," Liam says.

"Yeah," Micah adds. "We made a giant fort. It's so cool."

"So cool," Liam parrots.

"Come on, Zane. Let's start with the bedrooms," David suggests. I follow the man with the two boys bouncing along behind us.

Up the stairs are all the bedrooms. There's a long hallway that leads to another set of stairs.

"This one's our room,"Liam says opening the door. Inside the room it looks like a daycare center threw up in it. There are blankets and pillows arranged like a giant fort. The boys weren't kidding.

"Wait, where'd you get this extra cot from?" David asks.

"From mommy's room upstairs," Liam says.

"Oh," says David.

"Something wrong?"

"Eh, we'll figure it out. Let me show you upstairs."

We head up the tiny flight leading to a big room with its own en-suite. The ceilings are vaulted but there are plenty of windows that make the space feel open and airy.

"Saved this room for you, Liam and Kessie. Though, it looks like Liam might've stolen away your cot."

I look around and walk up to the couch. The blue and white nautical theme makes it look inviting.

I stretch out onto it. It's tiny. "This'll do," I say, smiling at David.

"So Zane... you and my daughter. What's going on there?"

I sit up. He seems genuinely interested.

I want to tell him. I want nothing more than for Kesley's family to know just how much I want her. Just how *mine* she is.

"I'm waiting on Kesley to decide that, sir."

David sticks his hands in his pocket and nods. "Brooks women. Stubborn as they come. But they have hearts of pure gold."

"If they're anything like you and Sherrie, I can see that."

* * *

"The guys will love you," Kesley says, emptying her luggage into the dresser under the TV.

I'm handing her the clothes as she puts them away.

"I'm not worried about them."

"Really? Then notify your face," she says.

"Hey, I can already tell that half the family is Team Zane."

"That's because you haven't seen my sisters yet."

I look at Kesley as she bends down to fill the last drawer. I get up from the bed and stand behind her.

"There's only one Brooks sister I'm concerned about, and right now she's bent over in front of me." I place my hands on the small of her back and reach for the ponytail swinging behind her.

She stops what she's doing as I tug on it and get her to straighten.

"Why don't I help you out of those shorts," I say into her ear when she's pressed up against me.

"Zane," she whispers.

"What? You scared your parents will hear you whimpering my name, little lion?"

She licks her lips and lets out a sigh.

"You want it, don't you?" I whisper into her neck.

She turns around to face me.

"We can't let on that we're anything... until I talk to Liam," she says sternly.

"Mmhmm. But that doesn't mean we can't have a little fun, wife."

I pick her up by the waist and she wraps her legs around me as I push her up against the nearest wall.

I look up at her. Begging her to kiss me.

"Such a caveman," she says through a grin.

I shake my head. "You want caveman?"

I take both her hands into one of mine and pin them above her head by the wrists. And take her lips into mine. She moans at the sudden movement.

"I'll give you caveman." I slip my tongue against hers and she rocks her body against me.

With lips parted she leans her head back against the wall, giving me access to her neck.

I run my tongue along the side of her neck and she lets out a whimper. "I'm going to let you go, little lion. And when I do... I want you to strip out of these clothes and get on that bed wearing nothing but that pretty smile. Do you understand me?"

She bites her lip and nods her agreement.

"Good girl."

I drop my hand from her wrists and set her feet on the ground. "Go."

In an instant, she's unzipping her shorts and sliding them down her legs followed by her panties. I watch as she reaches for the hem of her shirt and tugs it over her head followed by the bra she lets fall to the floor.

She looks at me before going to the bed and getting on her hands and knees.

"Open your legs wider, Kesley."

Her knees go further apart. I come up behind her and run a finger over the folds of her open slit. Her very wet, slit.

I remove my finger and bring it to my lips. She looks back at me as I suck off the juices she just released for me. "My wife has the sweetest pussy. I'm convinced of it."

She draws in her bottom lip and lifts her ass even higher for me.

"What's this? Are you begging for me to fuck you, little lion?"

When she doesn't respond, I give her ass a smack.

"Yes," she gasps. And I watch as her pussy clenches for me.

I get down on my knees before her and grab onto her hips. I dig my face into my wife's backside, lifting her hips just enough to give me access to her clit with my tongue.

Kesley lowers onto her elbows making sure to open wide for me and the second she feels the first flick of my tongue she's moaning into the sheets.

"You're wound up tight, baby. I'll make sure to take care of you," I say against her skin and continue licking her until she can't help but push against my face, giving herself more friction. At her request, I push a finger into her entrance and she moves her hips back and forth, letting me fuck her with it.

"I love seeing you come apart from my touch."

At my words, her legs start to shake and she lets out her release in my mouth. Rocking against me before she goes still and collapses.

I wipe my mouth on my arm before climbing into the bed next to her and rolling her over to look at me.

She looks sated and relaxed.

"That's better," I say to her.

She smiles and throws an arm over me. Pulling me closer to her so that our lips meet. "Thank you," she says between kisses.

I pull back to look at her.

"Never thank me for me having my way with you, little lion."

She looks confused. "I'd say, judging by the fact that I'm the one that came... I was the one that had my way with *you*."

I shake my head. "That's where you're wrong, wife. Anytime I get to be the reason you shatter. I win."

She kisses me one more time before peeling herself off the bed.

"We should get cleaned up and head down for dinner. Mom will have her spies sent up any minute now," she whispers and motions to the door.

"You think so?"

She stands up at the side of the bed. "Nope, I know so."

There's a faint knock at the door. Kesley and I both stare at each other. I motion for her to answer since it's her room.

"Um... he-hello?" She says.

"Hey Kes. It's me, Becka. Can I come in?"

"Uh, just give me a minute, Becks. I'm changing," she grabs a fresh t-shirt from her drawer and tries to pull on her shorts.

I get up off the bed and sneak into the attached bathroom. Quietly shutting it, just as Kesley pulls open the door to the bedroom.

Chapter 19
Kesley

"Hey Becks!" I try to smooth out my hair quickly realizing I probably look like I've just been railed.

Her eyes swipe up and down before she crosses her arms and tilts her head.

"You alone in here?"

"Yep, yeah. Sure am." I glance back at the bathroom and hope she doesn't venture in there.

"So..." She goes to the bed and smooths it out, patting it for me to sit. I close the door and follow her lead. "Tell me about this Zane dude."

"What? There's nothing to say."

She scoffs. "You've never once brought a guy on a Spring Break trip. There's something there."

"You don't even know him," I say matching her inquisitive look.

"No, but I don't have to by how much Liam has talked him up. I feel like I know him already. Which brings me back to the fact that Liam knows him. That's kind of a big deal."

"He's my best friend's brother. Of course, Liam's met him."

"Huh. So there's *really* nothing there?"

I don't know if it's the way she's looking at me like she can see right through my facade or if I'm just overwhelmed with feelings and can't bring myself to lie.

"Actually..."

She perks up. I don't even have to say anything and she already knows. "I knew it. Mom called me up last week and was *so* excited going on and on about how you're bringing a guy home. So tell me, how long have you guys been fucking?"

My eyes must bulge out of my sockets because she laughs uncontrollably.

"You can come out, Zane," she calls out in the direction of the bathroom.

A second later the door clicks open and Zane steps out, a towel wrapped around his waist. "Hello, Becka." His voice is like honey.

She rises and goes to him. I stay watching the interaction in shock. *What the hell is happening?*

"You know, Benny's not a big fan of you," she says to him.

"Well aware. We may have bumped heads a little in high school. Regardless, It's nice to see one of Kesley's sisters."

"Yeah, well I'm the nice one. It's Kira you have to worry about."

Zane shrugs. "I'm up for the challenge."

"Well, aren't you a cocky one?" Becka says, she straightens her glasses and assesses him. To which he just stares at her right back. "So... what are your intentions with my sister?"

"Becka!" She puts a hand up to me.

"No, Kes. You may be my older sister, but if this dude plans to be around you and *my* nephew. Then he needs to be vetted."

"My intentions..." Zane begins. "Are to make sure she and Liam are the two most cherished individuals on the entire planet. To make sure that every day is the best day and that they never regret letting me into their lives."

Becka crosses her arms over her chest. "Those sound like big commitment words. You trying to lock her down?"

My heart is beating violently in my chest, but I speak up before either of them says another word, "We're married."

It's word vomit. I can't even control it as it leaves my lips.

Becka whirls to face me. "What? Are you kidding me?"

I shake my head. "We eloped. We weren't going to tell anyone until I was able to talk to Liam. I don't want him finding out from anyone but me."

Becka turns to look at Zane. "Is that true, hockey boy? Are you my new brother-in-law?"

Zane says, "Is that a problem?"

"Is that your motorcycle up front?" she asks.

He lifts a brow, "Maybe."

"Then yes. Any man that plans to be in my nephew's life long-term should not be putting his life at risk riding that death trap daily."

Zane looks at me and I just shrug. I've never seen my sister so overprotective of me.

"That's fair," Zane says.

"Good. Glad we can agree," Becka says.

And they both turn to look at me.

"I don't know what's happening right now."

"I'll tell you what's happening. Tomorrow we're planning on a family outing with all the kids. The guys are going golfing with Dad. Which means Zane... welcome to the family. I hope you can play more than just hockey."

She turns to face me. "If you're going to tell Liam, you better do it fast. I'm the least astute of the Brooks women and I was able to sniff you two out. You won't last long pretending you're not anything to each other under this roof."

With that, my sister walks out the door shutting it behind her.

"Shit," I say.

"That was pleasant," Zane says with a grin.

"Are you delirious? Becka can't keep a secret to save her life. We need to talk to Liam tonight."

* * *

My son is swinging on the back patio with his cousin when I open the screen door.

"Hey boys," I say to them.

"Hey!" They both say.

I join them on the swing. "What are you guys doing?"

"Mom, Micah says that those things going in and out of the water all the way out there are flying fish. I told him that's impossible because fish don't fly, they swim. So they're probably birds."

"Flying fish *are* real!" Micah cries out.

"Hate to break it to you, snooks. But your cousin is right."

Liam turns to face me. "What?"

He makes a mind-blown motion with his hands over his head. Micah practically beats his chest.

And I squint to the area they were pointing to. "But also, those are not flying fish. They're definitely seagulls."

"Dang it," Micah says defeated. Liam lifts up his Hulk mask and sticks his tongue out at him.

"Ok, boys. Micah, I need to chat with Liam for a bit. Do you mind going inside while we chat?"

"Sure, Aunt Kes. But if you do see a flying fish, come and get me ok? I don't want to miss it."

"You got it, kid." I give him a thumbs up and he jumps off the porch swing, satisfied.

When Micah is inside I turn my attention to the green-suited little boy that has my whole heart. "Hey, snooks."

"It's about Zane, isn't it?" He takes off his mask and sets it next to him then turns to look at me.

I think my heart just sank. "It is, yeah."

"Is he going to be my dad?"

That question. It's the same question I've asked myself a million times since I saw the two pink lines on the pregnancy stick as a college student.

"He wants to be, snooks. You see, Zane and I are... well, we're kind of more than friends right now."

"He's your boyfriend? So Micah was right?"

"About what exactly?"

"He said Aunt Kira said that you and Zane are boyfriend and girlfriend and that means you're pretty serious."

How do I tell a six-year-old that mommy and Zane are not boyfriend and girlfriend but husband and wife?

"Grown-ups sometimes get together because they want to share a life together. It's good for both people so they become more than just a boyfriend and girlfriend."

"Oh... so you guys love each other." The way he says it, it's not a question.

"Uh..." Just then, Zane appears at the screen door. "Mind if I join you two?"

Liam scoots over and pats the space between us.

"Zane?" Liam asks.

Zane slips onto the porch swing, making it pause for a moment to adjust to his weight before we keep swinging. "Yeah, big man?"

"Since you and mom love each other... does that mean we're all going to live together? You, me, Mommy, and Aunt Lib?"

Zane can hardly hold back his amusement. "Well, obviously that would be ideal. But what would we do about *my* roommate?"

Liam and I both look at Zane. "Muppet," he says to us.

Liam brings a hand to his head. "Oh, my goodness. I forgot about Muppet. Well, I can make space in my room and he can live with me."

"That's really thoughtful of you, bud. And you know you're right," Zane turns to look at me. "I do love your mom. Which is why I asked her to be my wife."

Liam stops swinging for a second as he thinks on Zane's words and then resumes swinging his feet. "Oh, like Memaw and Pop-Pops. They love each other. So they're married."

Zane smiles at him. "That's right. But we kind of want to surprise the family with the big news. You think you can keep it a surprise for them, Incredible Hulk?"

"Of course," Liam says with certainty. He's quiet for a moment before he says, "Mom?" He looks over at me and I brace myself for a deep philosophical six-year-old question.

"Yeah, snooks?"

"Micah says that since he's on Spring break Aunt Kira is

going to let him and Luca have ice cream before bed. Can I have ice cream before bed, too?"

Zane and I both exchange relieved glances.

I chuckle. "Sure, kid."

"Yaay!" He jumps up and grabs his mask. Puts it on and does a quick superhero pose in front of Zane before disappearing back into the house.

I turn my attention back to Zane who has a sly grin.

"Should I smack that look off your face or will you be able to remove it on your own?"

"You love me," he singsongs.

I hold up a finger. "*Liam* thinks I love you. I never said I did."

Zane looks back out onto the ocean. "It's okay. You don't have to say it for me to know it's true."

I shake my head. "You're impossible."

"No, I'm your husband. And I'm going to bury myself so deep into that... heart of yours, little lion," he smirks. "Or die trying."

I smile at his words looking out at the setting sun over the ocean. Maybe, this is as simple as Liam thinks it is.

Maybe, there's a future that exists for us all to be together.

Chapter 20
Zane

Golf sucks ass. Frank tried to teach me when I was a teenager and I still remember practically falling asleep on the golf cart waiting for him to make the perfect shot.

I realized early on that a sport that makes you play by yourself just wasn't for me.

"I played hockey as a kid, you know. I was pretty good," John, Kira's husband, is carefully selecting a club. He glances over at me to read my reaction.

I don't say anything. I've heard this line a million times.

"I could've gone pro if I wanted."

"If it wasn't for that career-ending hit, that would've been me."

John seems like the kind of guy that would say he's good at anything. Even if he's not. It's kind of irritating. But from what Kesley told me about Kira Brooks, she has high expectations of everyone in her household.

He lines up his club and sticks his tongue out the side of his mouth to focus. Just as he's about to swing, Benny coughs loudly at his side and throws him off.

John looks at him with dead eyes.

"What?" Benny asks and smirks at his back when he lines up to swing again.

"So what exactly do you do, John? Don't think I caught that?"

"Oh, I run the advertising division of a chip company. You might know it. Starts with a *Fri* and ends with a *tos*."

I pretend to be oblivious. "I don't eat chips so I'm not familiar."

Benny laughs to himself.

"Well, judging by the abs I saw this morning on your run, I wouldn't think you eat chips," John says. "Checks out."

"Checking out Kesley's hockey beau?" Benny asks.

"Not like that, you idiot," John says as he watches the ball he just hit barely miss the hole.

Benny tsks. "You're always almost there, J-dawg."

"Shut up, I'd like to see you even get close."

I watch the two of them interact. The women they've chosen to marry have surely rubbed off their competitive nature on their men. Either that or like attracts like in this family. And if that's the case, then what the hell happened to me and Kesley? We couldn't be more different but something just clicks with us.

Benny lines up his club, looks out to the hole, swings and the ball careens in the direction of the hole. It drops just a few feet in front of it and rolls right to the edge before coming to a complete stop.

John looks at him with a toothpick now hanging from his mouth. And I can't help but think he reminds me of my team captain and his red lollipops and dares.

"What would you call that, Zane? I'd say that's pretty damn close, wouldn't you?" Benny coaxes.

I'm leaning on my club which is apparently a huge no-no. And straighten to get a good look.

"Wow, how did both of you get *almost* there? No wonder your wives are so uptight," I say without even thinking.

"Excuse me?" John says.

"What the fuck is that supposed to mean?" Benny says, dropping his club and looking like he's about to pounce on me.

Corporate dudes. Can't handle a fucking joke to save their lives. Just then David comes strolling up to us.

"Thanks for waiting up, boys. Whose shot is it?" He looks at the scene of men about to throw punches and his smile drops.

"What is it now?" David says looking at his son-in-laws.

"Nothing. Zane here just happens to be a big talker. Maybe he's willing to put his money where his big mouth is?" John says.

Is he related to Keelan? Now I'm really wondering.

I roll my eyes. "I can back up anything I say." I send him a wink knowing it'll set him off.

His eyes narrow on me. "If that's the case, then why don't we see if you can make a hole-in-one, hockey boy?"

I crack my neck. I didn't wake up this morning thinking I'd be getting into a pissing contest with my new brother-in-law's but... here we are.

"I can finish anything I start," I say confidently.

"Good," John says. "If you get the hole in one, Benny and I will do whatever you want for the rest of the day."

"Whatever I want?" I ask.

"Whatever," John repeats. Benny gives him a disapproving look for including him without his consent but he crosses his arms and gives a terse nod.

"Deal," I say.

"John, let's not do this now. We're here to get to know Zane and have fun, not piss him off," David says.

"It's cool, David. I don't mind embarrassing your son-in-laws. I find it quite fun actually."

I grab a ball and place it on the ground.

"Wait, don't you want to hear what will happen if you miss?" Benny asks me.

I turn my attention to the hole. Already calculating how hard I'll need to hit it at this distance.

"Nope," I say. "I won't miss."

I pull the club back and swing.

* * *

David is sitting back with his feet up on the lounger when I arrive with his drink.

"Gotta admit, Zane. You have quite the artistic eye."

The two men who challenged me earlier are sitting ten feet away with half their bodies in the sand. The soundtrack to *The Little Mermaid* is playing in the background and the coconut and seashell tops I got for them are wrapped perfectly around their chest. The mermaid tails David and I carved out of the sand covering their legs, came out pretty great.

Strangers walking by gawk at them. And a group of college boys stop and take selfies with my sand prisoners.

"Keep singing," I yell to them.

And the boys look at each other and groan before going back into *Under the Sea*.

David takes a sip and spits it out when he hears them get louder at my request.

"I know better than to mess with a professional athlete,"

he says to me. "But you taught those two a valuable lesson today."

I take a sip of the Pina Colada I got from the beachside bar shack up the way. It tastes like pure sugar and pineapple juice.

David watches me as I pour it out into the sand. And I laugh when he does the same.

"Wanna get something stronger?" I ask him.

"Hell yeah," he grins at me.

"What should we do about Tweedledee and Tweedledum?" I motion with my head toward the mer-men.

"Ah, let them keep entertaining the beachgoers. Serves 'em right." He slips on his shades and starts heading toward his Jeep rental without looking back.

I think I like Kesley's dad.

"Louder," I yell to them, before following David's footsteps.

Chapter 21
Kesley

I'm typing like a madwoman on the lounger behind the beach house when Kira appears out of thin air.

"Jeez, Kira. You scared the shit out of me," I say with a hand to my heart.

"You've been avoiding me," she says blankly.

I shut my laptop and take a deep breath. "No, I haven't."

"Yes," she takes the empty chair next to me. "You have."

"I've just been busy with work, ok. I have a project due in a week and my boss asked for the first five hundred words last night. I just barely got something down."

"Wow," she takes her glasses off and looks at me. "So, you're like a real journalist? Look at you go, Kes."

She sounds so sarcastic it irritates me.

"Is there something in particular you want to get off your chest or can I get back to work now?" I glare at her.

"No, please. Don't let me bother you. If I have any questions about why you're sleeping with your enemy, I'll just ask him directly."

She slips on her sunglasses and relaxes back into the lounge staring out into the sea.

"Kira," I say.

"Did you tell him?" she asks.

"Of course, not. He's not ready for that."

She turns facing me. "Your baby's daddy is on vacation with us, Kesley. He's claiming to be in love with you and wants to be Liam's dad. And you're telling me he's not ready?"

I swing my legs over the lounge to look at her.

"What I do about this situation is none of your business, Kira. I am a grown woman and can make decisions without you or anyone else in this family trying to meddle in something that is none of your concern."

"Is that why you married him?" she asks, giving me a side glance.

The heat in my neck rises to my face and I can feel the fire there.

"Becka told you."

"Not directly. But you just confirmed my suspicions. So what's he offering you for this little ruse?"

"It's not a ruse, Kira. We're really married."

"Please," she scoffs. "You two don't *love* each other. What does he have on you?"

I stand up and grab the laptop off the lounge chair.

"You know, this is exactly why people don't like you. You think you're so much better than everyone because you have Johnny and the kids under your lock and key... well, Earth to Kira! You aren't anything special. You're just a sad woman who takes out her disappointments on everyone else around her so she doesn't have to come face to face with the fact that you're just a grade-A bitch."

I don't look at her to see her reaction. I've never spoken to my older sister in this way. But the way she's judging me and Zane. I can't take it.

I hear her gasp but don't turn around to engage anymore. I stomp off kicking up the sand behind me until I get to the back door leading into the kitchen. I open the door and kick off my sandals trying not to drag in more sand.

My mom takes one look at me and drops the ladle in her hand. "What is it?"

I just shake my head, trying not to let the tears even begin to form.

"Kesley," she says sadly. "I'm so sorry. I was going to tell you."

She comes up to me and pulls my face into her chest. "I wanted everyone to be in our happy place. Relaxed and... hopeful. I told your father that's the only way I felt comfortable letting all my kids and their significant others know."

I pull away from her, the confusion impossible to wipe off my face.

"Mom?"

A tear rolls down her cheek. "The doctors are hopeful she says. We caught it early enough that I have a fighting chance."

Oh... my... god. This can't be what I think it is.

"And I'm okay letting go of these girls," she says looking down at her chest, "if it means I get to keep on living. I'll be happy that I just get to be here with you kids and my beautiful grand-babies."

Her voice cracks and I'm standing before her in shock.

This can't be real. My mom is the healthiest person I know. She's always exercised. Always ate good food. Stays as hydrated as a professional athlete. How could she be saying this right now?

The front door opens and the familiar bickering of all the cousins fills the quiet space. Mom lifts a finger to her lips as a sign to keep it quiet. I nod solemnly, in understanding. Just as my sweet boy comes bouncing in dressed in all green.

"There's my superhero grandson," Mom says as she bends and takes Liam into a bear hug.

"Memaw, Memaw, you won't believe it. Mom," he turns to me excitedly. "I beat Micah in the frog game in the arcade. The one where you have to cross the street and make sure he doesn't get squished. You know which one that is?" He looks from me to my mom and back to me.

"I-uh... you mean, Frogger?"

"Yeah, Frogger," a tired Becka says behind the four other kids arguing over prizes in a little black bag.

"How were they?" I ask her. She took one for the team since the boys were out golfing. Kira was sulking. And I had to finish my initial work for Jeremy, the terrible. Which is due in exactly... thirty minutes. On a Saturday.

"We survived. I will say, I don't know how you did it, Mom."

Three girls always bickering. Always trying to outshine the other. It had to be a lot. And we haven't changed all that much.

"Thanks for taking Liam, Becks."

"Yeah, no prob. But Mama needs a nap."

"No nap!" Her twin daughters yell in unison.

"Not you," Becka clarifies. "*Mama* needs a nap."

She drops all the bags onto the kitchen table and plops onto one of the chairs. "What's for dinner?"

I look over at Mom who's watching all her grandkids dig through the prizes excitedly. "I was getting ready to make everyone's favorite."

"Shepherd's pie?" Becka and I both ask perking up.

She nods. Shepherd's pie was Mom's comfort food

when we were growing up. She and Dad honeymooned in Europe as newlyweds and he had the best shepherd's pie he ever tasted in a small quaint town near London. She swore to make it her mission to perfect her recipe until she got it to taste exactly like the dish that she and Dad fell in love with.

She did. And every time we got together she made it for us. A family favorite.

We've gathered around Mom's shepherd's pie and shared some of the toughest moments as a family. Comforted by the blend of warm potatoes and savory meat and veggies, perfectly piled on top of each other into a tasty meal to remember.

The thought of my mom fighting cancer weighs very heavily in my chest. And I wonder who else besides Dad and Kira knows.

I look at Becka, fanning herself and looking oblivious. I get the feeling she doesn't know.

"Come on, kids. Let's go put on a movie in the living room so Memaw can cook and Aunt Becka can get some rest."

I usher the gang out of the kitchen and grab my laptop off the table where I left it.

Becka whispers a *thank you* to me and I nod to her. Grateful she gave me some time to at least type out the gist of what I needed to send to Jeremy.

It's been one week. I still barely know anything about hockey. Zane has been teaching me more about *unrelated* things than the reason why I agreed to this marriage in the first place.

But in talking to Izzy, Rina, and Candace. And with the private tour of the facilities. I'm able to put a few things down. I'll expound more in the completed article.

And jeez, does Jeremy not do Spring Break? Who in

their right mind is working on a Saturday afternoon when it's so beautiful out?

I get the kids settled and choose a Laz-E-boy chair in the corner of the living room to set up my laptop and finish my write-up.

I'm typing out the last sentence when the front door opens and Zane fills the doorframe with his muscular build. I panic and hit send on the email.

"Hey guys!" My voice comes out in a squeal.

Zane smiles when he sees me and looks at the TV to see the kids watching The Lion King. "Good pick."

My dad closes the door behind them. "Wait, where are John and Benny?"

Zane grins. "You'll be happy to know they're having a kid's movie jam sesh of their own."

Dad slaps Zane on the back and they both chuckle like it's an inside joke.

I look at them with scrunched brows. "They're still at the beach," Dad offers. "Hey, kids!"

"Hey, Pop-Pops," the five of them say, just as Timon and Pumbaa are coming onto the screen.

Dad disappears into the kitchen and Zane hangs back next to my chair.

I shut my laptop and place it on the floor. Standing up to get a good look at him.

"Wanna tell me what really happened, caveman?"

He looks to the kids who are busy with the movie and pulls me by the waist to him until our bodies are touching and my breath hitches in response.

"Your family is really something, little lion." He brushes a thumb over my lower lip. "And I'm so happy to be a part of it." He whispers that last part so only I can hear.

I push off his chest and he chuckles. "So, we gonna tell them tonight?" he asks.

"Uh..." I hesitate. "Mom has bigger news that I think will trump what we have."

"Is that so?" he asks concerned.

"I'm afraid so. We might have to hold off on it."

"That's if Hulk over there didn't already blab off to his cousins," he smiles at the little boy in his costume lying on his stomach and his legs bouncing playfully behind him.

"Kira knows," I whisper to him.

"So not much of a secret then?"

"I can't take the attention off of Mom tonight. Let's get washed up and ready for dinner."

"Hmmm, by washed up do you mean...?"

I slap him on the arm. "Not everything has to involve our bodies connecting, Zane."

"Says you," he rumbles from behind me as I walk up the stairs.

I turn to him. "I'm serious." The tears start to well up on the rims of my eyes and I quickly swat them away.

He looks around before approaching me on the stairs, puts a hand on my cheek, and leans in. "What's wrong, Kes? What happened?"

I just shake my head and turn to go up the steps, but he grabs my wrist and turns me to him. "Tell me."

I motion for him to follow me upstairs and when we're safe behind the closed door of our shared bedroom, I put my back against it and slide down to the floor. Covering my face as the lump in my throat makes it impossible to breathe right. I'm sobbing.

He sits next to me and wraps a strong arm around me, pulling me into himself.

I cry into his chest. I can't help it. He's given me a gentle place for my emotions to just land.

He doesn't say a word. But just holds me as I cry. And when I can finally gather my wits and form words. I tell him.

"It's breast cancer."

He breathes out, "Shit."

I sniffle. "Yeah, shit."

"I'm so sorry, little lion. That's... that's horrible news."

"I can't believe it's her. Of all people. She's so good, Zane. She's always so loving and uplifting. She loves Dad. She loves her kids. She gives so much of herself. She doesn't deserve this."

Zane shakes his head. "Nobody does, baby."

The way he says *baby* sends warmth down my spine and feels so good. He pulls me closer to him.

"Sometimes really bad things happen to really good people," he says. "And it's for no other reason than the fact that bad things just happen in this crazy, messed up world we live in."

"It doesn't make sense," I sob into his chest.

"No, it doesn't. And it sucks. And I'm so sorry to hear this. But your mom is loved. It shows in the way your dad talks about her. In the way everyone in this family wants to be around her. Even Liam."

"I don't know how to look at her without thinking of that terrible disease inside of her," I admit.

He pulls away to examine my face.

"Yes, you do."

I look at him, shaking my head. "How could you be so sure?"

"Are you serious? Because Kes... it's what you did with me."

I pull my knees into my chest. And rest my head on them as I look at him.

"My disease wasn't like your mom's. It was more hidden. Most people wouldn't be able to see it. The depression. The self-hatred and sabotage. The guilt. But you saw me," he continues. "Despite it. You saw me, Kes."

"What are you saying?"

He reaches forward and tucks a loose strand behind my ear.

"I'm saying... I didn't just want to marry you because it was convenient, Kesley. I wanted to marry you... to make you mine."

I lift my head up and kick my legs back out in front of me.

"I love you, Kesley O'Connor."

Those words wrap around my heart and squeeze it more than anything I've ever felt before.

Zane... loves... me. He actually loves me.

"I love you, too." I whisper to him.

He cracks a smile and tilts his head, watching me.

"Then let me take care of you, my little lion."

He pushes himself up off the floor and bends down to peel my body off the floor. Safe in his arms, he tucks my head under his chin and walks me to the bathroom where he carries me to the shower. Still holding me, he reaches in and turns on the water testing it to make sure it gets hot.

When he's satisfied, he sets me on my feet and tenderly strips me out of my clothes. I lift my arms up as he pulls off my t-shirt. He unbuttons my shorts and lets them slide down my legs.

I'm overwhelmed with love and other emotions I can't even pinpoint at the moment. How is this beautiful, damaged defender taking care *of me*?

When I'm standing before him, completely naked he leads me into the shower. It's nice and warm. I let the water hit me like a massage as he strips out of his golf clothes and joins me. I watch intently how his muscles coil when he reaches for the shampoo above me and squeezes some into his big hands.

He lathers it up and then brings it to my head, giving me a scalp massage as I stand under the water.

"Relax, baby. I got you." And with that everything I've carried into this weekend with my family, all the angst. All the expectations. All the worries. They melt away. Carried off down the drain along with the shampoo that he rinses out of my hair.

He continues to work it with the conditioner next and then takes some shower gel and squeezes it into a washcloth.

He turns me around and works the cloth down the length of my back. Hitting every curve until he reaches my heels. He lifts each foot and washes them clean. Then comes back up and cleans every surface of my body.

His lips come to my neck and he whispers, "I don't care what's happened between us before. There's only here and after. And I want it with you, Kesley."

He kisses me softly. "Do you understand? I don't want any other woman, but you."

I nod and turn to face him. He rinses the conditioner out of my hair and I close my eyes as I savor the feel of his hands on me. When all of it is washed out he grabs my hair and wraps it into his fist pulling it back so that I'm forced to look at him.

"You are mine." He says matter of factly. "And whatever you have to face... we'll face it, together."

My heart swells. And at that moment I want to tell him the truth. I want to tell him everything. To come clean about my job. About Liam. About how I've felt about him all these years since the accident that took away the joy in his life.

But he pulls my lips to him and drinks me in. And every thought in my head vanishes.

Except one.

I want my husband.

Chapter 22
Zane

My hands glide down her slicked skin and I try my damndest to keep my attraction to this woman under control. But I see it in her eyes the moment the switch flips.

She goes from reserved. Scared. Withholding.

To a woman who knows exactly what she wants. She reaches down between us and moves her wet hand to my pulsing erection.

"You don't have to..." I say to her. Her eyes meet mine with a heated glare.

"I want this. I want you, Zane."

And those words are all I need to stake my claim on the woman I love. I lift her up and press her against the shower glass. Our tongues in a desperate dance to claim the other. She wraps her legs around my waist and pulls me to her.

I reach in between them and feel the slippery wetness gathering there.

"I know you're not just wet from this shower, little lion. Is this all for me?"

She sucks in her bottom lip and nods seductively.

"Mmm. And what exactly would you like me to do about it, Mrs. O'Connor?"

She licks my neck up to my ear and bites it, forcing a growl to release from my throat. "I want you to fuck me like I'm yours and only yours."

I shake my head slowly at those words.

"Well, then I won't be gentle, little lion. There won't be a single part of your body I won't claim."

She swallows and nods her understanding.

I bend down and suck in one of her nipples popping it off and giving her a little bite. She gives me a tiny yelp and a teasing smile spreads across her face.

"Do you like that?" I ask her.

She nods and commands me, "Do the other one."

"That's my girl," I say in a growl, as I bend to take in the second one in the same way. She leans her head against the glass and moans slightly. I'm about to go down on her when we hear a small knock on the bathroom door followed by a mousy, "Mom? Are you in there?"

I straighten instantly and Kesley covers my mouth to keep me from saying anything. I tilt my head at her.

"He-ey, snooks. Mommy's just... taking a quick shower, okay? I'll be right down."

"Okay! Memaw says dinner will be ready in ten minutes," Liam announces.

"Yep, I'll be down as soon as I get dressed."

"Okay," Liam calls out. "Hey mom? Do you know where Zane is?"

She looks at me with wild eyes and mouths, "Shhh".

"Uh, maybe check downstairs?"

I smile wickedly behind the hand that's still covering my mouth and bite her.

"Okay, I want to show him the prize I won. He's going to freak!"

Kesley's features go soft and I can tell that impacted her.

"I'm sure he will, snooks. See you downstairs, okay?"

"Okie doke."

She waits for the door to the room to shut before letting my mouth go and dropping her feet to the floor as she slides down the glass.

"You gotta go," she tells me sternly.

I nod. "I know. But don't you dare touch yourself. That's mine," I say putting my hand between her legs and pulling her to me for one more kiss.

She swats at me. "Go."

Stumbling out of the shower like a horny teenager I grab the nearest towel and try my best to dry as quickly as possible. I peek into the room to make sure Liam isn't somewhere hiding and I slip into some fresh clothes.

In a few minutes, I'm able to sneak quietly down the stairs. Everyone is distracted by the movie and I'm able to squeeze out the front door, unnoticed.

John and Benny are just getting out of a ride-share service as I lean onto the banister of the porch.

"Well, hello there, my little mermaids. How was your beach day?"

They both glare at me as they approach.

"Some dude asked me for my number," John admits.

Benny scratches his butt. "I have sand up my ass crack."

I laugh a little too loud, "Sounds like a successful day, then. Let that serve as a reminder not to fuck with me."

They brush past me, sad and defeated, and enter the house. When the door swings open Liam pops out of the kitchen and sees me on the porch.

"Zane!" He calls out running past his uncles and straight

to me. I open the screen door and meet him at the bottom of the steps.

"Hey," I ruffle the hair under his Hulk mask.

His muffled voice under his mask sounds more excited than usual.

"Zane, check this out! I was playing bubble hockey with Micah—"

"What positions?" I stop him.

He thinks about it and scratches the back of his head as he does. "I think all of them."

It's bubble hockey, so that's true. "I guess that's fine."

He chuckles. "So anyways, I was playing on the red team. He was blue. The game was tied. The puck popped up and Micah's player won the face-off and stole the puck away. He passed it to the right winger that dropped it back toward one of his d-men—"

"Wait, wait, wait," I say to the boy, looking around and deciding to take a seat at the bottom of the steps facing him. "Liam, how do you know so much about hockey? Do you play?"

He shakes his head. "Not really, Aunt Libby gave me a hockey stick to practice and she takes me skating a lot. It might be fun to be a goalie," he admits.

I purse my lips at the comment. Ryker would be beside himself at this moment.

Liam continues, "But I watch all your away games with her on TV. She teaches me everything she knows."

"Is that right?" I'm surprised I didn't know this about Liam and Libby. They seem to be pretty close. Way closer than I thought.

"Yeah. She taught me what an offside call is and every time they put you in the sin bin she tells me what the refs are saying you did. Even when they're wrong."

I laugh and pat the space next to me for him to join me on the steps. He bounces up to it. "The sin bin?"

"Yeah, that's what she calls the penalty box. Is that not what it's called?"

I spend enough time there to know every single name that box is called.

"No, that's definitely it," I chuckle, looking at the little boy who now has his hands bouncing excitedly on his knees.

"Hey, I noticed you still have on the Hulk costume. Don't you normally switch every once and a while?"

He nods and seems happy that I noticed, "Yeah, but Aunt Libby said that the Hulk is your favorite because he's strong and he defends the people in his world."

I crack a smile. "That *is* why I love him."

"Well, me too."

"You're a protector, Liam. That's a big deal."

"I guess so."

"I know so," I tell him.

Liam peels off his mask and holds it between his legs. His brown tousled hair is smushed onto his head on one side from wearing the mask all day. He looks like he's about to say something but then stops himself.

"Liam?" He looks up at me. "Something on your mind?"

He shrugs and looks to his cousins still distracted in the living room. "The kids in school always make fun of me," he says softly. "I'm smaller than most of the boys in my class. So I guess wearing the costume makes me feel... I don't know. Stronger, I guess."

"Do they bully you?" I frown, feeling a sense of protectiveness over the boy.

"They just call me names. Pip squeak. Liam, the little. It makes me sad. I wish I was big like you."

"Liam, boys can be mean. Especially when they don't have any good role models in their life. I know for a fact you're such a great kid because you're surrounded by people who love you. Your mom. Your grandparents. Even your cousins. That's something special and not a lot of kids have that, you know? Besides, what they don't know is that good things take time to grow. You'll have your moment, big man. And maybe next year, you'll be the tallest kid in class."

"You think so?"

"I know so. When I was your age, I was the smallest kid in my class, too."

He shakes his head in disbelief. "What?"

"It's true. And when I came back from summer break and went into the second grade. I had hit a growth spurt and was no longer 'Zaney the Wee One'. I was taller than most of the kids. Especially the one that coined that stupid nickname."

He smiles, looking hopeful just as I see Sherrie's head pops out from the kitchen area. "Dinner's ready. Everyone outside, please."

"Outside?" Micah asks from his place in front of the TV.

"You heard me, giddy-up kids. That means you, too." She says pointing to me. I raise my hands in surrender.

"Where's Kessie?" Sherrie asks.

The blonde beauty descends the steps. "I'm here. I'm here."

My eyes track toward her voice and the moment I see her, I can't take my eyes off of her. She's dressed in an all-white sundress that hugs her curves in all the right places. Liam and I both stare.

"You have a really pretty mom," I whisper to him loud enough for her to hear us.

"I know," he says, smiling.

"Wow, you two are going to make me blush. Come on, let's go eat," Kesley says, a slow grin spreading across her face.

We get up and step back to let her lead the way.

"Mom... mom. Do you think it'd be okay to ask Zane if he can come to Career Day for my class next week?" Liam bounces behind her.

Kesley quickly turns to see my reaction.

"I'd be honored," I say to them both.

She smirks, "I think you got your answer, snooks."

Outside the family is slowly gathering. David had arranged a long family-style setup using all the tables and benches that were scattered around the back of the property. I wait for Kesley to choose her seat before picking the seat next to her. Liam takes the seat to my left.

"I can't wait to tell my friends you're going to be there," he whispers, excitedly.

"Wouldn't miss it for the world," I muss up his hair and he giggles.

Across from us, Kira hesitates to choose a seat. But ultimately picks the one at the end of the table. John watches her and puts Micah and their older son, Luca, between them taking a seat further in.

Kesley and Kira exchange heated glares before bringing their attention to the head of the table.

"Just waiting on Becka and her family," David announces. "Memaw's been cooking up something really yummy for us all."

"Should I go check on them?" Sherrie asks her husband.

"I'll go check on her," Kesley says, swinging off the bench and straightening her dress as she gets up.

When she's disappeared inside, an awkward silence settles in over the table.

John and Kira don't look at each other. David and Sherrie are seated on the other end. And the kids are playing footsies under the table.

"So, your boys are on quite a winning streak this week," David says, breaking the silence.

I crack a smile. "Yeah, probably has something to do with the fact that I'm not there."

He tosses his hand out. "They're probably playing harder to make up for you not being there."

"Do you love what you do, Zane?" Sherrie asks from her place next to him.

I look at Liam who is now watching me intently. His mask is still abandoned.

"Yeah. Hockey was the thing that saved me when I was at my lowest. As a kid *and* as an adult. I didn't have much of a family growing up. So that's where I gained one."

Liam speaks up, "You have Aunt Libby."

"I do. And she's always been there for me. I owe her a lot."

"And you have us," Liam adds.

I turn to face him. "And that has got to be the most special thing ever."

Liam smiles. I can tell Sherrie is soaking up the moment when Kesley comes bursting through the back door.

"She's so sick. She won't stop throwing up!" Kesley announces, concern dripping from her voice. "She needs to go to a hospital."

David and Sherrie both stand. "What's wrong?"

"I don't know," Kesley says, in near tears. "She needs to go now."

She disappears again with both her parents on her tail.

"What's wrong with Aunt Becka?" Micah cries out.

"I don't know, sweetie," Kira says. "John, stay with the kids." She gets up and runs behind her family too.

So John and I are left sitting on a near-empty picnic table with three boys.

"Hey Zane, I bet my dad can beat you in a race," Micah says.

"What? Zane is much faster than Uncle John. Sorry, Uncle John," Liam says.

"Micah, Liam's right. I'm not challenging Zane to anything else ever again."

"What?" Micah pouts.

I chuckle to myself.

"Sorry, I was such an..." He looks at the two young boys at the table. "A-s-s-h-o-l-e."

His older son cracks a grin.

"What's that spell?" Liam asks.

"Liam, why don't you and Micah race? Just from here to that tree," I offer.

"Ok, but I gotta warn you. I'm small, but I'm really fast," Liam says to his cousin.

"Pfft. I've got you beat," Micah says in response.

Boys.

They both take off. I turn my attention back to Kira's husband. "Sorry for embarrassing you in front of your father-in-law."

He shrugs. "I deserved it. I've just been in such a lousy mood lately. You just happened to be in my path of destruction."

Is John being nice to me? After the embarrassment I put him through?

"Zane?" I look at the man in front of me. And it's the first time I see it. The hopelessness in his eyes. I think he's about to say something serious but he just asks, "Is it true you have a parrot?"

I give him a nod and grin. "Is it true you almost played pro?"

He gives another weak shrug. "Like you, I loved hockey as a kid. I met Kira when we were young. She always insisted I needed a real job if we were going to have any chance at a life together. So I went into the corporate world instead."

"You aren't missing much," I assure him.

"Still miss the smell of the ice. The sound of the crowds cheering. You must love that."

I do love that. But I'm realizing... I might love something even more than all of that.

Chapter 23
Kesley

I'm pacing around the waiting room. When Zane reaches a hand out and takes mine, stopping me mid-pace.

"Sit down," he orders. "She's going to be okay."

I'm freaking out. I can admit it. Becka is strong. Probably stronger than Kira and I combined. But seeing her weak and unable to move on the bathroom floor? That was scary.

Benny pops through the double doors of the waiting room. And we all stand.

"What is it?" Mom asks first.

He shakes his head in disbelief. "Looks like you're getting a new grand-baby, Sherrie."

It takes a moment for the news to register. But when it does, Mom jumps for joy and hugs her son-in-law. "Oh, Ben, that's fantastic!"

"So, the vomiting...?" Dad asks. "That was due to her pregnancy?"

"The doctors think she may have hyperemesis gravidarum. Some pregnant women get more nauseous and vomit more frequently than what is normal. She was dehydrated when she arrived."

"And you guys didn't know?" Mom confirms.

"Noooo," Benny says shaking his head. "Total surprise. She thought she had food poisoning. I mean, the twins just turned two, we weren't even trying."

"What?!" Kira says from the back corner of the waiting room. "You've got to be kidding me?"

She grabs the purse next to her and storms off to the hall. We all look at John who just takes a seat, watching the door where his wife just walked out of.

"Congrats, Benny," John says drily.

Benny nods at him. I get up to give my brother-in-law a hug. "The family keeps growing."

"Well, since we're making announcements. I have a bit of an announcement to make," John says, rising to his feet and making his way toward us. "You guys should know... Kira and I... well," he sighs. "We're getting a divorce."

My eyes go wide and I immediately look to the corner of the room where the boys are all playing their Nintendos with headphones on, completely oblivious to the conversation. Becka's twin girls are asleep on the couches next to them.

"You're what?" Mom says, bringing a hand to her mouth in disbelief.

"We were going to tell everyone at the end of the trip but," he motions to the door. "You all would find out sooner or later."

"Oh, John," Mom tsks. "I'm so sorry."

Kira comes back in holding a can of coke she must've retrieved from a nearby vending machine.

We all look at her.

"What?" she says to us. Then it registers, "Oh my god, John. Did you... did he tell you guys?"

Dad gives a soft nod.

"I walk away for five seconds and you have to go and blab our business to everyone?" she says to her soon to be ex-husband.

"The way you just stalked off kind of gave it away, hon." John says *hon* like he would rather say another word in its place.

"Okay, well since we're now just blabbing out information. Did you all happen to know that Zane and Kesley are married? Yes, *married.* Tied the knot. Sealed the deal. And didn't tell anyone."

The confused faces in the room now turn to us.

"Kira," I say. "That's not your business to share."

"What does she mean, you're married?" Dad asks.

"It's a long story," I tell him turning back to Kira.

"Oh is it not mine to share? My bad. Mom do you want me to just go ahead and tell everyone about how you've been getting chemo and didn't want to tell you're own family because you didn't want to worry them?"

The men in the room look at my mom.

"You... you have cancer, Sherrie?" Ben asks.

"Kira!" I say louder.

"Oh, and Zane... while we're at it. Congratulations. It's nice to know your son finally has his father in his life."

"Kira, enough!" I say with rage filling my body so much that I don't realize when I'm walking up to her and slapping her across the face.

The entire room gasps and I'm frozen in place by what she just revealed and how I just reacted.

"You all want to make me out to be the bad guy here?" Kira spits out holding her cheek. "Well, all of you have your little secrets and hidden things you don't want people to know. So there. I just did everyone a service. Micah, Luca... let's go."

"No," John says sternly. "They're staying with me. You need to go home, Kira. Go take a breath."

Her jaw drops and she looks around at all the chaos she just unleashed. Still not pleased with herself, she turns on her heel and walks out.

"It's the IVF hormones. She's... not herself," John excuses her.

But all eyes are now on me as Zane stands to face me.

"What is Kira talking about?" he asks me.

My eyes glide back to Liam in the corner with his cousins still playing video games. I don't say anything. I just shake my head.

"I think everyone needs to take a beat. This is a lot for one night," Dad says, turning to Mom and consoling her.

Mom is now seated with her head buried into her hands on her lap, tears streaming down her face.

John sits down next to the boys. Benny hasn't moved from his spot near the double doors. And Zane... he's just staring at me like I'm some kind of ghost.

"Zane," I whisper.

"What is she talking about, Kesley? Who is Liam's dad?"

I rub a hand down my face. "Zane, not here. Please."

The eyes in the room shift away to give us some privacy. I can tell this is just all too much for everyone. It's a lot for any family.

Zane walks toward the exit brushing past me. "Outside, then."

I cast a glance at my dad and motion to Liam. He nods his understanding and we go outside.

The wind is picking up and the humid sea air swirls around us. "I don't know how to say this," I begin.

"Just start with the truth." Zane's voice is rough. Like he's trying to withhold his anger. His arms are crossed over his chest and he looks nothing like the guy I married under a thousand year old oak just the other day.

I bite my bottom lip nervously.

"Kesley, *who* is Liam's father?" he asks again.

Taking a deep breath and closing my eyes. I say the only thing I can. The truth.

"It's you, Zane," I choke out. "You're his dad."

Chapter 24
Kesley
Seven Years Ago

L ibby knocks on the door of my new room.

"You all settled in?" she asks from the hall.

"Yeah, come in." She bounces excitedly onto my bed and spreads out over it.

"You have *the best* taste in comforters."

"What can I say? I'm a thread count snob."

"Mmm, and I love you for it. Can we just switch beds?"

I give her a blank stare. "Seriously?"

"Yes," she says snuggling into a pillow. "You go deal with the black cloud that is Zane out there. I need a break."

I throw a pillow at her. "That's your brother."

"I know, it's just... ugh... I'm sorry I'm such a bitch. He's just way too hard on himself. Like he's somehow responsible for something that was beyond his control. There's no getting through to him."

"Libby!" I can't believe the words coming out of her mouth. "His fiancee and baby passed not even two months ago. That's a really big deal. You can't just expect him to... get over it."

"No, you're right. Like absolutely right. It's just... how do I put this without sounding like the biggest asshole?"

"I'll be honest, you already do."

She rolls her eyes at me. "I'm all Zane has. His friends have abandoned him. Dad has distanced himself even more. Two months of being his only shoulder to cry on, I'm just..." she pauses for the right word. "I'm just tired, Kes."

I can see it in her eyes and I know it's true. Zane lives across the hall from us. He's been here every single day since the accident. The only time he leaves is to go feed Muppet and he comes back. Part of me feels guilty for even moving in with Libby when she offered. I wonder if maybe he wanted the spare room himself.

"Listen, I'll go check on him. You just enjoy these brand new sheets for me, okay?"

Libby doesn't say anything.

"Lib?... Hello?"

I lift the pillow from her face and realize the girl is asleep. I feel sorry for her. She's been playing nurse, friend, and life coach to her brother for months. I know she's exhausted.

So I close the door behind me and tip-toe out into the living room.

Zane is sitting on the couch, sipping a beer and watching a documentary about the Sahara. I feel uneasy as I approach him. I have ever since he announced his engagement to Mallory Bennett earlier this year. It came as a surprise to us all. But especially to me, the girl who's had a secret crush on my best friend's brother for years.

I don't know exactly when it started. The day I met him, I was flustered, nervous, and new to the area. So many guys talked to me that day. I didn't even know who he was when he approached me. Only that he was yet another hockey player who was trying to shoot their shot with me that day.

I let him know I wasn't interested. And back then, I really wasn't. I just wanted to survive the day in a private school that my parents held with such high regard. But he took my rejection as law and never tried again.

Now the brown-haired, blue-eyed object of my desires is here. Sulking. Over a woman who was supposed to be his wife. And a child he'll never get to meet.

I don't think I'll ever have the right words for him. So I just approach him and take the seat next to him on the couch.

He glances at me but flicks his gaze back to the TV just as a lion pride is going out on a hunt. I look at the empty bottles sitting on the table. There are at least seven not including the one he's currently working on.

But who am I to judge how someone deals with grief? I sit and watch with him quietly. He's the one to break the ice.

"I wanted to be a zoologist when I was a kid."

I lean my head back on the couch and look at him.

"Wanted to know everything there was to know about the animal kingdom," he continues. "Cuddle with lions. Wrestle crocs. Communicate with birds. All of it."

I chuckle thinking of little Zane trying to sing to a mockingbird.

"What changed?" I ask.

He shrugs. "Dad said there's no money in zoology. That's for men who want to pursue passions and not build a legacy. Told me it was a pipe dream that needed to be replaced with something more... tangible."

"That's why you went to school for business?" I ask him.

"Yeah, had to please dear old daddy." He takes a swig

from the bottle in his hand. "The man hasn't visited me once since the funeral but he somehow thinks that buying things and directing my life is showing me his love. Last I saw, he was getting divorced... again. Marriage is so fickle."

"Not all marriages."

"No. I guess not." He leans back and rests his head on the couch in the same way I am. "My Granddad and Nana had been married all their lives."

"My parents too. They've been married longer than they were single. They're basically the same person at this point."

He smiles. "That's nice. To have someone you trust to share a life with."

I think about what he would've had with Mallory. Despite growing up with a bad example, this man wanted what his grandparents had. Otherwise, he would've never proposed.

"I'm... so sorry about Mallory, Zane."

He closes his eyes and when he opens them again he turns his neck to face me. "You know what the shitty part is?"

"Sounds like the whole thing is shitty."

"It is. But... I don't think Mallory loved me."

I shake my head. "Why would you say that?"

He takes another swig of his beer and sets the bottle down in front of him on the coffee table along with the others.

"Correction, I *know* she didn't love me. She said yes because I needed her to. I think she just felt sorry for me."

"Zane... there's no way she was going to marry you out of pity."

"You'd think, right?" He shakes his head again. "It wasn't out of pity. Mal was pregnant. But the baby wasn't mine."

My heart drops. The baby Mal was pregnant with wasn't her fiancé's.

"How... how do you know that?"

He runs his hand over his face like he regrets saying it. But the truth is out and I need to know what he means.

"Zane, how do you know it wasn't your baby?"

"Because Mallory and I... never had sex."

"What?" I think I'm in shock.

How was he going to marry a woman who was pregnant with some other man's baby?

"She cheated on you?"

"It's a little more complicated than that, Kesley."

"More complicated than your fiancee sleeping with another man? How could it be more complicated?"

"Because, I didn't love her either," he says matter-of-factly.

"But you guys were together. You dated and you proposed to her. Why would you propose to someone you don't even love?"

He sighs. "I needed to be married. For my family's sake, I needed a wife. I didn't need her to love me. I just needed her to agree to the terms. And Mal did."

"You needed a wife?" I scoff. "Why?"

"When my grandfather passed he put an inheritance clause in his will and to get it, I have to be married by thirty."

"But... you're only twenty-three. You have the rest of your twenties to find the woman you want to marry. Someone who loves you and you can be happy with. Why the rush?"

"I don't need a wife to love me. My mom loved my real dad. So much so that when he died, she was never the same. Love makes people vulnerable. I just needed someone to stick it through long enough that I could get my grandfather's legacy passed down to me so my family wouldn't lose it. Then we would split ways and find our real happiness once it was done... without the pressure."

"I don't understand. So that was your agreement with Mallory?"

"Yes, we would stay married until we both turned thirty. That year, we'd get divorced. She'd get to keep one of the homes in the area to raise her kid and I'd give her money for the time we were together. There was a pre-nup. I would pursue professional hockey. She and her baby would be taken care of. The inheritance clause would be fulfilled."

"And that would be that?"

"Well... she was on her way to see my Nana the night of the accident. Granddad made it clear we could only marry the one we loved. She was going to put on the whole song and dance and once Nana gave her blessing..."

"You'd get married."

He nods.

"Does... Libby know?"

"About what?"

"The agreement with Mallory. This... inheritance clause? Any of it?"

"Libby knows about the inheritance clause. She found it to be sexist and archaic. But no... she doesn't know about Mal. Nobody does."

Except me.

Nobody, except me, knows that Zane O'Connor wasn't in love with his pregnant fiancee. And that the baby she carried, wasn't his.

"I made a mistake," he sighs.

I look at him again. He's leaning forward with his forearms on his knees.

"I should've waited for the right time. The right..." His eyes shoot in my direction. "...person. Not try to force anything. Not try to take matters into my own hands. Now two lives are gone... because of my stupidity."

"Zane, you can't say that. The accident wasn't your fault."

"That's what everybody says."

"Because it's true." I scoot closer to him and rest my hand on his bouncing knee. It stops.

"She was driving to *my* Nana's house. To fulfill the duties *I* laid out for her. She'd still be alive. Her baby would've had a chance to live." He's shaking his head.

"Zane," I grab his chin and force him to look at me. "What happened is not your fault, you hear me? And you deserve to be happy. You deserve to find real love. I'm sorry that all this was forced on you. But you have a choice."

His blue eyes take in my every feature. I watch as they slowly drink me in.

"I don't," he says.

"Why?"

"Because the one woman I want, never wanted me." I drop my hand from his chin and watch him as he raises a hand to my face and brings me closer to him. "The one woman I've dreamed of. Desired. Wished could be mine. *Never* wanted me. So I had to go find something... anything."

I feel his breath tickling my cheeks. And I want so badly for him to kiss me. I want this. I want him.

"And... who was that, Zane?" I say gently.

He pulls me closer to him. Our lips barely touch and he whispers, "You."

And in one moment, everything changes.

225

Chapter 25
Zane

"What are you doing?" Keelan asks from the front door of his house, hands on his hips.

"Here's your bike. Congratulations." I throw him the keys to my Hayabusa and he catches them with ease.

He looks at me in disbelief and crosses his arms over his chest. "You shittin' me?"

"I'm not. I don't want it. But for the record... I did win."

Keelan shakes his head, confused. "You won? You got your sister's best friend to be your girl... and you're still giving me your bike? What the hell is wrong with you? What happened this week?"

A black Mustang Shelby comes to a screeching halt behind me. Hicks gets out of the driver's side followed by Fergie in the passenger's side.

"What's going on here?" Hicks asks. Looking from me to Keelan and back to my bike. "Holy shit. O-zone lost the bet?" he asks.

"Jar!" says Fergie.

"We're not inside the house, you nut. Those are house rules," Hicks fires back.

Fergie rolls his eyes at his missed swear jar opportunity.

"Actually, *I* lost," Keelan says walking up to me. "But he's giving me his bike anyway. Why?" The way he squints his eyes as he assesses me reminds me of a cop trying to nail a criminal.

"I don't need it," I say.

"So how are you going to get around? You don't drive," Keelan points out.

"I'll figure it out."

He sighs. "Zane, come inside."

"I think I'm good. My ride's coming to pick me up."

"Is your ride your girl?" Keelan asks.

I hesitate to answer. But finally say, "No."

"Then come inside," he orders.

I drop my arms and place the helmet on top of the bike, following him inside, like a sad puppy. Hicks and Fergie join us, too.

When we're in the middle of his lavish living room he points to a big chair sitting in front of a fireplace.

"Team meeting," he announces.

Hicks and Fergie groan.

"Seriously, now?" Hicks asks, "I'm hungry."

"Get Ryker on the line," Keelan orders.

"What the hell is happening?" I ask them, taking the seat he pointed out.

"An intervention," Keelan says pulling the couches closer in.

"A what?" I get up. "I don't need an intervention, Landry. I'm good."

"Zane, sit your ass down. You don't get to talk. You just

listen. When we're all done. Then you get to say your piece. Capeesh?"

Keelan takes the seat nearest me.

Hicks comes back in from the kitchen with a beer in hand. "Ryker's on his way," he announces.

"Good. Who's coming to pick you up, Z?"

I think I'm at a loss for words at the moment. "Uh... um..." I shake my head trying to remember. "Sincaid."

"The rookie. Great. Looks like the gang will all be here."

"Landry, I don't need this—"

"Shut up," he says with a hand in my face. "We've all been talking about doing this forever. We decided it would take you doing something really stupid to convince us you needed it. And you giving away your precious bike. Yeah, that's the final straw."

What sounds like a roaring space shuttle comes to a stop in front of the house.

"Ryker's here," Fergie announces.

"That was fast," I groan.

The front door opens and shuts and Ryker's heavy footsteps ring out through the hall. He rounds the corner and crosses his arms. "We finally doing this?"

They *have* been talking. How long have they been planning an intervention for me?

There's a ring at the door. "We are now," says Keelan, rising to go answer the door.

Ryker smirks and sits across from me. "Don't look so uptight, Z."

"Easy for you to say."

"We all deserve a good punch in the gut at some point in our thirties. You're getting an early start," he says.

I run my hand through my hair and groan. Keelan walks back in with Trevor behind him.

"Rookie, take a seat. Gang..." our Captain begins."We are gathered here today because our top defender needs our help."

"No, I don't," I protest.

"What did I say?" Keelan shoots me a death glare. I run my fingers over my lips and pretend to zip them shut.

"This, my friends, is the talking puck," he holds up the dingy signed puck he received as a kid at his first hockey game. I know that's what it is because he brings it everywhere he goes. We've all seen the puck signed by his favorite player.

"Whoever holds the puck gets to talk. So who would like to go first?" Keelan asks the group. Hands shoot up all around me. Everyone, except Ryker.

"You're all assholes," I tell them.

Keelan sighs out loud. "Hicks, you got any more of that duct tape?"

Hicks chuckles. "Sure do, Cap."

"Great. Go get it."

I raise a brow. "What the hell are you doing?"

"Since you don't understand the concept of rules. We're going to *make* you follow them. Fergie. Rookie. Hold him down."

"What?" I roar standing up from the chair. In an instant, Fergie and Sincaid have me by the shoulders and are forcing me back into the seat.

"You guys can't do this."

Ryker rises from his seat just as Hicks pops back into the room waving the duct tape, triumphantly. Ryker raises his hand and Hicks tosses it to him. He unrolls a strip and bites it off as he stalks toward me. I jostle in my seat but my captives hold me down harder.

Just before Ryker leans in lining the duct tape up to my mouth I look him in the eye and say, "Et tu, Ryker?"

He scoffs and says, "Stop being so dramatic." He proceeds to cover my mouth with the tape. I narrow my eyes at him and he just turns around chuckling to himself as he walks back to his seat. I'm going to hate removing this shit with the stubble on my face.

He hands the roll to Keelan who rips up two longer strips and ties my hands to the arms of the chair so I don't budge. Fergie and Sincaid are still holding me in place.

"Get his legs, too," Hicks says sipping a beer on the couch with his legs up.

"Well, get up and help me," Keelan says.

Once I'm bound, tied, and practically gagged in my team captain's living room. Keelan claps his hands. "Alright, places people. Just like we practiced."

The boys all pull in their seats. Keelan produces the puck. Hands go up. And he tosses it to Fergie first.

My muffled sigh is now joined by an eye roll.

"Zane," he turns to face me. "You're like the grouchy uncle at family Christmas. I love you. I want you around. But you're just kind of a... bummer. And I get it. I do. You've been through some serious crap. And I never want you to think that I take that lightly. I met you after that all happened so I get that this is the only version of you that I know. But I also know that if you just put aside you're own pride, not only would you be able to get the healing you need. But you'd be a better teammate, man. And we all need you to be at your best. Especially right now. Not pretending to be at your best, but actually *being* at your best."

There are nods all around the room. I don't say

anything. Well, I *can't* say anything. So I just nod my acknowledgment.

He tosses the puck to Hicks. He doesn't see it coming so it knocks his beer out of his hand and splashes onto the floor.

"You're cleaning that up," Hicks says to Fergie. Fergie just laughs. He definitely did that on purpose.

"Alright, where do I start?" Hicks says, tapping the puck into his palm. "You're mean, Zane. Like every time I try to be myself, you shut me down. It's not cool, man. I don't know if I trigger something for you that just pisses you off. And if I do, I'm sorry bro. But it'd be nice to just be accepted for who I am."

"Which is an idiot," Fergie adds.

"He's not an idiot," Landry says.

"No, I am. But this isn't about me," Hicks says. "It's about Zane being the villain in his own story. I see glimpses of someone who could be a good friend. But it disappears behind your sadness and self-loathing. And don't think I haven't noticed that you can down a twelve-pack in less than two hours, all by yourself. You can't do that forever, bro. You *will* get a beer belly. Guaranteed. Happened to my dad. One day six-pack," he motions to his belly for emphasis. "Then one morning after a binger... he was never the same again. Didn't even see it coming."

"You're drinking beer right now," Fergie points out.

"Yeah, *in moderation*. Anyways, that's all I got," Hicks finishes. "Oh, and for the record, girls love my ball deodorant. So suck it!"

"Thank you, Joshua. Very insightful and thank you for that highly unnecessary cautionary tale. Ok, who's next?" Landry asks the group.

Sincaid raises his hand. My eyes shoot to my defensive partner.

"Catch, Rookie." Hicks tosses him the talking puck.

Sincaid sighs. "You need to get serious help. You're a thirty-year-old man who can't drive a car because he's scared of what might happen. But then you ride a motorcycle like your life isn't important in the least. We all want you alive and well, Z."

Ryker's phone goes off in his pocket. "Shit, sorry," he says fishing it out.

Fergie points to the swear jar on the kitchen island. Ryker answers his phone and opens his wallet as he says, "Hello?"

He crumples up a twenty and throws it at Fergie.

"Phones are supposed to be off, Ry," Keelan says from his place on the arm of the couch.

Ryker holds his hand up. "Wildfire, slow down. What are you saying?"

We all watch him. "Turn on the news," he says to Keelan.

"Now?" Keelan says. "Kinda in the middle of something here."

Ryker nods still talking to his fiancee. "Are you sure?... Fucking hell."

Fergie shakes his head and takes the twenty dropping it into the jar in the kitchen. Our straight arrow always catches the swear words.

Keelan grabs the remote from the table and looks for the local news.

"Turn it up," Hicks says jumping to his feet.

"...from an article written by journalist, Kelsey—I'm sorry—*Kesley* Brooks with The Houston Pulse."

My eyes shoot to the screen behind me and I strain to

watch. The news anchor looks serious and the graphic shows a Heatwave jersey with the headline, "Is this bye-bye for Hockey's bad boys?"

"The exposé, written by Brooks, reveals a history of player impropriety and bad management by the Houston Heatwave owner, including firing previous staff members solely on the basis of their gender. Actions that are taken seriously in the world of professional sports. Sexism toward men in leadership roles is what the article claims..."

"Well, what did Rina say?" Ryker asks his fiancee as the news report continues.

"We've reached out to the owner of the Houston Heatwave, Mackenzie Stratton," the anchor adds. "And have been denied a comment."

"What the hell is going on?" Sincaid asks.

"Wait, did she say Kesley Brooks? As in *your* Kesley Brooks?" Keelan asks me.

I attempt a shrug but my hands are locked in place.

"Izzy says Rina's been trying to get a hold of Kesley. Zane, do you know anything about this?"

I tilt my head to the side and spread out my fingers.

"Shit... uh... we're kind of in the middle of something, Wildfire. And Zane's... a little tied up right now."

Understatement of the century. But all I can think of is Kesley. I haven't talked to her since leaving the hospital a few days ago. I jumped on my bike and rode home without a second thought. Because if what she said is true... and Liam is my son... then life is even more unfair than I thought it was.

But this. This is just taking that dagger she dug into my back and twisting it.

"Zane!" Three of the guys call out at once.

I give them a muffled, "What?" behind the duct tape.

"What happened with Kesley?" Keelan asks.

I drop my head back and try to get the kink out of my neck from the lack of sleep I've had the last few nights.

I don't even know what happened with Kesley. I left before we even had a chance to really sort things out.

She's my wife. She has my kid. And apparently, she's single-handedly taking down the NHL hockey team I play for.

But I can't say any of that with the duct tape on my mouth.

My phone is on mute in my pocket but my watch is picking up on the call and vibrating on my wrist. I see *Rina Lopez* on the small screen.

"Should we..." Fergie asks Keelan pointing to my mouth.

My eyes widen and I shake my head and give my muffled protests.

"Rina needs to talk to him," Ryker confirms.

Keelan stands up. "Sorry, bud. This might hurt you more than giving away your 'Busa."

He tugs on the side of the tape and I pull away. "Stop moving, Zane. Boys," he calls out. Fergie and Sincaid are on either side of me, holding me still.

Keelan takes a deep breath and rips it off like a band-aid.

I roar out the most colorful array of expletives I have ever combined in one sentence from the pain it causes. I feel the tears welling up in my eyes and I blink them away.

"Sorry, man," Keelan grimaces.

"What... the fuck... is *wrong* with you people! You don't even give me a chance to explain myself before you go jumping to your damn conclusions. Shit. A lot happened this week, okay. A lot of things that I didn't tell any of you because I know how meddling you guys can get and I didn't want to have to explain my actions to anyone. So there, okay," I yell out.

The boys are all quiet around me, staring at me as I pant like a restrained wild animal.

"Did you get that?" Ryker asks into the phone. He listens to the voice on the other line and nods. "Zane," he says to me. "Mack needs to see you."

Chapter 26
Rina

I'm swishing the wine in my glass, savoring the flavor from the bottle my dear friend sent me from her family's vineyard.

It's pretty good. I'll have to let her know when she's back in town that I like the new flavor.

The knock on my door jolts me from my state of relaxation. There's no game tonight. No press conferences to worry about. All my ducks are in order for the week ahead. What could someone possibly want right now?

I'm off duty.

I laugh to myself because that's a complete and utter lie. If I've learned anything this last year, working for the Heatwave, it's that I'm never *truly* off-duty. Especially not with the walking PR disasters just waiting to happen that are the stars of our precious franchise.

"It better be important," I say to whoever is at my door, before taking another sip of the wine.

The door swings open and in walks... my boss.

Her blonde hair is nestled on top of her head in an elegant updo and the wide-legged pants she's wearing flow effortlessly behind her as she walks to my desk. The sound of her Jimmy Choos punctuate each step.

She takes a seat on top of my desk, crosses one leg over the other, and turns to me. "We have a problem, Rina."

I sigh. "Who is it this time? Balinger? Hicks?"

She shakes her head.

I hesitate to say this one, but honestly, he's the most likely culprit, "Landry?"

She leans back and smirks, "Us."

If I had the wine in my mouth, I would've spit it out right on her chiffon blouse. "What? What do you mean, Mack?"

"It's the Pulse," she says with disdain. "They released an exposé and they are naming you and me, specifically, as the perpetrators. Just received a call from the commissioner."

"The Pulse?" I sneer. "As in the *Houston* Pulse? They've never had any interest in reporting on us. Never seen one of their guys in the press room. Not once."

Mack holds out her manicure, inspecting it before placing her hand back down on the desk.

"Seems like Clark sent in one of his rats. Do you know a reporter by the name, Brooks? Kelsey Brooks?"

Shit.

"You mean Kesley? O'Connor's girl?"

Mack raises a brow. "O'Connor's sleeping with the press?"

"Not really," I groan. "The girl writes clickbait. She has nothing to do with the journalism side of things."

"You sure about that?" Mack reaches for my laptop and turns it to her. Typing away until she finds what she's looking for. "Just released, not even fifteen minutes ago." She slides it back to me.

"Jesus. And you already got a call from the commissioner?"

I'm speed-reading through the article. "This is ridiculous. Everything's twisted. There's no mention of your father's responsibility in all this. And they're saying I slept my way into my position?... Mack." I stare at her blankly. "This is bullshit. Salacious gossip, not... news."

"Well aware, Rina. So, tell me, Ms. PR manager. *What* are we going to do about it?"

I shake my head at the words on the screen in front of me before shutting the laptop and rising from my chair. "Clark wants to play dirty. I'll show him dirty. I have some phone calls I need to make."

"Keep it aboveboard, Lopez. You know how I operate," Mack says, walking back to the door and turning to make sure I got it.

I nod, picking up my phone as she shuts the door behind her.

I dial a number I haven't called in years. The familiar voice greets me on the line, "Well, well, well. Gotta admit, never thought I'd see the day Rina Lopez would be calling me."

"McEvoy, always a pleasure. You still practicing Law?"

My college buddy answers back, "Depends. You still getting in trouble?"

"Runs a little deeper than just me. We got a situation with the team I represent here in Houston."

I hear kids screaming in the background.

"Uh, hold on a sec, Rina..." he whispers to someone near him. "I gotta take this. Can we let the kids go run outside?"

I smile. "How's Kenna doing lover boy?"

He chuckles. "She's got me whipped for life. And how's... you know who?"

I clear my throat, "Still very single." I announce. "But we're not here to talk about him."

"No, of course not. What can I do for you, Ms. PR Queen?"

"I need your help getting us the best legal team around. We're suing for slander."

Chapter 27
Kesley

"**M**om, did you hear anything from Zane yet?"

My baby boy is pacing in the hall worried that the man who promised he'd be here, his father though he doesn't know it, won't be coming after all.

"Snooks, it's just very unlikely that he'll be able to make it. Let's cut him some slack."

"But he promised he'd be here no matter what."

And I wish he hadn't.

Liam's teacher approaches the door just as the surgeon that Jimmy Campbell's dad invited to speak starts wrapping up his spiel.

"Ms. Brooks, any word yet from your guest?" The teacher whispers.

I check my phone again. Still no response. I shake my head, reluctantly.

"It's okay this kind of thing happens. I'll just give the kids a reading break."

Just as I'm about to give up. The double doors leading from the hallway open and in burst not one—*but six*—hockey players, dressed in pads, helmets, and jerseys and carrying their sticks. Even Ryker is dressed in his full goalie gear pulling in the rear.

And there, leading the pack... is Zane.

"You made it!" Liam jumps up excitedly.

"Hey, big man. I almost didn't recognize you without your Hulk gear," Zane says, smiling at our boy.

"I'm not allowed to wear it in school."

Zane looks at me from behind his visor. He lifts it and I'm met with piercing blue eyes.

"Hi," I say, nervously playing with my necklace.

"Hi." He's short with me and quickly turns his attention back to Liam. He might as well have punched me in the gut by the blow I feel. But I try to ignore it for my son's sake.

"Big man, this is the Heatwave starting lineup. Boys, *this* is Liam."

The way he says Liam's name lets me know he's been talking to his boys about him.

Keelan high-fives him first. "Heard you like superheroes."

"Hulk's my favorite. He reminds me of Zane," Liam says.

"That checks out," Hicks says from behind him. "He does go kinda hulk mode on the ice."

"It's true," Fergie confirms. "He's like a legend when it comes to hulk smashes."

Liam's eyes are bright, admiring everything about the man in front of him.

I hate to break up this little reunion but I knock on the door signaling to the teacher that our guests have arrived. In the few seconds it takes her to get to the door, I can feel my body heating up just being around him.

Zane and I haven't talked since he found out that Liam is his son. And so much has happened since then. So much we need to discuss.

"Oh my, you just brought the whole team with you, didn't you? What a pleasant surprise! Please come in," Liam's teacher says, ushering them in through the door.

Zane wraps an arm around Liam's shoulders. "Come on, big man. Let's show your classmates who's the coolest kid in this school."

Liam does a little happy dance before leading Zane and the guys inside. They're huge and take up every available space in front of the class, but I squeeze in after them.

Each player takes a turn talking about the position they play. Keelan leads the discussion. A true team captain.

When Zane is done with his part he comes to stand by me in the corner near the entrance. His voice is barely above a whisper so I lean in to hear him.

"We need to talk," he says sternly.

"You can start by answering my calls," I whisper back.

"I think we both know I'm not the one in the wrong here, Kesley." His eyes don't meet mine. They stay glued on our son, who is sitting at his desk nodding excitedly with each word the Heatwave players say.

I heave a sigh. "When?"

"Tonight. I'll come get you." That's all he says before stalking off to rejoin his teammates.

* * *

There's a knock on the door and Liam jumps up from the couch screaming, "I'll get it."

"Liam... wait!" I quickly dry my hands on the kitchen towel hanging from the oven and run my hands over my hair.

The door swings open and an excited female voice shouts, "Well, if it isn't my favorite nephew!"

Libby?

"What are you doing here?" Liam screams, jumping into her waiting arms.

"Yeah, Lib. What *are* you doing here?"

She squeezes the small boy until he complains and she finally lets him go.

"I had a little break between shoots and figured it's as good a time as any to come home for a few days." She slowly rises and picks her bag off the floor.

"Is that so?"

"That *is* so," she says. "Now, do you want to tell me why my brother called me saying that his wife has pitted the media against his beloved team?"

She puts a hand on her hip and cocks her head. "Starting with the *you're his wife part*, please," she says in a stage whisper.

Liam is back to watching his favorite show and oblivious to our conversation.

I cock my head at her and motion toward my bedroom. I can't believe she flew halfway across the world for this.

She drags her luggage in and leaves it by the door. Dropping her bag on the kitchen island as we walk by it. She jumps onto my bed and leans back on her hands, tilting her head at me. "I'm all ears, Kes."

"What did Zane tell you?"

"Everything. From his point of view, of course. And I gotta say, I know exactly what you guys are doing. And I'm not mad. I honestly couldn't be happier." She puts a hand on her chest. "What *I* don't understand is why you didn't wait for me to tell him about Liam. I thought we had a plan for that?"

"It was Kira who told him."

"What? How the hell did Kira know?" she scoffs. "I

thought you and I were the only ones who knew about that?"

"She put two and two together a while back. Promised me she wouldn't say anything... and then just lost it at our Spring Break trip."

"What the hell?"

"Liam still doesn't know that Zane's his real dad," I inform her.

It's a lot to recap. But I fill her in on what happened. The concussion scare. The proposal. The... ahem... wedding. Leaving out specific wedding night details, of course. And how Zane insisted he go with me on the family trip.

"I fucking knew you two loved each other!" she snaps and gives me a knowing smirk. "Nobody hates a person that much without feeling something more for them."

"Excuse me? Did you forget the whole, your brother slept with me and didn't remember the next morning piece? I had my reasons, Lib."

"Kes," she deadpans. "You can't hold something against someone when they didn't even know about it in the first place."

"That's the thing, Lib. We've been making excuses for him all these years. Both of us. Thinking he was too damaged. Too hurt. To be able to handle the truth. And I was the one in the wrong... I know that. I should've come clean that morning he woke up here."

I'm frustrated at this point. I haven't slept much in days and it feels like everything around me is falling apart and there's nothing I can do but watch it come crashing down into a pile of ash.

"Ok, so you're married to Zane. Congrats, by the way. Wish I would've received an invite but I get it. You eloped," she rolls her eyes. "And he knows Liam is his son. You guys can finally be one big happy family... so what the hell is the deal with this Heatwave media scandal?"

I sigh. "Jeremy."

"Jeremy, your boss, Jeremy?"

I nod. "He put me on an assignment. Told me he'd fire me if I didn't take it. I was backed into a corner, Lib."

"The asshole. He can't do that!"

"Well, he did. I sent him what I had as a preliminary piece. And he took what I had and wrote an entire article using my name and released it."

"Are you kidding me?"

"No. I've talked to Rina. She's working something out. Turns out that Jeremy was friends with the guys who were fired by Mack Stratton when she took over as the owner."

"Bobby *whatever his name is* and that other guy?"

"Yeah, the old PR manager and chief of marketing."

"Ugh. Those guys deserved to be fired. I heard all about them," she says with disgust.

"Anyway, it's all just blowing up in my face."

"A steaming hot pile of doo-doo." She shakes her head slowly.

I go to sit next to her on my bed. "I don't know what to do. But Zane will be here any minute now."

"He still wants to talk—so talk. What's the big deal? You guys are *married*. Must I remind you?" She picks up my left hand and ogles the sparkly ring. "Very married, according to the size of this ring. Yowza."

I pull my hand back and hold it to myself. "He probably just wants to call the whole thing off and let me know he found some other gullible simp to be his wife."

"Kesley Brooks, you are anything but. Stop talking about my friend that way."

Liam's voice calls to me from down the hall, "Mom, Zane's here!"

Shit. I quickly jump to my feet.

"Easy there, Seabiscuit. It's just my brother."

Yeah, *to her.* To me, he's become so much more. He's my son's father. My husband. The man I love. And right now... the man who hates me.

I reach for her and take her into my arms for a hug, "Thanks for coming," I say, squeezing her. "I know you canceled plans to be here."

She snaps her wrist at me, "Had to be here for all my favorite people. I couldn't just watch your world come crashing down from across the pond. I need front-row tickets to this shit show." She winks.

When we step into the living room, Liam and Zane are chatting excitedly in front of the TV.

"That had to be the funniest part of the whole movie," Liam says.

Zane is laughing with him. "I watched that part like fifty times and laughed every single time he smashed him."

I clear my throat to get their attention.

"Hi, Mom."

"Hi, snooks. Hi... caveman."

Zane turns to face me from the couch and gives me a nod.

"I gotta go, big man. But we'll watch that together soon, yeah?"

Liam laughs, "Really, Zane?"

"I promise. And you know I keep my promises, right?"

Liam nods enthusiastically. "Good. Now me and your mommy are going to go talk for a bit. We'll be back later."

He rises and motions with his head for me to follow him out the door.

"Uh, I was going to bring Liam with us," I whisper to him.

He shakes his head. "That's why I asked Lib to come. She's staying with him for the night."

That little sneak. She and Zane planned this?

I say bye to Liam and give Libby a silent *what the fuck.* She giggles before closing the door behind me. "Zane... what's going on?" I say following behind him.

The elevator dings open and he steps inside facing me. "Come on, Kesley."

He does it again. He uses my first name. Not little lion. Not Simba. Not wife. But Kesley. It irks me.

I step inside and cross my arms over my chest.

"Do you plan on just ordering me about and not giving me any answers?" I say.

"I'd like to, yeah." He seems unbothered. We get to the parking garage and Zane pulls a set of keys from his pocket. He hits a button and a sleek black SUV's lights blink.

I follow him to it and he presses another button. I hear the doors unlock. "Get in."

I stop abruptly. "We're not going to do this, Zane."

"Do what, Kesley?"

"This thing where you keep telling me what to—" Then it hits me. "Wait. Zane, where's your motorcycle? You don't own a car."

He smirks, "I do now."

He goes to the passenger side and opens the door for me, waiting until I'm in before he shuts it.

Once he's settled in the driver's seat I say, "Look, I'm sorry. I should have told you about, Liam. It wasn't right for me to keep that from you."

He holds a hand up for me to stop. "I want you to know, that I'm obsessed with you. I always have been. And in another life, our situation would've been very different. But it's not. It's shitty and messy and honestly, Kes. I don't know what to believe. But tonight, I don't want to talk about it."

He's gripping the steering wheel now and running his hands around it slowly.

"Okay. So what *do* you want to talk about then?"

He turns the ignition, starting the car. "About me taking you to meet, Nana."

Grandma O'Connor?

"What for?"

"She needs to confirm the marriage," he says matter-of-factly.

"Confirm?"

"Yes, Kesley."

"Zane, we need to talk about Liam."

"Libby already told me what happened, alright. I'm dealing with it. But I will tell you this, Kesley. If you think you'll be keeping him from me any longer, you are sorely mistaken."

"Zane, I didn't want to keep you from him to begin with. I just never found the right—"

"Time? Yeah, when would it ever be right? To tell the guy you slept with one drunken night that he got you pregnant with a child and that he's been around that child and never put the pieces together. Do you know how much of an idiot I feel like right now? To not recognize that my son has lived in the same building as me... for *years*, Kes? That I mourned losing a child that wasn't even mine when my own flesh and blood walked by me, day in and day out?"

He's grips the steering wheel tightly but still hasn't backed out of the parking spot.

"Maybe I should drive, Zane."

"No," he barks. Then softer says, "I've got this."

He puts a hand behind my headrest and looks back to make sure no cars are coming as he backs out.

"Are you sure you're good to drive?"

"Kesley, let's just get through tonight, okay? Once everything is signed over. I'll give you your money." He pulls out of the parking garage and looks both ways before exiting past the garage gates.

"This whole thing was just a means to an end anyway. Like you said, we could never be a thing. Not for real, anyway."

My gut tightens. I did say those words. But that was... *before.*

Before I realized how Zane felt all these years. That our one night together *was* real. Not just some drunken mistake. And that he does want to be in Liam's life.

"My grandmother is an astute woman," he says breaking through my thoughts. "She'll be very slick with her questions and will watch our every move, I can guarantee it. She already has her reservations about the fact that we made it official without her blessing. But I told her about our history," he explains.

"What about it?" I ask him.

"About... our son."

Our son—not *my* son—but *our* son.

"And she can't wait to meet her first great-grandson," he adds.

"So your family all knows that Liam..." I can't finish the question.

"I don't think my dad knows, unless Nana told him." He keeps a firm grip on the steering wheel and carefully checks all his mirrors before switching lanes.

"Zane... what did you do with your bike?"

He glances over at me and looks at me for a beat longer

than he has at any other point today before bringing his attention back to the road.

"Lost it in a bet."

"A bet?" I choke out. "That bike cost more than most people's yearly salaries."

He shrugs.

"Well, what was the bet?"

He shakes his head. "You don't want to know."

"Seriously, what could have been enticing enough for you to bet your custom bike on it?"

He's on the main highway now. I don't know where his grandma lives but it must be nice based on the direction of town that we're going.

"I have a better idea. Let's talk about how you almost blew up my hockey team." His eyes shift to me briefly again and then back to the road.

"It was a bad call. I thought I could spin it for the sake of the team, but my boss had other plans."

"So you agreeing to this marriage, it was all for you to gain access to the Heatwave?"

I can feel my shoulders slump and all I want to do is to be swallowed up by the seat I'm currently in. "If I could go back in time. I'd do so many things differently."

"Trust me, so would I."

"What's that supposed to mean?"

He shakes his head. "Let's just focus on what we need to do tonight."

I get it. He's pissed. I betrayed his trust. I even had his sister cover up for me for years. But I think he forgets just how messed up he's been all these years. Even so, he's right, this would all be for naught if we can't even accomplish the purpose of our marriage in the first place.

"So... I'll play the doting wife that can't resist your

charms. And you'll be the loving husband who can't find a single flaw in me?" I shoot him a glance and he cinches his brows.

"Are you kidding me? Nana would smell our bullshit from a mile away."

"Well, what do you expect us to do then?"

"This! Bicker! Be mad at each other. Act like a real, fucking couple."

Is he serious? He wants me to bicker in front of his grandmother? How is that supposed to convince her?

"We're newlyweds, Zane. Shouldn't we be on cloud nine?"

He barks out a sarcastic laugh. "That cloud has long since passed, Kesley. Welcome to life beyond the honeymoon."

"That was short-lived."

"Seems like most things between us are."

I cross my arms over my chest and look out the window. Yeah, bickering will be no problem.

"Liam wouldn't stop talking about the Houston Heroes. That's what he calls you guys," I say, changing the subject.

I look over at Zane and see the tiniest of tugs on the corner of his mouth. "It was fun being there for him. Though he'll be sad to find out we're more like a pack of rabid animals than anything resembling heroes."

"To him, you're a hero."

Zane sighs. "Have you told him, Kesley?"

I shake my head. "He doesn't know you're his dad... not yet."

"When are you planning on telling him?" His question comes out rough and accusatory.

"I was hoping we'd tell him together."

He stays quiet and doesn't look in my direction at all for

the remainder of the drive. When we pull up to a long winding driveway leading to a beautiful brick mansion, I know he's done talking about it.

He parks the car and shuts off the engine.

"Let's just get through tonight okay? Everything else... we'll just have to see."

I look over at him. Both hands still gripping the steering wheel. He looks defeated. More than I've seen him in a while.

And I decide at that moment. That I won't be the reason he keeps breaking.

Not anymore.

Chapter 28
Zane

The candlelights in the middle of the dining table flicker as Nana's butler walks by. The table is silent. I'm sitting on the far end with Kesley to my right. The man I call my father sits on the complete opposite side.

His hair is greying at the roots. I don't remember seeing grey hairs last time I saw him. And I definitely wasn't expecting him to be here tonight. Much less with yet another new wife. She's young. Probably even younger than Kesley. A bubbly and busty brunette that could pass as an escort if I've ever seen one.

He reaches for her hand and gives her a swift kiss, just as Nana walks in with the help of her maid. She slowly takes her seat in the middle of the table facing the two new wives.

"Thank you, Brenda," my grandmother's raspy voice says in a near whisper.

Kesley looks nervous. Fidgeting in her seat.

I didn't think I'd be competing with my own father for

who gets Granddad's inheritance. The will is pretty clear. So I don't know what his angle could possibly be.

Once Nana is situated, Frank goes in for the kill.

"Mam, I want you to meet, Stacia. Stacia O'Connor."

The regal woman before us clears her throat as she tilts her head slowly and assesses her new daughter-in-law.

"It's a pleasure to meet you, Mrs. O'Connor. Frank has told me so much about you." The brunette reaches a hand out to my grandmother who glances at her son briefly before taking her hand.

"Stacia has lived near Dublin for a good portion of her life, Mam." Frank is playing up his Irish accent.

"Is that right?" Nana asks, with dry interest.

"Oh yeah," Stacia says excitedly. "I grew up on *top of the mornin* and J*aysus, Mary, and Joseph.*"

Stacia quickly looks at my father for approval and I can already tell he's put her up to this. He's not fooling anyone. Especially not Fiona O'Connor.

Kesley and I exchange glances. Just as Grandma turns to us. "And you must be Kesley," she says, disregarding Frank and Stacia. "Zane has told me so much about *you.*"

I feel the heat rising to my neck. I didn't think I talked *that* much about her.

"Oh," Kesley lifts a brow to me. "Well, all good things I hope."

Nana cracks a rare smile. "All good things, child. How is my great-grandson?"

My father drops his fake smile. "I beg your pardon, Mam?"

"Oh, Hi Dad," I wave sarcastically at him from the far end of the table. "Welcome. I know it's been a while so just to catch you up... Kesley and I have a six-year-old. His name is Liam." I turn back to my grandmother, "And he's doing great, Nana."

"I hear he's smart as a whip."

"He is," Kesley confirms. "And has a heart of gold."

"Since when do you have a son?" Frank barks out.

Nana looks at him. "Francis, please. You really should stay in touch with your own family. Is this what you're looking forward to in your marriage, Stacia? A man so disconnected that he doesn't even know when his child has a child?"

Stacia's face goes pale and looks to my father for help.

"Have you had a DNA test?'" My father asks. "Are you sure he's yours?"

Kesley looks like she's about to combust. Her hands grip the tablecloth under her knuckles.

"Francis, why would you ask such a thing?" Nana scolds him.

"That's why he came here, right? To claim his son as the heir to Dad's inheritance?"

"Your son is the rightful heir to your father's inheritance," Nana fires back. "He's married in the allotted time. To a woman he so clearly loves. My question to you is, why are you here, Francis?"

Stacia looks at my father confused. "I thought your name was Frank?"

My dad loosens his tie with agitated movements. "This is ridiculous."

"So let me get this straight," Kesley says. "You came here knowing that Zane was going to be introducing his new wife to his grandmother and you felt the need to come parade yours as well? Knowing full well that inheritance belongs to your son."

"Nobody asked you, gold digger," he spits out.

"Enough," I pound a fist to the table making the drinks in front of us slosh. "Nobody speaks to my wife in that manner. Especially not someone I would've considered family. Though judging by the way you're acting, *Father*, you need to stay as far away from *my* family as possible."

I turn back to my grandmother. "I'm so sorry. This was supposed to be a pleasant evening."

"Oh, don't you worry, my child. That's not on you."

My grandmother raises a finger and in an instant, five servers enter the dining room from the kitchen area. Each one holding a plate of food.

A server pauses next to each of us, awaiting my grandmother's instructions. She nods and they place the covered plates on the table in unison and open the lids to the meals prepared for us.

Kesley gasps. "This is my family's favorite."

A grin pulls at Nana's mouth. "So I've heard." She sends me a wink. "In honor of my newest granddaughter-in-law."

Frank throws his napkin onto the plate and stands. "This is absurd, Mam. You know good and well that I've given this marriage thing a fair shot. The entire inheritance clause is a joke. A big fat, fuck you to the world joke."

Nana clears her throat. "Francis, I know this doesn't mean anything to you. But I'm going to let you in on something. The point of your father's inheritance clause was to encourage our family's legacy to continue. Past your father and I. Even past you and your brother and your children. It was never about any one person, my child. It was about the O'Connor name living on through generations and continuing to build on everything we started when we arrived from Ireland all those years ago."

"Unfortunately, you chose the pursuit of gains over the pursuit of your wife's heart. And I'm sorry, Stacia, I know this must be difficult to hear. But Frank's heart was never in the right place. Always putting business before... well, any of his marriages. He's done the same with his children. And he'll do the same with you if he doesn't change."

Stacia swallows hard and stares up at Frank. Kesley and I exchange quick glances.

"What you speak of doesn't exist, Mam. Even you and Dad had your issues. There is no perfect love marriage," he yells.

Nana nods. "Because you never gave anyone all of you, my son. You didn't give the ugly truths about your pain and struggles. You didn't trust your wife to know the broken pieces of you, as much as the accomplishments. We humans are multi-faceted creatures. We're complex. And until you own the part you played in your sad story, you'll never experience..." she turns her face to Kesley and me and nods in our direction, "This."

We look at each other. Nana doesn't know we're on rocky ground right now. She doesn't know that we're still trying to figure out our places in each other's lives. In our son's life. The role we ultimately must play. Or even the roles we wish to play.

All that is up in the air.

But she knows real love. She and Granddad had it. So she can see it when it's there. And that in and of itself, is reassuring.

Frank huffs, pushing himself off his seat and calling back to Stacia, "Come Stacia. We don't need to be here."

Stacia hesitates a moment before slowly rising from her seat. The poor woman. Used as a pawn by my father. All for his gain.

My father glares at me as he waits for his wife to join him.

"Thank you for... your time, Mrs. O'Connor," Stacia says quietly. Nana gives the woman a soft nod.

"And it was nice to meet you, Zane. Kesley. My best to Liam." We both acknowledge her but my father storms off and doesn't say another word. She follows behind him.

When they're both gone, Nana reaches for her fork and looks over at us.

"Some people would rather blame the world for their problems. But it's the one's who take responsibility and learn to grow from their mistakes... those are the ones who are truly in control of their destiny. I'm sorry about my son."

"It's okay, Nana. I've long since given up on that relationship."

She dips her fork into the shepherd's pie and pauses at my words, "You know, the best part of learning and growing is giving others the time they need to do it too. He'll come around. You did," she says to me. "And I can't remember the last time I've seen you this happy, Zane."

Kesley dips her head but I can tell she's watching me. I reach for my fork as well.

"But next time, I'd love to meet my great-grandson," Nana says with a smile, and takes a bite of her meal.

"I tried to tell him we should bring Liam," Kesley says.

"And *I* told her, I flew Libby from Milan just so my son's favorite aunt could watch him tonight. But yes, next time, Nana."

Nana looks down at her dish smiling and nods her head, "Good. So tell me, what will you do with the estate now that it's yours?"

* * *

Kesley is quiet as we walk back to my car. I should be relieved. My family's estate will stay with us. Libby will be so happy. Almost as happy as Nana was to learn that she was able to live long enough to meet her great-grandson.

"I want to spend time with Liam. Maybe take him skating at the arena."

Kesley looks at me as we walk.

"Of course. You're his dad, you have every right to spend time with him."

I nod. Upset that I've missed out on so much time with my boy.

"We can come up with a plan to let him know about you. In his mind... he doesn't have a dad."

That makes me even more upset. I know what it's like to grow up without a dad. Or to have a father figure that did little to care for me. I would never want that for my own boy. I'll do everything in my power to make sure I'm always in his life. Regardless of what might happen between Kesley and I, Liam's my priority.

We get to the car and my wife looks up at me. "Maybe... we can try to make this work? For real. Like you said at the beach house."

I stay quiet. I gave her all of me at the beach house. And she took it, even keeping all these secrets from me. I can't trust her. That's it in a nutshell. Kesley used me to get ahead in her career. She withheld my son from me and involved my own sister.

Trust is hard to earn. And right now... despite my feelings for her, I don't trust her.

"Let's just focus on our son right now, okay."

She doesn't say anything else the entire ride home. I don't either. And when we walk down our shared hallway, she turns to me as I'm unlocking my door.

"Goodnight, Zane."

I look over my shoulder. "Goodnight."

Once I'm inside and behind my closed door, I can finally breathe. It's impossible for me to be around that woman and not touch her. I've known deep pain, but this betrayal—I'm finding it hard to get over.

"Hello big boy. Hello big boy," the parrot squawks when he realizes I'm home.

I go to the kitchen and grab his snacks.

When I pull the sheet off his cage, Muppet looks at me frantically like he does every night.

"What? Don't look at me like that."

The bird mumbles to himself.

"Listen, if you got something to say, just spit it out," I tell him.

"Oh, shut up you big oaf," he replies. "Come give me a kiss. Muah. Muah. Muah."

I shake my head at my only companion. "I don't know what Mal ever saw in you. You're annoying as hell."

I open the cage door and he flaps his wings backing up further into the cage.

"Don't you get tired of being holed up in here all by yourself?"

The bird mumbles to himself again.

"Wouldn't you rather be free? This little prison, it's so sad."

He turns his neck every which way and his pupils dilate as I speak to him.

"There's a whole world out there, you know. People to enjoy. People to hate. People to love with everything you have left."

Muppet's wings settle at his sides again and he takes tentative steps toward me.

"You know… there's a little boy that thinks you're the coolest thing around. I think you guys would get along pretty well. He's pretty great."

The bird steps onto my arm and reaches for the snack in my other hand.

"And if he wants to be a zoologist, or a hockey player, or the freakin' president of the United States. I'm going to be there with him, every step of the way."

Muppet looks at me as he munches his snack. When he's done, he stares at me and mumbles to himself.

"What was that?"

He stills before squawking, "Oh shut up you big oaf."

I roll my eyes. Message received, Muppet.

Message received.

Chapter 29
Kesley

I can't sleep for the life of me. I flip over in my bed and huff out my frustration.

The conversation at dinner is still fresh in my mind. The way Zane defended me. The way his own grandmother could see what we have even if we might be too stubborn to admit it ourselves.

I know because that night all those years ago, we made love at our most broken and vulnerable... and it was the most *real*.

He might not remember, but I know every detail of that night.

I remember the way he looked at me. Like he could see right into me. The longing on his face. The softness of his touch.

He told me I wasn't a rebound. That I was always his first pick. But I didn't see it then. I didn't see it even when I dated other men and he got jealous. I didn't see it when he and Liam got along so well, before they even knew they were father and son.

I missed all the signs because I was mad at a man that I had pushed away. And he didn't deserve that.

I wish I could turn back time. Say yes to that confident jock that approached me in the library. The one I would later learn was my new friend's brother. The one who would become the most important person in my life, next to Liam.

I close my eyes shut to try to get thoughts of that man out of my head. But the smell of burning wood has me sitting up in an instant. We don't have a wood-burning fireplace so what is that?

I jump out of my bed and reach the doorknob just as the fire alarm in the building goes off.

"Liam! Libby!" I call down the hall. They're already awake opening their doors at almost the same time that I do.

"Where's it coming from?" Libby asks throwing on a robe.

Liam comes running down the hall to me. "Why is it so loud?"

"I don't know, snooks. It might be a fire in the building. We gotta go."

The three of us, find shoes and open the door leading into our shared hall with Zane.

Liam goes to press the elevator button but nothing happens. Libby runs to Zane's door and pounds on it.

"Mom, the elevator isn't working!" he screams out.

"It's okay, we'll take the stairs."

Libby continues to pound on her brother's door. "Zane! Open up!" she calls out to him.

But all we hear is Muppet and his outbursts.

Libby grabs the handle and quickly retracts her hand. "It's hot!"

I push past her and place my hand on the doorknob, smoke billows out from beneath the locked door.

"Oh shit, it's Zane's place. There's a fire."

Libby pounds on his door with both fists, "Zane, wake up, there's a fire! Please, wake up!"

Please God don't let him be drunk and passed out. I imagine the worst. This can't be happening.

I pull Libby back. "I'm going to kick it down."

"What?" Libby cries out.

"Take Liam and get to safety," I say to her. She nods and runs over to Liam.

"Is he going to be okay?" Liam cries out.

"Go with your Aunt Libby, snooks. We'll be down soon, I promise."

Liam nods and they both disappear down the stairwell.

I draw in a breath and do my best to get oxygen flowing to my extremities.

"Ok... on the count of three, I'm doing it," I say to myself.

One. I hear Muppet squawking behind the door.

Two. There's coughing. He must be in there.

Three. I use every ounce of strength I have to force the door open with just my leg strength.

The door bursts open and I see Zane on the balcony. Between us, a fire burns the window dressings and is spreading to the furniture.

He has Muppet on his shoulder and is looking for ways to get down.

The wall of fire won't let either of us pass.

"Zane!" I cry out.

He turns to look at me. "There's no way out. Not without getting toasted."

There has to be a way out. I'm not losing him. I look around for anything that can diminish the growing fire.

I grab the throw off Zane's couch and head for the kitchen sink. I turn the water on and try to get the throw as soaked as I can. Then I go back and toss the wet blanket over the fire raging toward Zane. It gives him a temporary open spot through the fire.

Without a second thought, he runs from the opening of the balcony and right to me.

The blanket keeps the fire away just long enough for him to cross to me. I grab his hand and we run out to the hallway just as something explodes inside his apartment. The smoke detectors are blaring, and the sprinkler heads go off.

"What caused the fire?" I huff out. Zane is running down the stairs step in step with me. "Zane?"

"I don't know."

"Was it a cigarette?"

"No! I... quit smoking."

He has Muppet tucked into the crook of his arm.

I stop and look at him. The momentum carries him in front of me and he looks back, "What?"

"Why did you quit smoking?"

He shakes his head, not wanting to answer.

"Zane!"

"Because... I want to live as long as I can... for Liam."

My heart bursts in that moment. This is what I've wanted to hear him say all these years. To have a reason and a purpose to live. And what better reason than our son.

"So let's go get him!" he says taking my hand.

Halfway down we see the firemen coming up the steps. They're fast.

"Top floor, apartment on the left," Zane tells them. They nod and continue on up past us.

Zane watches as they take the steps two at a time and then turns to me. "We gotta go. Hold Muppet." The bird squawks as I take hold of him and without asking, Zane bends down, picks me up, and throws me over his shoulder.

* * *

When the fire chief arrives he gets briefed and comes to talk to our small group of neighbors.

"Which one of you is Zane O'Connor?"

Zane has Liam in his lap and sets him down next to me before rising. "That would be me."

"Sir, are you aware of any faulty wiring in your apartment?"

Zane's face is perplexed. "No, why would you ask that?"

"Because either someone is out to get you, or you have a really bad maintenance crew. It looks like whoever did your electricity hasn't adhered to any safety codes. A kindergartner could've done a better job wiring your place."

Why would Frank skimp out on the building's electricity?

"Was that the cause of the fire?" I ask him.

"Looks like it. If I were you I'd be getting in touch with your landlord to find out why a renovated penthouse has trash wiring and no signs of any issues within the rest of the building. Seems weird if you ask me."

Very weird.

"Thank you, sir. I'll look into it." Zane gives me a sidelong glance.

When the fire chief is far enough away Libby reaches

for Liam's ears and covers them to whisper, "What the actual fuck?"

"It's not safe here," Zane says to us. We need to find somewhere to sleep tonight.

"I can call my parents," I offer. "They're just thirty minutes outside the city. They have extra rooms."

Liam jumps up and down, "Yeah, I love Memaw and Pop-Pop's house."

I look at Libby who's looking at the top of our building with pensive eyes.

"Lib?" I ask.

"Yeah, call them up," she says, taking her eyes off the building and giving me a half smile.

Then goes back to staring at the condominiums we all call home.

Chapter 30
Zane

I slowly open the cracked door to the room Liam is sleeping in.

"He just fell asleep," Kesley whispers.

She's folded around him and I walk up to them both and place a hand on his head, brushing back his brown hair.

"Goodnight, big man," I whisper to my boy.

I look at Kesley who's smiling softly back at me.

"You should rest," I tell her.

She nods and scoots off the small bed. We stop in the hallway and she closes Liam's door. Everyone else in the house is asleep, including Libby who insisted she sleep on the couch downstairs.

"Come on," Kesley says taking my hand.

She leads me to her bedroom. The same one she used to sleep in growing up. I grab the spare comforters that Sherrie left on her small desk and open them up spreading them out on the floor.

"What are you doing?" she asks, pulling the ponytail holder out of her hair and letting it cascade down onto her shoulder.

"I'll sleep on the floor. Get some rest, Kes."

I lie down on the hard surface and use the other blanket to cover myself. Kesley doesn't say a word and instead switches the light off. I watch her pad over to her bed.

A second later, she says softly, "You don't have to sleep down there, caveman. This bed is big enough for the two of us."

I gulp and hope she can't hear me. I can't sleep next to her. The things she's made me feel...

"I can't do that, Kesley."

"Why not?" I hear her rustling the sheets.

A low rumble climbs through my chest, "Because if I sleep next to you, I'll fuck you. And I don't want to. So goodnight."

She's silent a moment. Then I hear her footsteps in the darkness. I blink up at her standing over me.

She takes her shirt off and slips out of her pajama shorts, tossing them both aside. She stands before me naked. And I'm even more pissed.

"Don't. Do. That," I say through gritted teeth.

"Zane... I almost lost you today," she whispers into the darkness. I can hear the brokenness in her voice.

"And?"

She pulls the covers off of me and straddles my body before laying her head on my chest. I can still smell the hint of smoke that lingers in her hair.

"And I never want to feel what I felt tonight. Not ever again," she admits.

It takes everything in me to not wrap my arms around her and pull her lips to mine. I'm cracking with each passing second. This is Kesley. My safe space.

But it doesn't *feel* like that right now. She broke that.

"Kesley, what you did. Keeping Liam from me. That

was... the ultimate betrayal. I've lost so much and for you to just keep the greatest thing I didn't know I had. I... I can't just move forward from that."

Her head is tucked under my chin and she's clinging to me like a lifeline when I feel her gentle sobs. "I am so sorry. I wanted to tell you the second I found out. But I didn't think you'd believe me. You were so drunk the night I gave myself to you."

I could strangle my old self for locking away that memory for me.

"And Libby admitted she had given you pills to help you sleep. You were struggling, Zane. Telling you that you had a baby on the way...after everything you've been through. It... felt wrong."

"That wasn't your secret to keep, Kesley." My voice is clipped. I don't mean to sound like an asshole. But I can't hide that I'm upset.

"No... it wasn't."

"And Libby knew too. Do you get what a slap in the face that is to me?"

She lifts her head and even in the dark I can see her peering into my eyes. "It was wrong of us not to tell you. You should've been there for it all. I know that now." She goes back to resting her head on my chest.

I'm so confused. This is her giving me a sincere apology. I should be able to just accept it and move on.

But something in me wants to rage. I want her to hurt as bad as she hurt me.

"The bet..." I say.

She meets my eyes again, waiting for me to say something.

"It was to get you to say yes to being my girlfriend before the playoffs."

She pushes herself up and looks at me. "What?"

"The bet between me and Keelan... it was you."

She rolls off of me and sits up on the blanket. "What are you talking about? What was the bet?"

"If I didn't get you to say yes, Keelan would get my bike."

She's silent before she says, "But that would mean you won."

"Mmhmm."

"Then what did you get out of it?"

I reach down into my pocket and pull out the folded check Keelan gave me for my bike and hand it to her.

She reaches for the lamp on her desk and switches it on, unfolding the piece of paper.

"Are you fucking kidding me? Two hundred grand?" She looks from the check to my face and back to the check.

"It's yours. Consider it child support for all the years you kept me from my son," I say sitting up on my elbows and glaring at her.

She closes her eyes and folds the check, tossing it back to me. "I don't want your money, Zane. I never wanted your fucking money. I'm not Mallory," she spits out.

"Mallory accepted my help."

She reaches for the blanket she took off of me and wraps it around her naked body. "I don't need you. I don't need your money. I don't need any of this."

She stands and reaches for her clothes. "Good luck finding someone to marry your ass so you can have your family's fortune. That's what this was all about for you anyways."

"That's the thing, Kesley." I stand up and stalk over to her. She reaches for the doorknob and tries to pull the door open. But I reach forward and shut it again. She's trapped between me and the door. And I'm speaking to her back when I say, "I don't need you anymore. I have a son. He's the youngest O'Connor male. Liam will be the one to get the inheritance."

She slowly turns to face me. My hand is still pressed against the door right above her head.

She says like the mama bear that she is, "I will *not* let you put that burden on my son."

"*Our* son," I correct her.

"Look what this inheritance has cost you Zane! Your youth. Your mental health. You've done things you regret and all for what?"

"For my family."

"Please... what family? Libby? She's got more money than she knows what to do with? And Frank? He's set for life with his own fortune. God only knows how much longer your Nana has. So family? What family Zane?"

I growl out, "For you. For Liam. You two are my family now. And if I have to endure everything I went through to get you both. I'd do it all over again."

She looks at me through slitted eyes, "I don't understand. You just said you don't need me."

"I don't need you."

"Then what are you—"

"I *want* you, little lion. I want you to be my wife. I want you by my side, raising our son together. I want you... to want to be with me."

Her breath hitches as I reach for her chin and pull it up for her to look me in the eyes.

"Without the agreement. A real marriage. A real... family."

She doesn't move. For a moment I feel the air escape the

room. Like she might just say no. Instead, she reaches for the loops on my jeans and pulls me toward her.

I watch as she reaches for the hem of my t-shirt and pulls it over my head. Dropping it to the side. She runs her hands over my abs, up my chest and wraps both arms around my neck, drawing me toward her.

"Then fuck me like you want me to stay, caveman."

Chapter 31
Kesley

He reaches for my waist and pulls me toward him. I can feel the erection in his jeans.

"Of all my vices," he says to me in a low growl. "You're the worst one."

"Why's that?"

"Because you're the only one I don't want to kick. You're the worst of all my addictions."

I'm about to tell him that I can be the best thing that's ever happened to him, but the hand he has on the door slides down and takes hold of the back of my head pulling me to his lips.

He kisses me like I've never been kissed before. Like kissing me is the only thing keeping him alive. And I need it too. We barely come up for air. And when we do, it's only for him to put his mouth on my body.

He hoists me up and pushes me against the door, grabbing me by the neck and forcing me to look up at him.

"I'm still mad at you. You made a mess of my life. Thanks to you and your little exposé, Rina has the entire team on *Operation Win Back Houston*." He stops talking to kiss my neck, sucking on the sensitive spot just below my ear. It drives me wild. I buck into him and he secures my legs around his waist, pushing himself into me even more, giving me the pressure my body demands from him.

When he's done making his mark on my neck, he inspects his handiwork.

"I'm going to make you pay for what you did," he promises. "On the bed. Get on your hands and knees."

He steps back off the door and lowers me onto the floor. And like an obedient lion being tamed by her handler, I do as he says.

He drops his jeans and then his underwear and turns to face me.

"Uh-uh, face the wall," he says.

I oblige him and shift my body so that I'm facing away from him. And when I do, I see why.

He steps up behind me and runs a rough hand over my ass. "I'm going to fuck you until I have you seeing stars. And you're going to watch me do it," he says to my reflection. "Do you understand me, Kesley?"

I bite my lip and nod my agreement. He stops moving his hand and pulls back slapping my ass harder than he's ever done it before.

I yelp and he goes back to rubbing my sensitive skin. "I hear pink is your favorite color."

He looks down at my heated cheek and then back at my reflection. "You turn a beautiful shade of pink when I punish you, little lion."

Zane reaches between my legs and runs a finger over my slit. "And you get so wet for me when I do it, too. You like being bad, don't you my little lion? You like getting me worked up?"

My little lion. I'm his. He's claimed me.

I only whimper. I don't say anything and he slaps the other cheek just as hard as the first. I can feel my skin heating from his contact. "Say it," he growls out.

"I-I like being bad."

"Mmm," he hums his satisfaction. "And you take me so well, wife."

He notches his rock hard cock at my entrance and slowly pushes into me. My ass in the air for him. I watch his face in the mirror as he slides into my pussy from behind.

"Give me a safe word, Kesley." He works himself into me inch by delicious inch until he's buried to the hilt and I want him to drive into me so badly.

"Uh... I don't... I don't know one." He pulls back just as slowly as he entered me and withdraws. I feel the emptiness and want him back immediately.

"Pick one, or I won't fuck you. We can just call it a night."

I hurry to think of something. A safe word... a safe word. "Mufasa," I blurt out.

He cocks his head into the mirror. Then takes hold of my hips and drives into me in one quick motion causing me to cry out before he withdraws again.

"You say Mufasa and I'll stop whatever I'm doing. Do you understand me?"

He goes back to rubbing his hand over my ass. "Kesley?"

"Yes... yes! I understand," I breathe out.

"That's my girl. Now I'm going to make sure," he pauses to lean forward and kiss my back. "That you remember..." he kisses me lower. "Exactly whose you are."

His lips press against my ass and I feel him sucking my skin into his mouth. Marking me again. He reaches between my legs as he does and his fingers gently massage the wetness over my clit.

He pops off one cheek and goes to the other, still moving his fingers over my clit. Making me pant from his movements. From the feel of his lips on my ass. And I'm grateful to have already showered when I feel his lips between my cheeks. His tongue darting out and piercing that sensitive spot in the middle.

I jolt, shaking on my hands and knees from the feel of him claiming what's his.

"Zane," I breathe out. His finger moves faster between my legs and I can feel my entire body convulse.

My husband. The man I want more than anything. He knows my body better than even I do.

He knows what I need before I can even tell him. Still working my clit, he inserts a finger into me while his mouth works my ass. I'm going to lose it. I can't control the wave that's about to crash over me. I feel my orgasm about to crest. When suddenly... he stops.

My head shoots up to see him in the mirror. He withdraws from every surface he was working and steps back, arms crossed.

"What the hell are you doing?" I rasp. "Don't stop."

"I told you... tonight I'm punishing you."

I can't believe this man. He's infuriating to no end.

I flip over onto my back. Fine, he wants to play games. I'll play games. I drop my legs open in front of him. And touch myself while he looks down at me through hooded eyes.

"Don't you dare make yourself come, wife," he warns.

"Well, you're not doing it so..." I keep rubbing myself in front of him as he watches with rapt attention.

I can feel my orgasm building again. And with Zane watching me intently I'm about to go over.

He knows when it's about to happen, because he lunges

forward like a predator stalking its prey and pulls my hand away. Taking the other one and holding them in place above my head using one hand.

"I said... don't make yourself come," he repeats.

"You're impossible."

"And you don't listen." He pulls me up further on the bed so that he can position himself on top of me. Still holding my wrists in place above me, he drives his cock into me and I cry out.

"I'm the only one who will draw out your pleasure," he says thrusting into me and giving me what I want. I meet him thrust for thrust as I'm building again. About to feel that ecstasy. And he might let me have it this time. He's grinding into me. And there's nothing I want more than to come on him.

He leans in and takes my mouth into his. When he pulls back this time he doesn't stop driving into me. "Your parents are in the next room," he reminds me. "When I let you come... I want you to scream into my mouth so we don't wake them. Got it?"

"Yes," I pant out. *Ugh, finally!*

He pounds into me and just as I'm about to explode he seals my mouth to his and I scream out into his mouth just like he ordered.

He follows me over the edge, halting as he spills into me and I take everything he has to give me. We stay breathing hard, holding each other for what feels like an eternity.

He looks at me and whispers the words I didn't know I needed to hear. "I forgive you, Kesley."

Zane cleans me up and orders me to lay down on my stomach. When I do, I hear him squeeze lotion into his hand warming it up between his palms. Then he climbs into the bed behind me and and gently applies the lotion to my backside.

He pulls me to him when he's done caring for me.

"Thank you," I whisper into the arm he has wrapped around me. And finally, my body finds the rest it needs.

Chapter 32
Zane

Libby watches me as I pour myself a cup of coffee. "There's something I need to tell you," she says.

Kesley is still asleep in her bed. Sherrie and David took Liam to school to try to keep some semblance of normalcy for my boy.

"If it's another kid I don't know about... maybe just keep it to yourself," I smirk before bringing the coffee to my lips.

"No..." she sits down at the Brook's breakfast table, arranging her hair into a messy bun. "I don't think what happened last night was an accident."

"Why do you say that?" I take the seat next to her.

"When was the last time you talked to Frank?" she asks.

"At Nana's. He stormed off."

"And before that?"

"Just in passing."

"Right, isn't that weird? He'd visit me all the time. Just to check up on me, make sure I was good, that the apartment was good. He'd even ask me about you. Like, all the time. Like he was trying to keep tabs on you."

"Lib, what are you getting at?"

"I just find it funny that the man that practically raised us has done everything he could to avoid you."

I've never thought twice about him actively avoiding me. I chalked it up to him just being uncomfortable in my presence.

I set my coffee mug down as the realization hits me.

"You think Frank had a hand in my apartment fire?"

"They never found the guy that killed our father," she says solemnly, still deep in thought. "Or the driver that hit Mallory's car," she adds. "He owns the building where we live. And yours is the only apartment to be found with faulty wiring?"

We look at each other. Her eyes wide and I'm shaking my head.

"There's no way Frank is behind this. He has his own life to worry about."

Libby grabs my hand. "Zane, everyone who's ever gotten in the way of him getting that inheritance... is dead."

"Our Dad... uncle... whatever you want to call him—he wouldn't do that Libby. He wouldn't kill innocent people."

She shakes her head. "No, he wouldn't. But he has enough money to throw at someone who would."

In a moment of clarity, I remember the words he said to me at Mal's funeral.

"We can't all win in this life, Zane. Some people just have all the luck... or the means to get lucky. I'm sorry for your loss."

Maybe he wasn't talking about Mallory at all. Maybe he was talking about losing my shot at the inheritance.

But if Frank was behind it all... what would that mean for Kesley? For Liam?

I stand, and the chair scrapes behind me.

"What is it?" my sister asks.

"He knows about Liam."

The second it hits me. That all the things that have happened to us might have been planned... nothing feels safe.

"Kesley!" I call up the stairs taking them two at a time.

She doesn't answer.

I open the door to her room and she's on the phone. "Uh-huh. Are you guys ok?"

"Who is it?" I bark out.

"There was an accident on the way to school."

My eyes go wild.

"Liam's okay. Mom and Dad too. Their car might be totaled," she whispers.

Totaled? With my son inside?

That's enough. There's no way one family can have this many accidents. I grab my wallet and keys from the night-stand near Kesley.

"Where are they?" I ask.

"What are you—"

I reach for the phone still in her hand, "Sherrie, I need you to tell me exactly where you guys are and who hit you."

"Zane!" Kesley scolds me. But I ignore her and her mother explains the situation.

"Thanks Sherrie, can I please talk to David?"

Libby appears in the door and she and Kesley exchange looks as Kesley's mom puts her husband on the phone.

"Zane?"

"David, I need you to hear me. Somebody is trying to hurt Liam. The driver who hit you... where is he?"

"What? Who would want to hurt Liam?"

"I'll explain later. David, where's the driver that hit you?"

"They just took him away in an ambulance. He was pretty beat up."

"Which hospital?"

David asks around. "Grace Memorial," he finally says.

"Good. David, please keep Liam safe."

"I've got him."

"Thank you." I pass the phone back to Kesley who says goodbye to them and hangs up.

"What's going on?" she says rising from the bed.

"It's Frank. This whole time it's been fucking Frank."

"We don't know that for sure," says Libby from the door.

"What's been Frank?"

I grab Kesley by the hands. "I'm going to find out who's trying to hurt us. And if I find out it's him... he's as good as dead."

"Zane, don't do anything stupid!" Libby begs.

"Call Izzy. Get to a safe place. Lock all the doors. Whoever he sent to get Liam knows we're here."

* * *

The hospital is bustling. There are people everywhere. But I need to get to the ER.

"O'Connor!" I turn to see Ryker's older brother heading my way.

Rowan, the one Kesley had befriended at that first game she attended, comes up to me and slaps a hand on my shoulder in greeting.

"You sure, you can do this?" I ask him.

"You kidding? I can spot a rat the moment I see them. It's a gift," Rowan grins.

"I'll be just outside the room," I tell him. I can't risk being spotted by my uncle's potential hitman. Any of my teammate's could be recognized. So I called in for reinforcements.

We wait for a nurse to leave the room and when she does, Rowan slips in.

I hear the conversation from the door.

Rowan unplugs the machines. The man in the hospital bed gasps. "You're going to make this really easy for me," he tells the man with a vicious tone.

"Who sent you?" The man says, his voice shaky.

"Your worst fucking nightmare," Rowan replies.

I'm grateful for Ryker's older and fearless brother.

"Please... I-I didn't mean to get caught. It was going to be clean. In and out. Just like the last one. But there was a kid man. A fucking kid. They didn't tell me it was a kid."

"So you didn't finish the job is what I hear?" Rowan says drily. "Am I hearing that right?"

"Please, j-just tell Frank I'll get his money back to him. Tell him I can finish it. I'll find someone who can do it."

"You want me to tell Frank O'Connor that you'll find someone else to finish *your* job?"

The man pleads, "I'll make it right."

"Don't bother," Rowan spits out. "You're done."

He storms out and shuts the door behind him. And we both leave the hospital as quickly as we arrived.

When we get outside I pull out my phone. "Rina, hey. Tell McEvoy we got him. Bobby Lowe just confessed to being hired by Frank O'Connor to take out my son."

"I can't believe I'm hearing this," Rina says. "Did you get it recorded?"

Rowan pulls the phone from his pocket and replays the video. Rina listens in over the phone.

"So Frank O'Connor, Jeremy Clark, Bob Lowe... have all been working together? Unbelievable," she breathes out. "I'm going to really enjoy seeing those bastards all behind bars."

"Yeah. You and me both."

Chapter 33
Kesley

"Kesley, you're making us all crazy. Please, sit down," Ryker says from the couch.

I've been pacing back and forth in Izzy's living room. "I can't. I need to know that no one else will get hurt."

"Here, have some wine," Izzy offers me a glass.

Libby walks by and takes it before I get a chance to reach for it, "Thanks," she says before downing the entire glass. "I really needed that. Hey is that from our granddad's vineyard?"

Izzy smiles at her. "It's our go-to."

Muppet squawks from his place near the window. A dark SUV pulls into the roundabout driveway and I can finally breathe.

They're here.

I run to the front door and pull it open, sprinting to greet my family.

Liam jumps out first. "Mommy!"

"Oh, my sweet boy! Are you okay? Are you hurt?" I turn him every which way.

"He's a champ," Zane says coming up behind me. "Not even a scratch."

I wrap my arms around my husband's waist and he reciprocates the hug. Kissing the top of my head.

My parents both exit the vehicle too.

"I was worried sick for you guys."

Mom comes up and hugs me. "You've got quite a man here," she motions toward Zane.

"Proud to call him my son-in-law," Dad says, slapping him on the back.

Zane gives them a grateful smile.

"What's going to happen?" I ask him. "What's going to happen to Frank?"

"We won't have to worry about him or his co-conspirators. Nana was right. He needs time and he'll be serving it behind bars for his involvement in all this."

"I can't believe the lengths he's gone to just to keep you from owning an estate."

"That's the thing," Zane says. "Nana sent over all the documents listing out what Granddad had in his extensive portfolio. And I found something."

"What?"

"It's pretty big," Dad says.

My eyes jump to each of them. "Well what is it?"

"Looks like Zane is now the owner of the Space City Arena," Mom says.

I turn to Zane whose smiling ear to ear. "Just the arena. Not the team," he adds.

"Are you kidding me?"

"Frank knew it was in Granddad's portfolio all along, the prick. He made a deal with a group of men who worked there to do whatever it took for them to become the owners. Take down anyone they had to. When Mack took over for her dad and started cleaning up shop—they got desperate. Got Jeremy Clark involved and the Pulse."

"Oh my god... and...nI just fell right into their trap," I cover my mouth with my hand. Feeling sick. I knew something was off when Jeremy threatened to fire me if I didn't do the story. If I've learned anything, it's that I can trust my gut when alarm bells go off. He felt slimy from the start.

"I'm so glad you never dated him," Mom says, from the side of her mouth.

"That was never going to happen."

"You and your boss?" Zane asks, cocking his head to the side.

"Ex-boss. And don't worry, there was nothing there. His cologne was screechy."

They all look at me puzzled. "You had to have been there. Anyways, looks like I'll be needing a new job after all."

We all start making our way into Ryker and Izzy's place. Zane pulls me to his side as we walk up the steps, "You don't need a job, little lion. Not unless you want one. You're my wife and I'm taking care of you and Liam. You're not alone in this anymore." He pauses at the door. Everyone else goes inside.

"Whatever you want. Whatever you need. I'll make sure you have it."

In that moment, my entire world shifts. Zane and I are together, together. We are a family. And together, we'll be taking on whatever comes next.

He bends down and kisses me on the cheek. "But I do know someone who might appreciate your bar gig," he says.

"Oh yeah?"

"Rowan."

"Huh… that's interesting. I thought you didn't like the guy?"

He shrugs. "Kinda earned my respect."

Libby steps out of the house to meet us. "So?"

"He's guilty," Zane announces.

"Shit," Libby says. "I was hoping he wasn't. That really sucks."

"Can't always trust your own flesh and blood. They can end up being complete assholes."

I can't imagine what it must feel like to learn that the uncle that took you in as a kid, ended up being the same guy that had your dad killed.

Yeah, nobody is safe from the level of greed it takes for a person to do something like that.

"Speaking of assholes…." Libby says.

Zane and I turn toward her. "I have a teeny tiny confession to make."

"Okay," I say waiting for her to say it.

Her brother just glares at her. "Well, what is it?"

"Don't take this the wrong way but… the bet was my idea."

Zane and I exchange glances. "What?" We say at the same time.

"I know… I kept that from you guys, and that was a dick move. But I would just like to let the record show… that I am not sorry for getting your teammates involved. Look at you two. It was meant to be."

We both glare at Libby. "You can say *thank you* whenever you're ready," she says tossing her hair back before walking back into the house. She closes the door in our faces.

Zane and I just look at each other.

"So the bet with Keelan..." I say.

"The intervention..." Zane adds. This whole time, there was another criminal mastermind at play.

"Did she even really have modeling gigs lined up in Europe?" I ask him.

He looks just as puzzled as I do. How long has she been running this play?

Zane opens the front door to Ryker and Izzy's house and we both call out to her at the same time, "Libby!"

* * *

Weeks Later

The smell of the ice is becoming one of my favorite things. Though Zane's hockey gear... good lord... I could do without *that* smell.

But I'll take it, if it means I get live this life side by side with the man I love.

The announcer's voice comes on the loudspeaker and the lights dim in the arena as they introduce the home team.

"Ladies and Gentlemen, the moment you've all been waiting for...get ready for game four of the Stanley Cup playoffs and welcome our very own Houston Heatwave!"

The boys skate onto the ice as pyrotechnics shoot fire up into the air and the crowd cheers all around. Liam jumps up and down waving his sign that says *"My daddy is the best defender!"*

He's wearing one of his dad's number eighty-two jerseys. It fits him too big, but he wears it proudly.

One day my boy will be big enough to fill it in. And if he's anything like his dad, he'll be tall and strong. A defender on *and* off the ice.

I love seeing him having fun. Libby screams next to him and they draw our defenseman's attention. He looks up at us in the crowd and nods his head to us.

I see Izzy and Candace making their way down the seats.

"Hey girls! Didn't think you would make it in time for the anthem."

Candace is carrying snacks galore, most of them are probably for Izzy and her growing appetite. "Have you seen the crowd here?"

"It's absolute bananas out there," Izzy adds. "Half the city is here tonight. That's what we get for them having a three game winning streak. Tonight's the night, girls."

They take the two empty seats next to me. "Here," Izzy says, handing me a bright orange leather jacket.

"What's this?"

"You missed it when we were talking about playoff jackets," Candace says. "But we had one made for you."

I open it up and it has number eighty two stitched onto it on the arms and on the back along with, "Mrs. O'Connor?"

The girls look at each other and smile and say in unison, "Welcome to the Heatwave WAGS club!"

"It's a very exclusive club right now," Izzy teases. "Like literally just us three."

We all laugh. The Heatwave boys aren't known for settling down. But I'm grateful for the ones that have, because now I have new friends I never thought I'd get.

Rina comes down the row of seats in front of us. We usually don't see her until after the game.

"Uh-oh. Everything alright?" I ask her when she's close enough to hear me.

"New press release... check it out." She shows me her

phone and on it is an article from The Houston Pulse. "An apology released by the new editor-in-chief retracting the previously written article on the Heatwave now that the real perps are behind bars and awaiting trials."

"Wow, that's great news," Izzy says.

"What does that mean for *Operation Win Back Houston?*" Candace asks.

"Oh, it's still on. Full force. These boys are in the playoffs. They need all the community involvement they can get."

"So the youth skate night?" I ask.

"Still on," Rina says.

"And the Date-a-player charity auction?" Izzy asks.

"I mean, only the single guys of course. But yes, still on."

I look over at Libby. "I am *not* dating a player. That's a you guys thing," she says wagging her fingers at us.

"Alright, so what can we do to help?" I ask her.

"Tonight? Cheer your asses off. If these boys can make it to round two of the playoffs... let's just say Mack will be very, very pleased."

"Won't we all!" Libby says leaning over Liam.

The lights turn down again and we all rise up for the national anthem. And when I do, I slip on my very loud and noticeable orange leather jacket.

It fits perfectly. I look down at the ice at my husband, lined up with his teammates.

His eyes drift up to me and I smile at him. Then to throw him off I shoot him a middle finger and he bursts out laughing. The guys next to him try not to get distracted.

When he composes himself, he mouths, *I love you.* And I blow him a kiss.

Damaged Defender

Life has a funny way of giving us exactly what we need. Even when we don't know what we're looking for.

But standing here with all my girlfriends. My son by my side and my hottie hockey hubby on the ice... I can't help but think that everything happens exactly as it should.

Even if it's one wild ride to get there.

Epilogue | Zane
Five Years Later

"**D**ad, the twins keep messing with my gear!" Liam cries out through the intercom.

I turn to look at Kesley. "Did you hear that?"

"He called for you, not for me?" She smiles and it lights up the room.

"Is that a first?" I ask.

"Don't be so surprised, that's what happens when a dad retires and stays home twenty-four seven. How do you like your new role as snack bitch, by the way?"

She's bent over a box of dishes in our newly renovated kitchen when I come up behind her and stroke a hand down her spine, stopping to cup her ass.

"I'll be snack bitch any day, if it means I get you as my sugar mama."

She rises, setting the drinking glasses she's holding onto the counter and wrapping her arms around my neck.

"Is that so?" she says.

"That *is* so... Mrs. Editor-in-chief."

"I do like the sound of that." She gives me a tiny peck on the mouth.

In a few years, Kesley's gone from barely writing to being the final say for anything going online for The Pulse. And when it was time to decide whether or not to extend my contract with the Heatwave; well, I felt there was something much bigger for me to do in this next stage of life.

"Da-aad!" Liam cries out again.

"I think you gotta go handle that Coach Daddy."

I lean down and nip her bottom lip. She yelps, "Hey! Mufasa!"

"I'm going to go handle that. But when I get back... I'm going to handle you, little lion."

"I'd like to see you try," she teases.

A low rumble escapes my chest. And I can only imagine chasing my wife around the estate Libby and I held so dear growing up. The place our children now run around in and fill with laughter.

"I'll be back," I promise with one more kiss before I disappear around the corner.

I go up the winding staircase and head into the kid's wing. "Alright kids, what's going on here?" I enter the game room where I thought they were. Toys are scattered about. But there's no sign of them."Kids?"

"Get him!" I hear Liam say and suddenly I'm being covered by blankets.

"Hey, what the heck is going on here?" I try to claw my way out of it but they've piled several sheets and blankets over me and I fall to the floor.

"Hit the lights" Liam says and I hear the laughter of one of my twin daughters as she obliges.

"Fi, is that you? Mally?"

They both laugh from somewhere around me.

"Ok, dad. Listen up. We've got you surrounded."

"Me? What did I do?"

"We have several snipers with nerf guns trained on you so I suggest you just stay right where you are, buddy." Liam says like he's in some kind of war movie.

"Is somebody going to tell me what's going on?"

"Agent Nala, Simba has been captured. I repeat, Simba has been secured."

A moment later, my wife's voice comes on over the intercom, "Good work, Agent Zazu. Make sure Agents Timon and Pumbaa don't let him get away."

"We're on it, over and out," he says into the intercom. "Don't you dare move, Daddy," Liam warns.

"Yeah," Fiona says. "Don't move daddy."

"Or we shoot," says Mally.

"Since when have I been raising double agents?"

"We ask the questions around here," Liam cuts in. "Now, where were you the night of March 15th, 1994?"

"What?"

"Answer the question, daddy." Fiona says nudging me with the end of her nerf gun.

"Uh... I don't know... being born?"

"That's right, you were being born. So you know what that means?"

"What?"

"It means you're old," Mally says, matter of factly.

"I am not old!" I say with a laugh, struggling under the blankets.

"Oh shut up you big oaf," Muppet squawks from his perch in the back of the room.

"No one asked you, birdbrain!"

"Hey, nobody calls my parrot birdbrain. Especially not you, birthday boy," Liam sneers.

"Guys," I try to dig my way out of the blanket prison. "What is this all about?"

When I'm finally free and poke my head out I'm surrounded by faces I was not expecting to see. My teammates and their families have quietly snuck in and surrounded me, each person holding a nerf gun pointed at me.

"What in the world?"

"Happy birthday!' They all cheer together.

Libby steps out from the gathered group with a cake. Her pregnant belly is poking out further than it was the last time I saw her. "Make a wish, Z."

Kesley is behind her all smiles and Izzy is snapping photos from the corner of the room.

"I should've known when I was captured that the Heatwave had something to do with it."

"Just make the wish, bozo," Sincaid says. He's taken my place as Houston's top defender.

I roll my eyes and give them what they want. "I wish..." I pause to look at my people. And for the first time in my life, there isn't anything I feel like I'm missing. Except maybe one thing. "I wish... I had the biggest nerf gun a guy could ever get so I could blast all these suckers."

"Dad, you're not supposed to say your wish out loud!" Liam scolds me.

I blow out the candles and Kesley kicks a nerf gun to me. I pick it up.

"What's this? I can't defend myself with this puny thing!"

"You took hits for a living. You can't defend yourself against a couple of foam darts?" Kesley says with a scoff. "Weak."

The guys laugh. Their guns still trained on me. "Ok, ok. How about we work out a deal."

Keelan laughs, "No deals. This is war!" He shoots me with a dart and everyone else in the room follows suit. I wave my puny nerf gun in the air in defeat, as my kids pile on top of me.

Kesley kneels down beside me and lifts my head off the floor. "Hey team, I think we got him," she announces, giving me a kiss on the forehead.

Today is my birthday. But if you ask me, I don't need a birthday to celebrate the life I get to live.

The love doesn't end here...

If you love these characters—go read Michael and Libby's story in Offensive Plays. It's a brother's teammate, ex's brother, surprise baby romance with all the laughs and love from our Heatwave boys.

Read Offensive Plays on Amazon!

Here's a sneak peek:

Chapter One
Michael

"I can't believe I missed that shot!" The words rip out of my throat like a roar as I yank off my helmet and toss it to the waiting equipment manager.

"It happens to the best of us, man," Zane says from behind me.

I shake my head as we round the corner into the locker room.

Just before I took the shot, I could feel the reverberations from the crowd's cheers inside my chest. We were right there. The fans were counting on me.

And then, I saw... *her*. And I fumbled. One split second was all it took. Now, I've let my team and my city down.

We're all quiet as we take off our gear. I don't even bother to look at our team captain. We both know I screwed up. I don't need his heated glares reminding me.

Coach Murray doesn't even announce himself like he usually does. He strolls in, hands in his suit pocket followed by the assistant coaches.

"Chin up, boys. This isn't over."

"Sure feels like it is," the rookie defenseman says, looking defeated.

My eyes shift around the room. One shot. I had one shot. And I blew it—and worse, they all know it.

"It's not over until it's over. And even then... you fight to the last possible second, you understand?" Coach says. "One game isn't going to change the fact that this was the least likely team to make it to the playoffs at the beginning of the season. Well, look around. You made it. That's a packed barn screaming for their team to win this thing. Keep fighting." He holds a fist out to emphasize.

"We'll review tapes tomorrow," says one of the assistant coaches. "Tonight, just rest up."

Rest? Yeah, right.

I can already feel my brain doing re-runs of that stupid play. I look around the locker room and see our goaltender, Ryker Balinger, with his head hanging low between his knees.

He had a rough night, too.

"Rest up," Coach reiterates before walking out.

Our PR manager, Rina Lopez, steps in next. All stilettos

and business. "Landry, Balinger, and Ferguson. We need you for interviews," she says dryly.

And this is the worst part. Like rubbing salt in the wounds, the press will ask us how we feel and how we think we can improve. Our answers are always the same. But somehow today, it feels like an even bigger hit to my already bruised ego.

"Five minutes," Rina says, before clacking out into the hall and not saying anything else.

We're all quiet again. This group is never quiet, but we've been running ragged. We've played eleven games in the last twenty-two days with no break. Normally, with the regular season being over, we'd be enjoying a long-awaited vacation.

But it's our first playoff season and getting this close and potentially losing our chance of making it into the conference finals, feels wrong. The only sounds are the swishing of jerseys and the shuffling of tired feet, followed by the zipping of bags.

I can't let this awkward silence go on.

"I fucked up," I finally say.

Tired faces look up all around me from what they're doing.

"It's not just on you, Ferg," Ryker says. "We all had a part to play."

Ryker's one of the older guys. A veteran on the team. And if Ryker's okay with the loss, then maybe I should be too. But a bag slams onto the floor just as the thought leaves me.

I turn to my left to see Landry huffing as he rips off his equipment, replacing it with an orange heatwave tech shirt.

"What's *your* problem?" Ryker asks him. His best friend

doesn't mince words with the team captain like the rest of us might.

"Nothing," he says, turning to sit on his bench and unlace his skates with sharp motions. But his eyes meet mine in a quick heated glare.

"It was a mistake, Kee," Ryker says.

"Of course it was," Zane says on the opposite side of the room. "So we need to let it go and move on. Don't we, Cap?"

I don't even have to say much. My team's got my back.

"Yep, let it go. I'll just," he slams a fist into the wall of his stall. "Let. It. Go." He punches with each word. His chest is heaving, but he takes a few deep breaths and finally calms down.

Hicks says under his breath next to me, "I don't think he's gonna let it go."

We all get undressed in silence, knowing Rina will be waiting with her heel tapping in front of the press room if we're even a second late. Keelan and Ryker both head out the second they're done. And I take just a little longer, trying to delay the inevitable.

Zane is looking down at his phone when he gets up from his place on the bench and brings it over to me, screen first. He doesn't say anything but holds it out for me to see.

It's a clip of me when I hesitated to take the shot. A fan must've taken it from the stands because, from the angle... it's very clear what distracted me. My eyes trace back up to my teammate, who's looking at me with what I think might be pity.

"It's not..." my words trail off before I finish the thought.

He nods toward the hall, and we walk out into it, away from the rest of the team.

"Fergie," he begins. "Your little crush is about to cost us the playoffs." He sighs when he says it.

Is he serious right now? This is coming from the guy who avoided telling the girl he pined after for years exactly how he felt about her, until just recently.

He puts a hand on my shoulder, and I tense. "I'm telling you this as a friend, Ferg. Libby isn't easy."

I stare at him blankly. "I don't know why you're telling me this."

"Because," he says, lowering his hand and leaning against the wall behind him. "You're a good dude. And I don't want to see you risk it all for a girl who, truth be told, is kind of a man-eater."

I think my jaw just dropped. I run a hand over my chin... *yep. It did.*

"All I'm saying," Zane continues. "Is maybe to set your sights on someone that isn't going to make your life hell. Man to man? Libby will eat you alive and use your bones to pick her teeth."

"I'm not interested in your sister, Zane." It comes out a little too zealous, but he's got a lot of nerve.

Read Offensive Plays on Amazon!

You met Zane—the bad boy with a heart of gold. But our next Heatwave player is as good as they come. Stick around to find out what makes our good boy... go bad.

xo, Anne

Follow Anne Martin on Amazon to stay up to date with all her new releases.

Also by Anne Martin

Heatwave Hockey Series

Pucked Together

Damaged Defender

Offensive Plays

Scoring Chances

Penalty Shots

Holiday Power Play

Cedar Grove Series

My Best Friend's Billionaire Brother

Neighbor's Secret Baby

Secret Billionaire Protector

Silver Fox Boss

Standalones

Baby for Brother's Best Friend

Printed in Dunstable, United Kingdom